SKELETONS IN THE ATTIC

SKELETONS IN THE ATTIC

JUDY PENZ SHELUK

W☊RLDWIDE

TORONTO • NEW YORK • LONDON
AMSTERDAM • PARIS • SYDNEY • HAMBURG
STOCKHOLM • ATHENS • TOKYO • MILAN
MADRID • WARSAW • BUDAPEST • AUCKLAND

W☻RLDWIDE™

Recycling programs
for this product may
not exist in your area.

ISBN-13: 978-1-335-73625-3

Skeletons in the Attic

First published in 2016 by Imajin Books.
Revised text edition published in 2017 by Barking Rain Press.
Reprinted in 2019 by Superior Shores Press.
This edition published in 2021.

Copyright © 2016 by Judy Penz Sheluk
Copyright © 2017 by Judy Penz Sheluk, revised text edition

This edition published by arrangement with Harlequin Books S.A.

For questions and comments about the quality of this book,
please contact us at CustomerService@Harlequin.com.

Harlequin Enterprises ULC
22 Adelaide St. West, 40th Floor
Toronto, Ontario M5H 4E3, Canada
www.ReaderService.com

Printed in U.S.A.

In memory of my father, Anton "Toni" Penz,
a good man who died far too young

ONE

I'D BEEN SITTING in the reception area of Hampton & Associates for the better part of an hour when Leith Hampton finally charged in through the main door, his face flushed, a faint scent of sandalwood cologne wafting into the room. He held an overstuffed black briefcase in each hand and muttered an apology about a tough morning in court before barking out a flurry of instructions to a harried-looking associate. A tail-wagging golden-doodle appeared out of nowhere, and I realized the dog had been sleeping under the receptionist's desk.

Leith nodded towards his office, a signal for me to go in and take a seat, then followed me, plopping both briefcases on his desk. He leaned down to pat the dog and pulled a biscuit out of his pants pocket. "Atticus," he said, not looking up. "My personal therapy dog. Some days, he's the only thing that keeps me sane."

I nodded, slipping into a chair closest to the window. It wasn't a particularly large office, and you definitely got some street noise—horns honking, sirens, the occasional revving of a motorcycle engine—but it did offer a decent view of Bay Street. I watched as countless individuals of every possible size, shape, and color scurried along the street, as cyclists—completely insane in my opinion—weaved their way in and out of the endless stream of gridlocked traffic. In the heart of Toronto's financial district, everyone was always in a hurry, even if getting somewhere in a hurry wasn't possible.

Atticus took up residence in a chair by the corner. Going by the blanket that covered the fabric, this was his regular seating arrangement. It amused me to think that Leith Hampton, a criminal defense attorney known for his blistering cross-examinations and ruthless antics, both in and out of court, owned a goldendoodle, let alone one that was allowed on the furniture.

After a good fifteen minutes, a half dozen consultations with more harried-looking associates, and three telephone calls, all brief, Leith was apparently satisfied he'd sorted out what needed to be done and who was going to do it. He looked up at me, and I realized what made people gravitate towards him. It wasn't his five-foot, six-inch frame, mostly slender with the exception of a slight paunch, but his eyes; eyes so blue, so intense in their gaze, that they seemed electric.

He opened a drawer and removed a manila file folder along with a thin document bound in pale blue cardboard, the words LAST WILL AND TESTAMENT OF JAMES DAVID BARNSTABLE etched in black on the cover. "Let's go into the boardroom. We won't be disturbed there."

Apparently Atticus wasn't allowed in the boardroom, because he jumped off the chair and trundled back to his spot under the reception desk, sighing loudly as he flumped his curly-haired body down onto the floor. I followed Leith into a long, windowless room with a mahogany table surrounded by several black leather swivel chairs. I selected a seat across from him and waited.

Leith placed the will in front of him, smoothing an invisible crease with a well-manicured hand, the nails showing evidence of a vigorous buffing. I wondered what kind of man went in for a mani-pedi—I was surmising on the pedi—and decided it was the kind of man who billed his services out for five hundred dollars an hour.

Unlike his office, which had a desk stacked high with paperwork, a saltwater aquarium, and walls covered with richly embroidered tapestries, the boardroom was devoid of clutter or ornamentation. The sole exception was a framed photograph of an attractive blue-eyed blonde, mid- to late-twenties. She had her arms wrapped possessively around two fair-haired children, ages about three and five.

Mrs. Leith Hampton the fourth, I assumed, or possibly the fifth. I'd lost count, not that it mattered. My business here had nothing to do with Hampton's latest trophy wife or their gap-toothed offspring. I was here for the reading of my father's Last Will and Testament, an event I would have been far happier not attending for a good many years to come. Unfortunately, a faulty safety harness hadn't stopped his fall from the thirtieth floor of a condo under construction. The fact that a criminal defense attorney of Leith's reputation had drawn up the will was an indication of just how long the two men had been friends.

Leith cleared his throat and stared at me with those intense blue eyes. "Are you sure you're ready, Calamity? I know how close you were to your father."

I flinched at the Calamity. Folks called me Callie or they didn't call me at all. Only my dad had been allowed to call me Calamity, and even then only when he was seriously annoyed with me, and never in public. It was a deal we'd made back in elementary school. Kids can be cruel enough without the added incentive of a name like Calamity.

As for being ready, I'd been ready for the past ninety-plus minutes. I'd been ready since I first got the call telling me my father had been involved in an unfortunate occupational accident. That's how the detached voice on the other end of the phone had put it. *An unfortunate occupational accident.*

I knew at some point I'd have to face the fact that my dad wasn't coming back, that we'd never again argue over politics or share a laugh while watching an episode of *The Big Bang Theory.* Knew that one day I'd sit down and have a good long cry, but right now wasn't the time, and this certainly wasn't the place. I'd long ago learned to store my feelings into carefully constructed compartments. I leveled Leith with a dry-eyed stare and nodded.

"I'm ready."

Leith opened the file and began to read. "I, James David Barnstable, hereby declare that this is my last will and testament and that I hereby revoke, cancel, and annul all wills and codicils previously made by me either jointly or severally. I declare that I am of legal age to make this will and of sound mind and that this last will and testament expresses my wishes without undue influence or duress. I bequeath the whole of my estate, property, and effects, to my daughter, Calamity Doris Barnstable."

I nodded and tried to tune out the monotony of the will's legalese. I had expected no more and no less. I was the only child of two only children, and my mother had long ago left my dad and me to fend for ourselves. Not that the whole of his estate would amount to much; some well-worn furniture, a few mismatched dishes, and a small stack of dog-eared books, mostly Clive Cussler and Michael Connelly, with the occasional John Sandford tossed in for good measure.

The inheritance would mean clearing out my father's two-bedroom townhouse, a dreary example of 1970s architecture mired in the bowels of outer suburbia. I thought about my crammed studio apartment in downtown Toronto and knew that most of his belongings would wind up at the local Salvation Army or ReStore. The thought made me sad.

"There is one provision," Leith said, dragging me out of my reverie. "Your father wants you to move into the house in Marketville."

I sat up straighter and looked Leith in the eye. Clearly I'd missed something important when I'd zoned out. "What house in Marketville?"

Leith let out a theatrical courtroom sigh, well practiced but over the top for his audience of one. "You haven't really been listening, have you, Calamity?"

I was forced to admit I had not, although he now had my undivided attention. Marketville was a commuter community about an hour north of Toronto, the sort of town where families with two kids, a collie, and a cat moved to looking for a bigger house, a better school, and soccer fields. It didn't sound much like me, or my father.

"You're saying my father owned a house in Marketville? I don't understand. Why didn't he live there?"

Leith shrugged. "It seems he couldn't bear to part with it, and he couldn't stand living in it. He's been renting it out since 1986."

The year my mother had left. I'd been six. I tried to remember a house in Marketville. Nothing came to mind. Even my memories of my mother were vague.

"The house has gone through some hard times, what with tenants coming and going over the years," Leith continued. "I've done my best to manage the property for a modest monthly maintenance fee, but not living nearby…" He colored slightly and I wondered just how modest that fee had been. I glanced back at the photo of his vibrant young family and suspected such treasures did not come cheap. There was probably alimony for the other trophy wives as well. I decided to let it go. My father had trusted him. That had to be enough.

"So you're saying I've inherited a fixer-upper."

"I suppose you could put it that way, although your father had recently hired a company to make some basic improvements when the last tenant moved out." He flipped through his notes in the folder. "Royce Contracting and Property Management. I gather the owner of the company, Royce Ashford, lives next door. But I'm not sure much, if anything, has been done to the house yet. Naturally all work would have stopped following your father's death."

"You said he wanted me to move into the house? When was he going to tell me?"

"I think the initial plan was that your father was going to move back in there. But of course now—"

"Now that he's dead, you think he wanted me to move there?"

"Actually, it's more than wanted, Calamity. It's a provision of the will that you move into Sixteen Snapdragon Circle for a period of one year. After that time, you are free to do what you wish with it. Go back to renting it, continue to live there, or sell it."

"And if I decide to sell it?"

"Homes in that area of Marketville typically sell quickly and for a decent price, certainly several times your parents' original investment back in 1979. You'd have to put in some elbow grease, not to mention some basic renovations, but your father left you some money for that as well."

"He had money set aside? Enough for renovations?" I thought about the shabby townhouse, the threadbare carpets, the flannel sheet covering holes in the fabric of the ancient olive green brocade sofa. I always thought my dad was frugal because he had to be. It never occurred to me he was squirreling away money to fix up a house I didn't even know existed.

"About a hundred thousand dollars, although only half of that is allocated to renovation. The balance of fifty thousand would be paid to you in weekly installments while you lived there rent-free. Certainly enough for you to take a year off work and fulfill the other requirement."

Fifty thousand dollars. Almost twice what I made in a single year at my call center job at the bank. Leaving there would definitely not be a hardship. And my month-to-month lease would be easy enough to break with thirty days notice. "What's the other requirement?"

Leith leaned back in his chair and let out another one of his theatrical sighs. I got the impression he didn't really approve of the condition.

"Your father wants you to find out who murdered your mother. And he believes the clues may be hidden in the Marketville house."

TWO

I STARED AT Leith Hampton open-mouthed. "What the hell are you talking about? My mother wasn't murdered. She left us when I was about six." I may not have had a clear recollection of my mother, but I still remembered the way kids talked about it at school, their parents the obvious source of information. Small town floozy finds a new man and makes tracks for a better life. Until now I had no idea the gossip had surfaced anywhere other than Toronto.

"Apparently your father came to believe otherwise," Leith said, folding his arms in front of his chest.

This surprised me. My mother's name was seldom mentioned when I was growing up. Most of the time it felt as if she'd never existed. My natural curiosity about who she was and where she went had been far from sated. The few things my father told me about her, usually after a couple of beers, hardly counted. That her name was Abigail; that she liked to bake; that she loved old movies, especially musicals from the 1950s.

"So you're saying the Marketville house never used to be part of his will?"

"The house was always part of the will, and you were always the beneficiary. The codicil is the part where you have to go live in the house for a year and try to solve your mother's alleged murder, or failing that, discover the real reason behind her disappearance." Leith shook his head. "I'll admit I didn't support the idea, but he insisted. I did my best to talk him out of it, but you know how obstinate your father could be."

I did. Look up stubborn in the dictionary and you might just find a picture of James David Barnstable. It was a trait I had inherited, right along with his unruly mop of chestnut brown hair and black-rimmed hazel eyes. The hair I could straighten into submission, given enough product and enough patience with a blow dryer and flat iron, and the eyes were probably my best feature. But the stubborn streak had almost proved my undoing on more than one occasion. My father's, too. "Do you know what led to his fixation?"

"I know he hired a private investigator when your mother first left, but nothing came of it. It was as if she'd vanished into thin air. There may have been some other attempts that I'm not aware of. But it was his last tenant in the Marketville house that reignited the fire."

"How so?"

Leith gave a dry chuckle, but there was no humor in the sound. "Apparently the tenant was a psychic, or at least she claimed to be. A woman by the name of Misty Rivers."

As someone named after Calamity Jane, a Wild West frontierswoman of questionable repute, I wasn't about to criticize anyone else's moniker. I was just grateful my parents had the good sense to give me a different middle name. "What did this Misty Rivers do or say to get my father's attention?"

"She told him the house was haunted by someone who once lived there, someone who loved lilacs."

"And from that he reached the conclusion my mother had been murdered?"

"It's a reach, I know. But in the past another tenant had complained of weird noises. Creaking in the basement, footsteps in the attic, that sort of thing. We both dismissed the complaint as the tenant's attempt to get out of her lease. If that was the objective, it worked. She moved out early without paying a penalty."

"But then after the psychic—"

"Exactly. After Misty Rivers, your father wasn't so sure. When you moved out of the Marketville house, he'd locked up all of your mother's things in the attic. He said he couldn't bear to go through them after she left, then the years just ticked on by. Misty made him believe there might be clues hidden amongst your mother's belongings."

It was as if Leith was talking about a stranger. "He never told me about any of this."

"He wanted to be sure, to protect you from getting hurt. He didn't want you believing in what might only have been a fairy tale."

A fairy tale. Except this one didn't seem to have a happy ending. I fished around in my purse for my cocoa butter lip balm, found it, dabbed some on while I thought about it.

"What's all this about lilacs?"

"Over the years, folks have tried planting a variety of things, flowers, a vegetable garden, all without any measure of success. The only thing that grew on the property was an out-of-control lilac bush in the backyard. It didn't matter how many times it was cut back, the following spring it would come back full and bushy. Apparently your mother had planted it."

I rolled my eyes. "Lilacs are known for their indestructibility. And it would be easy enough for someone to see an old lilac bush and draw the conclusion the original owner had planted it." Another thought occurred to me. "This Misty Rivers, did she want money?"

Leith nodded, his expression grave. "I believe your father was going to pay her to investigate. Against my advice, speaking on the record. Unfortunately for Ms. Rivers, his premature death intervened."

Unbelievable. My common sense, union dues paying, hardworking tradesman of a father. Hiring a psychic. What had he been thinking?

It was as if Leith Hampton had read my mind. "I know it's a lot to take in, Callie. All I know is that in the past few months, your father became increasingly obsessed with your mother's…disappearance. I have to admit that I didn't see it coming. All these years, he refused to talk about her, and for good reason."

"What good reason?"

Leith clamped his lips together as if he wanted to bite back the words he said, or was going to say.

"What good reason, Leith?" I asked, again. "If I'm going off on this wild goose chase, at the very least I need to know everything there is to know."

Leith sighed, but there were no theatrics this time. "I suppose you're right, and besides, once you get digging into the past, you're bound to find out."

I know lawyers get paid by the hour but there was no need to drag this on. I leaned forward, standing semi upright while my fingernails tapped on the polished mahogany surface. "Bound to find out what?"

"Although your mother's body was never found, no one ever saw or heard from her again. The police suspected foul play. Although your father was the one who reported her missing, he soon became the prime suspect. There was a lot of neighborhood gossip."

"Because the spouse is always the first one police suspect," I said, thinking of the countless episodes of *Law & Order* I'd seen over the years.

"Exactly. Eventually, the police moved on, but the case was never closed. The damage it did to your father's reputation in Marketville…he just couldn't stay there. He also couldn't bear to sell the home. Hence, the rentals over the years."

"And going back now? Revisiting ancient history, opening old wounds. What was he hoping to prove?"

Leith shrugged. "Maybe he just wanted to clear his name, Calamity. Maybe adding the codicil was his way of asking you to do the same. I wish he'd confided in me more than he did. When it came to his legal matters, he didn't treat me as a friend, he treated me as his lawyer. I encouraged that view of our relationship."

"I work at a bank call center. The only thing I know how to investigate is customer complaints." I tried to process everything Leith had told me. "You said I needed to move into the house. What if I don't find out anything?" What if, as was entirely likely, there was nothing to find out? What if I found evidence that implicated my father?

"Your only obligation is to try, and of course, to live there."

"If I don't want to?"

"Fifty thousand dollars would be held in escrow for renovations. Misty Rivers would be allowed to live in the Marketville house, rent-free for the period of one year, with the proviso she investigates your mother's disappearance. I would be given weekly progress reports, for which she would be paid one thousand dollars per report. The same sort of progress reports you would be expected to give, should you agree to take this on. The entire fifty thousand dollars would be paid outright should the mystery of your mother's disappearance be solved before the year was up."

Weekly progress reports saying what? The lilac was back in bloom? I wanted to scream. Instead I asked, "What happens after a year?"

"Misty Rivers moves out. The house will come into your full possession, to do with what you like. No more strings."

In the meantime, some swindling psychic would be pawing through my mother's belongings and living rent-free, probably without any interest in clearing my father's name. Not on my dime and not on my time.

"As I mentioned earlier, your obligation ceases one year from the date you move in. After that, you're free to do what you wish. Sell the house, continue to live there, put it back on the rental market. The fifty thousand dollars for renovations would be available from the moment you move in. Any dollars not used for renovations will come to you free and clear."

"And what becomes of Misty Rivers?"

"She's on a five-thousand-dollar retainer, should you decide to consult with her." I couldn't imagine doing any such thing.

But it looked as if I was moving to Marketville.

THREE

SNAPDRAGON CIRCLE WAS a cul-de-sac within an enclave of 1970s bungalows, split-levels, and semis. The occasional two-story home dotted an otherwise predictable suburban landscape, although closer inspection revealed upper level additions to the original structures.

Every road within the subdivision had been named after a provincial wildflower, starting with the central artery of Trillium Way and branching out to symmetrical side streets with names like Day Lily Drive, Lady's Slipper Lane, and Coneflower Crescent.

Most of the homes appeared to be well cared for, the lawns lush and green, the windows gleaming. Sixteen Snapdragon Circle, a yellow brick bungalow with a badly sagging carport, was the one notable exception. The roof had been patched in a half dozen places with little attention paid to attempting a match in the color of the shingles. The windows were caked with years of dirt and grit, and quite possibly, a few eggs from Halloweens past.

To say the house needed a little bit of TLC was putting a gloss on things. What this house needed was a good coat of fire.

It took me a minute to realize that a man had wandered over to the bare scratch of front lawn to join me. I pegged him to be about forty, good looking in a rugged handyman sort of way, the kind of guy you'd see on one of those TV home improvement shows. Well-defined biceps, sandy brown hair cropped close to his scalp, warm brown eyes. He wore jeans, work boots, and a black golf shirt with a gold logo advertising Royce Contracting & Property Maintenance. I imagined a six-pack under that shirt and tried hard not to blush.

"Royce Ashford," he said, extending his right hand. "I live next door." He gestured to an immaculate back-split, gray brick with white vinyl siding. The siding looked new.

So this was the contractor Leith Hampton had mentioned—the contractor my dad had hired.

"Callie Barnstable."

"Are you the new tenant?" There was something in the way he said it, a hint of "here we go again" and "poor you" implicit in the words.

"Even worse. I own this place. Quit my job to move here."

For a brief moment, Royce raised his eyebrows in surprise, but he recovered quickly. "I heard about his accident. I'm sorry. He seemed like a good man."

"Thank you. I understood from Leith Hampton—my father's lawyer—that you knew my father."

"I wouldn't say I knew him, exactly. I met him for the first time a few weeks ago. I gather he hadn't been here in a few years—all the rentals were handled through Hampton & Associates. He seemed quite shocked at the state of disrepair." Royce smiled. "I'm afraid tenants don't always respect a property the way they might if it was their own."

"I noticed."

"Your dad was planning to renovate. I'd given him a few ideas and an estimate. I got the impression he was planning to move back in."

So Leith had been right, my father had planned to

come back to Marketville. I wondered if he had planned to sell the townhouse. I thought about the postcards from Realtors addressed to "The Estate of James David Barnstable" that I'd tossed in the trash. I was definitely going to sell the townhouse once probate cleared, but I wasn't about to list it with someone so tactless. Now I wondered if any one of those Realtors had talked to my father. I heard Royce clear his throat and realized he'd been talking to me.

"I'm sorry, I was off in my own world."

"I expect it's all a bit overwhelming for you. I was saying that you're free to find another contractor. Whatever you decide, I'd suggest getting the roof re-shingled before you get leaks inside the house. Your father had already gotten quotes and selected a company. I could set that up for you, if you'd like."

"Thank you, that would be great. The sooner the better, from the looks of things. I'd also like to discuss the rest of the renovations once I get settled in." I just hoped it wouldn't take up the entire fifty thousand dollars. Leith had mentioned that whatever was left over would come to me. It could buy me a little more time to figure out what I was going to do once my year was up. I couldn't imagine going back to the call center.

"I'll see how soon I can get the roofers in. As for the other renos, there's no rush. You can let me know when you're ready. In the meantime, if you're up for a drink or dinner—no obligation to discuss business— let me know. It can't be easy coming to a town where you don't know anyone."

"Thank you." I pulled out my cocoa lip balm, dabbed a bit on my lips, and wondered about the best way to approach Royce. I decided to go full at it. "Do you mind if I ask you something?"

"Not at all. Ask away."

"Did you happen to know the last tenant?"

A slow grin spread across Royce's face. "I assume you mean Misty Rivers, psychic extraordinaire. She was convinced the house was haunted, tried to convince your father of the same."

Just as I had suspected. It wasn't just *I think it's haunted*. The woman had done her best to mess with my father's head, and it seemed to have worked, although why he had believed her was another matter entirely.

"Do you believe in such things?" I studied Royce through narrowed eyes.

"I'll tell you the same thing I told your dad," Royce said, shrugging his shoulders. "I was born and raised in Marketville, and in the late 1970s, the population would have been roughly 20,000, less than a quarter of what it has today. These houses were built to entice first time homeowners with young families. Folks who couldn't afford to buy in the city. Back then the building code wasn't as stringent as it is today, and to be fair, a lot of the technology and energy efficiencies that we now take for granted hadn't even been developed. Add to the mix that the house has been tenanted for thirty years, with minimal attention paid to upkeep, and there's bound to be some squeaks and squawks."

"So the short answer is no."

That slow grin appeared once again.

"I suppose, Callie, that you're about to find out."

FOUR

THE INSIDE OF Sixteen Snapdragon Circle wasn't much better than the outside. I went around the house, opening the windows to get rid of a musty smell that seemed to infuse every room. Then I went back to the entrance and took stock of my inheritance.

Avocado green and gold linoleum flooring in the hallway carried through to a small eat-in kitchen, the cupboards painted a gloss chocolate brown, the walls sunshine yellow. Harvest gold appliances. A laminate countertop, gold speckles on off-white, a pot ring burned into its scarred surface. A window over the sink overlooked the sagging carport. Welcome back, 1980.

An old memory came to mind. Me, as a little girl, four, maybe five years old, curly brown hair in a messy bob, standing on a footstool and staring out of that very same window. I was wearing a red and white striped apron with tiny heart-shaped pockets. I used to hide tiny pieces of beef liver in those pockets so I could flush the bits down the toilet after dinner. My parents had a strict "eat your dinner or there's no dessert" policy, and no amount of gravy or fried onions made the liver tolerable to my taste buds.

I closed my eyes, hoping to remember more.

Popped them wide open when I heard a creak in the attic.

A shiver ran through me. I found the furnace control and turned up the heat. To the left of the hallway was a combination living room-dining room. I wondered if there was hardwood underneath the threadbare gold carpet that covered the floor. I knelt down, lifted up a heat vent, and pulled back a corner to reveal a strip of pale blonde hardwood. Small mercies. That rug's days were seriously numbered, and stripping carpet was something I could do myself. It would save a bit of renovation money for another project. From the looks of this place, fifty thousand dollars wasn't going to go far. If I wanted to sell in a year and get a decent amount for the place, I'd have to put in a lot of elbow grease.

Another hallway led out of the kitchen and dining room and into a main bathroom in shades of 1970s pink, and two bedrooms painted builder's beige. The smaller room was barely larger than a walk-in closet; the master bedroom was just large enough to fit a queen-sized bed if you were the kind of person who didn't care about night tables. The eyesore of a rug continued throughout. I lifted up another heat vent and found evidence of more pale blonde hardwood.

Both bedrooms had decent-sized windows, with the master affording a view of the backyard. I noticed the sprawling lilac, not yet in bud. It was early May after an unseasonably harsh winter. It could be at least another month before it would be in full bloom.

I opened the master bedroom closet and made note of a small footstool and attic entry. According to Leith, my mother's things would be stored there. I wasn't looking forward to rummaging around an attic—thoughts of mouse poop and spider webs sprang to mind, and I really hated closed-in spaces—but it would have to be done, and sooner rather than later. If I could solve this supposed "mystery" or prove there was no mystery to solve, I could go back to my life in downtown Toronto.

It might not have been exciting, but it was cloaked in anonymity, something the recluse in me relished. Five years in my condo rental, I had yet to get to know any of my neighbors. One hour in Marketville and my neighbor had already invited me over for a drink or dinner.

I continued with my investigation of the house. A narrow stairway led to the basement. I'm not a huge fan of basements. They always feel vaguely creepy to me, and the low ceilings and dark wood paneling did nothing to warm me to this one. There was a separate room with an ancient washer and dryer not long for this world. It wasn't a wringer washer, but it wasn't far off. A second room housed the furnace, original to the house from the looks of it. It would probably need to be replaced before next winter. I mentally tallied up the renovation expenses I'd made note of so far and tried to shake off a feeling of gloom. It looked like I had inherited a money pit, and maybe a haunted one at that.

As if on cue, the furnace made a strange, belching noise before shuddering into submission.

"I hear you," I said, and scampered up the stairs, taking them two steps at a time.

FIVE

THE MOVERS WEREN'T expected to arrive for about an hour, which gave me time to hang up the clothes I'd brought, along with some basic kitchen essentials—kettle, tea, mug, and a package of chocolate chip cookies. I also managed to find a spot for three tubes of cocoa butter lip balm, one in a kitchen drawer, one in the bathroom, and another in the bedroom, temporarily on the window ledge until my bedside table was in place. The fourth tube I kept in my purse. Maybe it was a little neurotic, but there are worse addictions.

Thankfully, the movers were on time. It was a relief given all the horror stories I'd been reading in the papers about various moving companies scamming customers. Most of the scams seemed to involve movers who refused to unload a person's belongings unless they agreed to demands for hundreds more in additional fees, such as negotiating stairs—I'd heard as much as fifty dollars per stair—and other miscellaneous charges. I'd been careful to get references, but you never knew if those were faked. I'd pretty much heard it all working in the bank's fraud unit call center.

A couple of burly guys hopped off the truck, surprisingly graceful given their bulk. The taller of the two, Marty according to the name tag on his coveralls, came up to meet me. The other, a heavily tattooed guy, went to the back of the truck and began unloading.

"It shouldn't take me 'n' Tim more than a coupla hours," Marty said. "You don't have much stuff."

That was true. My rental had been a 550 square foot, one-bedroom with a minuscule balcony. I suppose I could have supplemented my new digs with things from my father's townhouse, but I just couldn't bring myself to do it. In the end, I'd donated what I could to the Salvation Army and ReStore and hired a company to take the rest to the dump. The only thing I'd kept was his filing cabinet—jam packed with paperwork I'd have to go through and shred—and his toolbox, which was bound to come in handy. Until now, my screwdriver had been a bread knife and my tape measure had been my feet.

Marty and Tim worked in harmony, neither one showing the slightest sign of strain. After about ninety minutes, Marty handed me the release paperwork to sign and asked for cash or a credit card. I suppose given the state of the house, I didn't look like a good bet for a personal check. I looked at the invoice and decided I'd been in the wrong business all these years. I was just about to hand over my Visa when I noticed that tattooed Tim looked a tad squeamish.

"Is everything alright?"

"Sure, of course," Marty said. "It's just that Tim here thought he heard noises in the attic. Bit of a little girl when it comes to mice, Tim is."

"Weren't no mice," Tim said, the freckles on his pale face standing out like fireflies. "I'm sure I heard footsteps and then something like a lady crying. It was ever so soft, but—"

"Well, I didn't hear anything, and I was standing right there beside you." Marty sniggered. "You'd tell us if you were hiding someone in the attic, now wouldn't you, Ms. Barnstable?"

I folded my arms in front of me and tried my best to look annoyed, but the truth was Tim hearing things made me nervous. What was it Leith said? Something about one of the previous tenants getting out of her lease because of noises in the attic. And I had heard that creaking sound earlier. Not exactly footsteps and a lady crying, but still disconcerting.

"Do you mind taking a look inside the attic? I have to admit the idea of mice sort of freaks me out."

"We're on the clock," Marty said, shaking his head. "Boss only pays for the hours we invoice."

"Fine, I'll pay you another fifty dollars each." Tim and Marty shrugged in unison.

"Very well. Seventy-five dollars each. Cash. Just do me a favor and take a peek."

A furtive look passed between Tim and Marty, one that suggested I'd just been the victim of a scam, though I couldn't be certain.

"I'll look. Tim can stay down here and protect you." Marty gave Tim a not-so-playful punch on the arm. "Show me where the entry to the attic is."

I led them to the master bedroom and opened the closet door. "I noticed the laddered footstool earlier today."

Marty pulled out the footstool, folded down the stairs, and reached up. "There's a padlock on the entry way. Who padlocks an attic?" For the first time he sounded suspicious.

I didn't much care for his tone. "My father, that's who. He rented this place out for years. I guess he didn't want folks snooping in areas that didn't belong to them. Hang on a sec."

I came back a minute later with the key ring Leith had given me. "Has to be one of these."

Marty stared at the keys and the lock and somehow managed to select the correct key right off. He pushed open the wooden door, sticking his head and shoulders inside the opening.

"So far no evidence of rodents," he said, his voice getting increasingly muffled as he clomped through the space. Tim, the gutless wimp, went outside under the guise of needing a smoke.

"What is it?" I asked as Marty climbed back into the bedroom. If the stunned expression on his face and the pale white pallor was any indication, he'd seen something that went way beyond spiders and mice.

"I think you might want to go see for yourself, Ms. Barnstable, and you might want to call the cops."

"Call the police? Why? Has something been stolen?"

"Stolen? How would I know what's supposed to be up there? There are a couple of dust-covered trunks. I'm guessing you'll need a key to open them." He handed back the brass ring. "It's what's not supposed to be up there that's the problem. At least I don't think it should be up there."

"And that would be?"

"I'm no expert, but to me it looked like a coffin."

"A coffin? Did you open it?"

"Hell, no. I got out of there the minute I saw the coffin."

"If you didn't open it, why do you think I need to call the police?"

"How many times do you find a coffin in the attic?"

How many times, indeed. I just hoped there was a reasonable explanation. One that didn't involve a dead body.

SIX

THE ATTIC WAS every bit as creepy as I expected, a windowless, claustrophobic space, the walls and ceiling filled with pink fiberglass insulation, the air smelling faintly of mothballs. Given the padlock, I had expected it to be stockpiled with valuables. It wasn't. There was a large leather steamer trunk that looked like it might be vintage, a newer trunk, bright blue with brass trim, and what appeared to be a picture triple-wrapped in bubble wrap.

There was also a coffin, full-sized from what I could gather. I took a deep breath, resisted the urge to bolt out the cubbyhole entry, and inched my way over. Unlike the attic, there was no lock on the coffin. I almost wished there had been, if only to delay the inevitable. I took another deep breath, put on the yellow rubber kitchen gloves I'd brought with me—I'd watched enough episodes of *CSI* to know the importance of not leaving fingerprints—bent down, and gingerly lifted the lid. It was lighter than I expected, but that didn't stop me from dropping it abruptly. The thump echoed in the room, scaring me more than I could have thought possible.

Because what I saw lying against the cream-colored satin wasn't a dead, decaying body, but a skeleton. One that looked decidedly human.

I had been ready to uncover some skeletons in the closet. A skeleton in the attic was another matter entirely.

"SOMEONE IS PLAYING a prank on you," Constable Arbutus said after a thorough examination of the coffin and skeletal remains before her. "This skeleton is very high quality PVC, the sort that might be used to teach medical students about anatomy."

I didn't know whether to be relieved, terrified, or annoyed. I also didn't have a clue who could have put it here. Or why.

"A prank? Are you sure?"

"Well, I can't be sure it's a prank, but I can be sure that this skeleton isn't human."

"What about the coffin?"

"Nothing more than a stage prop. It's very lightweight, probably made from papier-mâché, painted to look like wood." Arbutus studied me for a moment, her gray eyes assessing my every movement. "It's obvious you're upset by this, and you have every right to be if you're not the one who put it there. Do you have any idea who might be behind this?"

I shook my head. "I just moved into the house this morning. For all I know it could have been here for years."

"Judging by the lack of dust on the coffin, versus everything else up here, it's a fairly recent addition. You say you just moved in this morning. Didn't you look in the attic when you were buying the house? What about the home inspector?"

"I didn't actually buy this house. I inherited it from my father. It's been rented out for years. What I don't understand is how someone could have gotten into the attic. It was padlocked."

"The lock is an older model," Arbutus said. "It probably wouldn't take a lot of skill to open it. There are tutorials online that give step-by-step instructions. The simplest explanation is that the person had a key."

Which meant either my father had put the coffin up there or a key had been hidden in the house somewhere. Arbutus interrupted my thoughts.

"You mentioned that the property has been tenanted until now. When was the last time the locks were changed?"

"I don't know if they've ever been changed. I can call the lawyer handling the estate. He might know."

"I'd suggest you do that, if only to try to figure out who might have had access. Regardless, you should also change the locks, replace them with deadbolts."

I nodded. Arbutus was right. I had no idea how many people had a key to Sixteen Snapdragon Circle. And deadbolts sounded like a good idea.

"Why did you go into the attic on your first day?" Arbutus asked.

I told her about the noises Tim the mover had supposedly heard and how Marty, the other mover, had agreed to check it out for me. I left out the part about thinking I was being scammed. "You're saying that this Tim heard footsteps and a woman crying?" Arbutus asked.

I nodded.

"Had you heard anything like that?"

I admitted I had not, although I had heard a creaking sound.

"Creaking I can understand. But footsteps and a woman crying, that's something altogether different. You say Marty checked the attic after you paid the bill. Did he do that as a favor to you?"

"I agreed to pay them seventy-five dollars each. In cash."

Arbutus chuckled. "Nice. They see a single woman

moving into a house alone, then they find a way to check the attic to earn a few dollars under the table. I'm willing to bet that Marty got the shock of a lifetime when he saw the coffin."

"He was the one who suggested calling the police. I thought if it was just an empty coffin, it might be strange, but nothing criminal. When I saw the skeleton, I decided he was right."

"To be honest, it's still not criminal. There's no law against putting a coffin with a PVC skeleton in an attic, and we have no reason to suspect that anyone other than your father put it there. I'm afraid there really isn't anything the police can do." Arbutus watched me through narrowed eyes. "Unless there's something you're not telling me?"

There was, of course, starting with my mother's disappearance in 1986, and my father's more recent suspicions that she might have been murdered. Suspicions fueled by a psychic named Misty Rivers.

Something stopped me from telling Arbutus. Maybe it was because I still believed my mother had run off with the milkman, or some other male equivalent. Or maybe it was because I was afraid Arbutus would think I had staged the whole sordid attic scene, just to get the police involved and save me the trouble of doing the legwork myself.

"Nothing important," I said.

I'm not sure if Arbutus believed me, but she nodded and handed me her card. "Call me directly if you learn of any deliberate attempts to frighten you, or if any other unusual happenings occur that concern you. Now how about we get out of this attic?" She didn't have to ask me twice.

SEVEN

I RANG LEITH the next day and grilled him about the locks. He admitted, somewhat sheepishly, that they hadn't been changed in a couple of years. "I'd have to look up the exact date to find out," he said, "but the tenants were required to hand in their keys when they moved out. It was in their lease agreement."

I wondered, not for the first time, just what Leith had actually done to earn his property management fees. The house was in disrepair, the locks hadn't been changed, and who knew what else I was going to find.

"It didn't occur to you that they might have made a copy and kept it?"

Leith didn't answer directly. Instead he asked why knowing who might still have a key to the house was important.

I filled him in on my attic adventure. That got his attention.

"A plastic skeleton in a papier-mâché coffin, which is in all likelihood a stage prop. Who would put something like that in an attic?" Leith let out one of his theatrical sighs. "Let me go through the paperwork. I'll call you right back."

"RIGHT BACK" MIGHT HAVE been an exaggeration, but Leith did call a couple of hours later. He was all business.

"In addition to myself and your father, two tenants

potentially have a key, the last one being Misty Rivers. My assistant has left for the day. I'll have her scan and email you both of the rental applications tomorrow. There might be something there you can follow up on."

"Thank you, I'll look them over. In the meantime, is there anything you remember, specifically, about the other tenant?"

"Her name is Jessica Tamarand. She's the woman I told you about. The one who complained about hearing weird noises and got out of her lease early."

Interesting. "Could anyone else have a key?"

"Royce Ashford, the next-door neighbor at Fourteen Snapdragon Circle. As the contractor your father hired, he might have a copy."

"I met him earlier today. He didn't seem like a nutcase."

"I'm not passing judgment, Callie. I'm just telling you who might have a key. They might also have made a copy and given it to a friend, or in the case of Royce, an employee."

"You're starting to make me nervous."

"And a skeleton in a coffin doesn't? Never mind, don't answer that. I've arranged for a locksmith to come to the house tomorrow. He'll replace the locks on the front and back doors with deadbolts."

Something that should have been done before I moved in, and after every tenant left. "What time can I expect him?"

"Between noon and three o'clock. I'd suggest you stay in the house until he's finished. You don't want any other unwelcome visitors while you're out."

"You're not making me feel any better."

"My concern with this entire scheme of your father's

has been exacerbated. I'm sure he didn't mean to put you in any danger, but I don't like what's transpired thus far."

"What do you suggest? That I hire Misty Rivers after all?"

"I think that might be the safest course of action."

I couldn't believe it. Did Leith actually think I'd walk away because of a skeleton in the attic? I vowed to be more selective about what I shared with him in the future. Give him the bare minimum to fulfill the reporting clause. What he didn't know couldn't hurt me. Or stop me. "I was being facetious."

Another theatrical sigh. "I was afraid you'd say that. You're even more stubborn than your father. Just promise me you'll be careful."

"I promise."

Somehow I managed to get a decent night's sleep and woke up feeling ready to tackle whatever challenges lay ahead of me. I wrestled my hair into an oversized clip and pulled on a pair of gray sweatpants and a Toronto Raptors tee shirt. Then I went around the house, checking every cupboard and drawer in the kitchen and bathroom and scouring the inside of every closet, upstairs and down. If there had been a spare key to the attic, it was no longer in the house. I'd be glad when the locksmith had come and gone.

While I waited, I decided to assess the amount of renovations required. Even with fifty thousand dollars, it was quickly apparent that I'd need to do some of the work myself. Getting rid of the ugly gold carpet and refinishing the hardwood floor beneath it would be a good first step. I fired up my laptop and checked the local regulations for disposal. I could put it out with my weekly garbage on Friday as long as it was tied into rolls no longer than four feet and no heavier than forty pounds. No problem. I didn't think I could even lift forty pounds. Which reminded me that I needed to find a local gym.

A check of my father's toolbox yielded a utility knife, just the thing to cut up carpet into manageable bundles. Pulling the carpet up, however, proved to be a more difficult and far dirtier job than I had anticipated. The thought that I should be wearing rubber gloves crossed my mind—who knew what disgusting things lurked in those wooly loops—but I'd left the only pair I had in the attic and I wasn't quite ready to go back up there yet. While I didn't consider myself overly vain, I wasn't about to head out shopping dressed the way I was. I push-pulled the sofa and chairs down the hallway into the spare bedroom and covered them with old sheets.

After the first few hard tugs on the carpet things got a bit easier, although no less messy. The underpadding had all but disintegrated through the years, leaving behind scraps of speckled blue foam, which I balled up and put inside a large green garbage bag.

I had just about finished stripping carpet off the living room and dining room floor when I came across my first discovery: a small brown envelope, wedged against the dining room wall. Someone must have lifted the heating vent and slid the envelope along the floor as far as they could.

The envelope had one of those tiny metal clasps to close it up. The lack of a glued seal meant that anyone, before now, could have added to or removed contents. But who would have hidden an envelope under the carpet, and more importantly, why?

I was just about to open it when the doorbell rang, a

chirpy sing-songy sound. I glanced at my watch. Eleven a.m. It was too early for the locksmith.

Some instinct told me to hide the envelope before answering. I was putting it inside one of the kitchen cupboards, behind a box of bran flakes, when the door-bell chimed again. Someone was impatient. I went to the front door and looked out the peephole. A plump fifty-something woman with a mass of fluffy bleached blonde hair, jet black eyes, and oversized silver hoop earrings stared back. She wore jeans, a long-sleeved navy blue jersey knit shirt, and a polar fleece vest with an abstract pattern of the moon, stars, and assorted astrological symbols.

Misty Rivers, I presumed.

I opened the door and gave her my best quizzical smile. "Can I help you?"

She smiled back and made a sweeping gesture with both hands, the fingernails a tad too long and painted an inky midnight blue, the tips of each garnished in gold glitter; a French manicure transformed to tacky. The scent of patchouli oil drifted in the air. "Misty Rivers, at your service."

"I've been expecting you." I realized, as soon as I said the words, that it was true. I *had* been expecting her, had in fact wanted her to come. As the last tenant of Sixteen Snapdragon Circle, Misty was my number one suspect when it came to putting the skeleton and coffin in the attic. "Come on in."

Misty swooped in, glanced at the disarray in the living room, and sashayed into the kitchen. "I see you have a tea kettle. I'd love a cup of tea. Milk, one sugar." She plopped into one of the two chairs at a bistro table that used to furnish my balcony.

Pushy. "I'm sorry, I don't have any milk. I don't drink

it, and I wasn't expecting company." I felt a perverse flush of pleasure, as if not having milk in the house was some sort of minor victory.

"Clear then," Misty said, apparently determined to stay for a visit.

I grabbed my cocoa butter lip balm from the second drawer—a drawer I suddenly remembered my mother calling the "junk drawer" for obvious reasons. It had been filled with everything from scissors to string. I plugged in the kettle and put out a plate of chocolate chip cookies.

"I suppose you want to know why I'm here," Misty said, reaching for a cookie.

"I can guess. Leith Hampton said you thought this house was haunted. Apparently you convinced my father of the possibility."

"That's one way of summing it up."

I poured the boiling water into my old brown and white teapot and placed it, along with two earthenware mugs, on the table. "I have to tell you, Misty, I don't believe in such things as ghosts and haunted houses. I believe there is a reasonable explanation for everything." I stared straight at her.

"Including anything unusual that might be in the attic."

If Misty knew what I was referring to, she didn't give any sign, not so much of an eye flicker. Instead, she nodded as if she knew what I was going to say all along.

"I could sense you were a non-believer the moment I set eyes on you. But rest assured, a few weeks of living in this house will alter that perspective. When it does, I'll be here for you."

"Leith also mentioned you were on retainer," I said,

determined not to be swayed or swindled. "He also mentioned the reward."

"Naturally I'd want to be compensated for my time, the same as you or anyone else would be," Misty said, her black eyes flashing. "However, my offer isn't contingent on money. It's about finding the truth about your mother and ensuring that no danger befalls you, as it did your father. I warned him to be careful, but of course he wouldn't listen. Obstinate as a bull. A typical Taurus."

As a Taurus myself, I didn't appreciate the commentary, but I chose to ignore it. What I couldn't ignore was the fact that she knew my father's astrological sign. Just how close had they become before his death? Instead, I tried to imagine whether a faulty safety harness could have been anything besides an accident. But surely the official investigation would have revealed, if not hinted at, foul play, had it existed? I made a mental note to contact the site supervisor and see what I could find out.

"There's no reason to believe my father's death was anything but accidental."

Misty fluttered her blue fingernails. "If it makes you rest easier believing that, Callie, then by all means, although I will say it's narrow-minded thinking on your part. If you're sincere about solving the mystery of your mother's murder, then you must also accept that your father may have been coming into the truth. That knowledge may have killed him."

I poured the tea, as much to settle my nerves as to play hostess. What the hell had I got myself into? If Misty was right, I could be in danger. Maybe I needed to invest in an alarm system in addition to new locks.

"It's only prudent to consider all possibilities, Callie," Misty said, interrupting my thoughts. "To take necessary precautions should the need arise. As I said before,

I'm willing to help you, should you decide to accept my offer in the future."

"I'll bear that in mind. I do have a question for you now that you're here."

"Ask away."

"Do you still have a key to the house?"

"A key? No, of course not. I returned the front and back door key when I moved out. Why?"

"I'm having the locks replaced today and it made me wonder who might still have a key. I gather it's been some time since the locks were changed."

"Really? I just assumed there were new locks when I moved in. It's disturbing to think someone else could have had a key while I lived here. You're wise to install new locks."

"May I ask you something else?"

"Of course."

"Have you ever been in the attic?"

"The attic?" Misty frowned, accentuating the already prominent lines in her forehead. "First you ask me if I have a key, which I do not, and now you want to know if I've been in the attic, which I have not. I'm beginning to feel as if you're accusing me of something, and I have to say I don't appreciate it."

Misty's indignation seemed genuine, though I suspected that her line of work required considerable acting skills. Still, putting Misty on her guard was probably not the best way to approach this.

"I didn't mean to offend you. I just wondered if there were mice up there. One of the movers thought he heard noises. It was probably nothing."

"Ah, that would be the ghost of your poor, dead mum, trying to get your attention."

"Since I don't believe in ghosts, I'm going to have to

look for mice. Now, if you'll forgive me, I really have to get back to work. That carpet won't strip itself."

"Of course. I apologize for dropping in before you got properly settled. It's just that I had a premonition. I wondered if you'd found it yet."

"Found what?"

"A brown envelope. I couldn't make out if it was addressed to anyone." A dark crimson flush spread up Misty's neck and across her face. "I'm still trying to refine my psychic powers. Sometimes my visions are a little clouded."

"An envelope?" I shook my head, forcing myself not to look at the cereal cupboard. "No, I haven't found anything like an envelope."

"Yes, well, as I said, I'm still trying to refine my powers. It could have been a symbolic message, although usually those come in the form of animals or birds." Misty stood up, brushed some invisible crumbs off her pants. "I'll leave you my card. Please call me if you find yourself needing any assistance, any assistance at all. And thank you for the tea and cookies."

I took the card and nodded politely. Then I escorted her out the door and into her car. I watched as she pulled out of my driveway, off Snapdragon Circle, and onto Trillium Way. When I was certain she wasn't coming back, I went back to the front door and peered through the peephole. The image was blurred and distorted, but there was no question about it: you could definitely see inside the house. Right into my brown and yellow kitchen.

So much for Misty Rivers' psychic vision.

EIGHT

THE LOCKSMITH ARRIVED a few minutes after Misty had left. I asked him about replacing the peephole with something less invasive. Thankfully, he installed those as well. He assured me that a modern peephole would allow me to look out, but not allow anyone to look in. He set about to work, telling me it would take a couple of hours.

As much as I wanted to find out what was inside the envelope, I didn't want to look at the contents with anyone around. Instead, I fired up my laptop and spent the time catching up on my email. As promised, Leith's assistant had scanned and sent the rental applications for Jessica Tamarand and Misty Rivers. I printed them off and was just about to review them when the locksmith came to tell me he'd finished. I paid the man, watched him leave, then sat down in the kitchen, staring at the cupboard.

It was time to find out what was in that envelope.

I'm not sure what I was expecting but it wasn't five tarot cards carefully wrapped inside a sheet of pale pink paper, the sort of paper you'd find inside one of those fancy boxes of stationary at the greeting card store. What I knew about tarot could fit in a thimble, but even I knew five cards was far from a full deck.

I unfolded the paper and took note of the handwriting, a softly swirling backhand slant in turquoise blue ink. The handwriting was unfamiliar, but to my eyes it looked feminine, which made sense given the color of the paper and ink. The cards were listed in order as follows:

III: The Empress
IV: The Emperor
VI: The Lovers
Three of Swords
XIII: Death

I laid the cards out on the coffee table and looked at them a while. I realized I had no idea what any of it meant, though the last card, Death, definitely freaked me out.

I could check for meanings online, but it was probably best to consult with an expert. I thought about Misty Rivers. As reluctant as I was to involve her in my life, she did have a five thousand dollar retainer and I might as well have her earn it. Whether she actually knew anything about tarot was another story.

There was one more thing inside the envelope, a small silk brocade pouch, the sort of thing you'd put jewelry in if you were traveling. I undid the snap and pulled out a rectangular locket with a silver chainlink necklace.

The front of the locket was some opaque glass, delicately encased with filigree silver in a swirling floral pattern. A solitary clear stone was inset in the center. A diamond? Or a rhinestone? The back was solid silver.

There was something decidedly old-fashioned about the style, as if it had been made in another era. I would take some photos and email them to my old school friend, Arabella Carpenter, to see if she could tell me any more about it. Arabella had just opened the Glass

Dolphin, an antiques shop in Lount's Landing, a small town about thirty minutes north of Marketville.

I opened the locket using the tip of my fingernail to find a photograph of a man with fair hair, serious brown eyes, and a chiseled chin tilted ever so slightly upwards. Something about the man looked familiar, though I couldn't place where I'd seen him before. Had he come to the house when I was a little girl? Or had my mother met him somewhere, with me in tow?

I removed the photograph out of the locket, careful not to bend or damage it, and turned it over to find a handwritten note, the writing small and cramped: *To Abby, with love always, Reid. Jan. 14, 1986*

January 14, 1986. Exactly one month before my mother's disappearance. Abby. Not Abigail. A lover's nickname?

More importantly, who was Reid? And what, if anything, did he have to do with my mother?

I took about a dozen photographs of the locket from all angles—the picture of Reid removed—and emailed them off to Arabella with a note saying I'd found the silver necklace in the Marketville house. I'd talked to Arabella at my dad's funeral, and called her when I was getting ready to move from Toronto to Marketville, so she knew some of the story, although certainly not all of it. She was a good enough friend to know I was holding something back, but she didn't press.

The tarot cards were another story. The natural contact was Misty Rivers, but calling her so soon after her impromptu visit was bound to raise her curiosity. I decided to wait until I'd explored the attic properly. As much as I hated the thought of it, there might be other things to show her.

I rubbed my temples and tried to ward off the migraine I knew was coming. What had started off as a bit of an adventure and a legal obligation—not to mention a year off work—was rapidly turning into a complicated commitment with some skeletal twists.

Tomorrow was garbage day. Manual labor might help me think. I'd face the attic tomorrow.

I MANAGED TO finish removing the carpet from the living room, dining room, and hallway, stopping only long enough to eat. No other hidden treasures or surprises, although I was pleased to find the floors were in decent shape. They'd need to be refinished, but it would be a lot less expensive than replacing them. I hoped the bedroom floors would be as promising.

For the moment, I was left with about a dozen rolls of carpet, two full green garbage bags, and one very sore back. I suspected my arms and legs would stiffen up overnight, and late as it was, I really wanted to sleep in without worrying about an alarm clock for the sake of an early garbage day pickup. I dragged out the vacuum, managed to get most of the remaining fluffy bits, then began schlepping the rolls out to the curb. I was on the third one when Royce Ashford came outside.

"Someone's been busy," he called out from his front porch. "Do you have any more to put out?"

"Only about another ten." I felt my back spasm and tried not to grimace. "All offers of assistance gratefully accepted."

Royce was ready, willing, and more than able, carrying two rolls at a time without a trace of discomfort. I started imagining six-pack abs under his Toronto Blue Jays tee shirt and mentally smacked myself upside the head. It would not do to get romantically involved with the next-door neighbor. Especially with my track record when it came to men.

"That's that then," he said, carefully arranging the last rolls of carpet into a neat pile. He handed me a newspaper rolled inside a yellow plastic sleeve. "Your *Marketville Post*, delivered every Thursday whether you want it or not. Filled with a week's worth of local news, which basically serves as wrapping paper for store flyers. Not too thick at this time of year, but you need a crane to lift it during the Back to School blitz and at Christmastime."

"I actually love going through store flyers, and I have a ton of things I need to buy. In fact, I'd offer you a drink after all your hard work, but I'm afraid all I have to offer is tea or coffee, without milk. I also plan to hit the liquor store tomorrow." I looked down at my now filthy clothes. "Plus I'm badly in need of a shower."

Royce laughed. "Yeah, you kind of are, though I will say I admire your work ethic. I could use ten of you at my company."

"If that's a job offer, I'll pass. I have the bedrooms to de-carpet and a host of other renovations I haven't even started to consider. I need to make a list. At least I got the locks changed today."

"It's a good idea to have new locks installed when you move into a place. You never know who might have a key."

"That's true. Leith Hampton thought you might have one."

"Really? Well, no, can't say I do. As for that renovation list, I'm happy to help you prioritize. No obligation to use my company. Just some neighborly advice to steer you in the right direction."

"Thank you, Royce. I'd love to take you up on your

offer. How about coming over for dinner one night and we can talk it over? I make a mean lasagna and Caesar salad. And I pour an excellent glass of Australian Cabernet Sauvignon."

"A home-cooked meal and a glass of wine in exchange for some renovation advice? How's Saturday sound? Or am I being too eager?"

I laughed. "You sound like a guy who could use a home-cooked meal without doing the cooking. Saturday works for me. How does six o'clock sound?"

"It sounds perfect. Right now, though, I'd suggest a good, long soak in a hot bath, preferably one loaded with Epsom salts." He stepped closer to me and for a brief moment I thought he might be leaning down to kiss me. Instead he pulled a strand of wooly carpet from my hair. "Good night, Callie. I'll see you on Saturday."

"Saturday," I said, when I could finally find my voice. But he was already gone.

NINE

I CHECKED MY email first thing Friday morning and was pleased to find a reply from Arabella Carpenter.

Subject: Locket

Hi, Callie,
Thanks for sending me the pix of your lovely locket. I have seen similar lockets over the years and as such, in addition to the photos you've sent, my email appraisal is based upon those examples. Here goes:

Based on the quality of materials and workmanship, along with its Art Deco style, your locket was almost certainly made in the 1920s. The opaque glass is camphor glass—clear glass treated with hydrofluoric acid vapors to give it a frosted whitish appearance, made to imitate carved rock crystal quartz.

From the mid-nineteenth century to the 1930s, camphor glass was used for many things, from lampshades to bottles. In jewelry, it was often cast with a star pattern on the reverse to give it a radiant appearance.

This is indeed the case with this piece, as you can see from the inside left of the locket when opened. There is one further mark on the back, a 14 with a semicircle around it, which indicates this is not silver, as you thought, but 14 karat white gold.

The stone in the center of the locket is almost certainly a diamond, although I'd have to see it in person to

be sure. Why not pop by the shop one day and bring it along? It's high time we caught up over lunch or dinner.
 Best,
 Arabella

A locket from the 1920s. Was it a family heirloom? Purchased secondhand from a jeweler? Found at an estate sale? Arabella's reply raised as many questions as it answered. I sent her back an email thanking her for her quick response. I promised to set up a firm date as soon as I had a chance to go through the rest of my mother's things in the attic. I finished up with, "There may be a few more things for you to look at! Dinner's on me! Callie."

With that taken care of, I made myself a mug of vanilla rooibos tea accompanied by a couple of chocolate chip cookies. Not that I made a habit of eating cookies for breakfast, but my cupboards were pretty much bare, and without milk the bran flakes were even more unappetizing than usual.

I remembered the *Marketville Post* and fetched it from the front hallway. Before long I was immersed in flyers and making a store-by-store list. I was almost starting to feel like a proper homeowner, instead of a daughter looking for clues into her mother's disappearance.

I headed out the door at nine, wandered up and down the aisles of four different grocery stores, and stocked up on essentials, non-essentials—note to self: never shop for food on a two-cookie stomach—and everything required for Saturday night's dinner. I even found a nice six-bottle wine rack, perfect for the kitchen counter.

My next stop was the Liquor Control Board of Ontario, known to everyone as the LCBO, and Ontario's only option if you wanted hard liquor. Started in 1927 after prohibition ended to control the sale and distribution of alcohol, it amused me that almost ninety years later the government still didn't trust the concept of privatization. Well, they were softening some on beer and wine, but the rules for selling either were arduous at best, and hard liquor was a definite no-go zone.

The city snob in me was surprised at how swanky this particular LCBO was, as nice or nicer than any of the Toronto area stores I'd frequented in the past. There were aisles and aisles of carefully laid out liquor, liqueurs, imported and domestic beer, assorted fruity coolers, as well as wine separated both by country and color. There was even a huge vintage wine section at the back of the store, though most choices were well outside of my rather modest budget. I made my selection of more affordable reds and whites from the Australia and Chile aisles. The man at the checkout counter was nice enough to put my purchases in a couple of boxes and carry them to my car. Civilized.

My final stop for the day was at an office supply store, which, according to its flyer, just so happened to have some paper shredders on sale. If I was going to go through the papers in my father's filing cabinet, I was going to need one.

A serious young associate was more than happy to discuss the pros and cons of cross-cut versus strip-cut shredders. Apparently cross-cut paper shredders sliced paper into small squares or diamond shapes, whereas a strip-cut shredder cut paper into long strips.

"The cross-cut is more expensive, but it's also more secure," the associate said, his expression grave. "The long strips created by the strip-cut shredder can be reassembled by someone with enough time and patience for the task."

I imagined Misty Rivers riffling through my garbage—anything to bolster her so-called "psychic" abilities—and opted for the cross-cut shredder. You can't put a price tag on privacy.

I GOT BACK to Snapdragon Circle just past noon, made myself a tuna salad sandwich, and prepared my first report to Leith. I'd already decided not to mention the envelope until I could find out more about the contents. Besides, it was week one. He wouldn't be expecting much.

To: Leith Hampton
From: Calamity Barnstable
Subject: Friday Report Number 1

Discovered a PVC skeleton in a papier-mâché coffin in the attic. Police believe it might be a prank. Have not been back in the attic since. On the to-do list. Had locks and front door peephole changed. Met Royce Ashford, next-door neighbor. Misty Rivers came by the house and offered her assistance. I declined for the moment. Began stripping old carpet. Revealed hardwood underneath.

I reread the email. It was a recap of what he already knew, but it would suffice. I hit "send" and pondered my next steps. I knew I should finish stripping out the carpeting, but I was too sore and tired to think about it. That left going through my father's papers, researching the best resource for figuring out the meaning behind the five tarot cards, or rummaging through the attic.

I opted for my father's papers. I carried the shredder into the living room. I remembered seeing a blue recycling bin in the carport, retrieved it, and put it next to the shredder. What didn't need shredding could be recycled. I went to the small bedroom and push-pull-dragged my father's filing cabinet down the hall and into the living room.

The first task would be weeding out the meaningless. The idea being, if it wasn't meaningless, it *might* have a meaning.

The first few file folders were devoted to household expenses: hydro, natural gas, telephone, internet, and cable. By the looks of it, he'd been saving them for the last decade. Since he hadn't owned a business where he could write expenses off, there had been no need to keep them. I shredded the bills.

The second batch of paperwork covered my father's income tax returns for the past six years. I went through them line by line, but the only thing of real interest was an annual deduction for a safety deposit box at a bank in Marketville. I went to the kitchen cupboard where I'd tossed the brass key ring. Sure enough, there was a key that looked like it could have belonged to a safety deposit box. I made a note to contact Leith to find out how I could access it as the beneficiary of my father's estate. People didn't keep safety deposit boxes without good reason.

Next up were a bunch of manuals, which covered everything from tools and appliances to lawn mowers and a home gym. I vaguely remembered the home gym, a contraption that had all sorts of weights and pulleys, but it had been a few years since I'd seen it at my father's house. So far, the filing cabinet was proving to be a bust.

I went through the manuals one by one, tossing them

into the blue bin after a cursory glance. Mixed amongst them was a travel brochure for Newfoundland and Labrador. I fought back tears, remembering Dad's bucket wish list to go whale watching.

I was just about finished when I came upon a small sales catalog selling anatomical models of all shapes and sizes. I flipped through it and found a skeleton named "Morton" who looked suspiciously like the one currently residing in my attic. The fact that someone had circled that particular model in blue ink pretty much confirmed that they were one and the same. The final nail in the coffin—pun fully intended—was a receipt, tucked inside the back cover, for "1 papier-mâché casket" from a Toronto store called Macabre Crafts & Ghoulish Creations. The receipt was dated less than two weeks before my dad's death. According to their letterhead, the firm specialized in props for the film and theater industry.

Someone is playing a prank on you, Constable Arbutus had said. The coffin is nothing more than a stage prop, the skeleton a PVC medical model. Surely my late father couldn't be the perpetrator of that prank. Or could he? Was the codicil in the will nothing more than an elaborate ruse? If so, why? I placed the catalog and receipt on top of my folder containing the rental agreements for Misty Rivers and Jessica Tamarand.

A search of the remaining files offered a few more useless manuals, but no answers. Maybe the safety deposit box would hold a clue, but it was late Friday and Leith wouldn't be back in the office until Monday. For the moment, that was a dead end.

I looked around the room and spoke out loud, as if someone might actually be listening. "Damn it, Daddy, you're really starting to piss me off."

I slammed the filing cabinet drawer shut and stomped

my way back to the attic, pushing back the tears that started to threaten. When I was finally ready to cry for my father, I didn't want to be angry.

TEN

I PULLED MYSELF through the attic entry, determined not to give in to my aversion to confined spaces. Unless I could enlist Royce to help me, it was unlikely I'd be able to move the trunks to the main level of the house, and I didn't think our friendship—if we could even define it as such—was at the point where I could show him I had a coffin in the attic. I was going to have to go through everything up here on my own.

But not right this minute. Today my only purpose was to see if there was a message from my dad tucked inside the coffin, or something—anything—that might offer a clue as to what the hell he'd been thinking.

Even though I knew that the coffin came from a theater supply company, and that Morton, as I'd come to think of the skeleton, was nothing more than a PVC replica, it still took me a few deep breaths before I could bring myself to open it. When I did, I was once again struck by how light the lid was.

Morton stared back at me with his cavernous eye sockets. I gently lifted him into a seated position—now that I knew his name I felt an odd connection—then checked underneath the satin headrest. Sure enough there was a letter-sized white envelope.

I opened it and took out four photographs, each one of a woman, man, and young girl. They were standing in front of a small maple tree, holding hands and smiling broadly for the camera. I recognized a mid-twenties version of my father, a decade or so younger than I was today. I felt my throat constrict at the image of him smiling back at me, so vibrant and full of life.

I'd never seen a photograph of my mother until now, but I knew without any doubt that she was the blue-eyed woman in the photos. I'd inherited her heart-shaped face, her slightly too-wide nose. I felt a touch of envy at her hair, glossy blonde and poker straight.

It stood to reason that I was the girl in the photos. There was certainly no denying the mass of chestnut brown curls untamed by hairbands or hats, or the serious black-rimmed hazel eyes. I looked to be about five, which meant these would have been taken the year before my mother had left us. I closed my eyes, tried to conjure up a memory, something, anything.

Nothing came to me.

What was interesting about the photographs—beyond the fact they'd all been taken in the same spot—was that each one had been taken in a different season. In one, the maple tree was leafless and covered in snow. In another, it was in full bud, a call to spring. In the third, it was covered in shiny green leaves, summer at its finest. In the fourth and final picture, the leaves had turned a deep crimson. Our clothing also depicted the seasonality, from coats, boots, and scarves, to light jackets, jeans, and running shoes, to tee shirts, shorts, and sandals.

I turned the photographs over, one by one, and noted the same backhand slant, in the same turquoise ink, that had been on the listing of tarot cards. *Spring 1985. Summer 1985. Fall 1985. Winter 1985.*

I was right. The pictures *had* been taken the year before my mother left. February 14, 1986, the date forever etched in my mind. Years later, when a boyfriend dumped me on Valentine's Day, my father lamented that

I'd fallen victim to the Barnstable curse. What I'd fallen victim to, I'd told him, was another classic example of my loser radar, a combination of poor judgment and lack of insight. I didn't tell him that I'd actually been expecting a ring, or that I'd spent hours picking out just the right Valentine's Day card, an adorable image of two porcupines kissing, with the message, *I love you so much it hurts*. It had hurt all right, just not in the way I'd expected.

I wondered who had taken the pictures, where they'd been taken, and why that particular spot had been selected. The maple tree, only slightly larger than a sapling in 1985, would be considerably bigger now, if it still existed. There was no evidence of it on this property, but then again Leith Hampton had said the only thing that grew was the lilac. So it was possible the tree had been here at the time.

I placed the four photos back in their envelope, but I didn't put them back in the coffin. Instead I continued my search to see if anything else had been hidden. Only when I was convinced there was nothing else hidden did I stop to wonder just why my father would have put these pictures inside a coffin with a PVC skeleton. My best guess was that Misty Rivers had talked him into some sort of bizarre ritual. I knew I'd have to talk to her, about this as well as the tarot cards, but I also knew I'd have to think through my approach. Something told me Misty was one very clever operator.

I looked around the attic, at the two trunks, and what looked to be a large, colorful poster wrapped in bubble plastic. It was getting late and I'd had enough of this attic's skeletons, real and imagined, for one day. I couldn't begin to imagine riffling through the trunks for another couple of hours in this dusty, claustrophobic space, and a quick try confirmed my guess that they would be too heavy for me to lift and carry out of the attic. The poster, though somewhat awkward, was light. Even if I couldn't face it today, I could take that back down with me and check it out in the morning. I picked it up and carefully made my way back to the main floor of the house. I wasn't a psychic, but I did see a large glass of chardonnay in my immediate future.

I MEANT TO ignore the poster until the morning, I really did, but as I sat sipping chardonnay and dipping veggie slices into hummus, it kept calling out to me. I finally relented and got a pair of scissors to cut away the bubble wrap.

It turned out to be a framed movie poster—the kind you'd find in a theater—for the movie musical *Calamity Jane*. The poster depicted Doris Day wearing a bright yellow shirt, pristine rawhide vest and tight-fitting pants, gold cowboy boots, and a wide brim hat. She was standing on top of a saddle with the words *Calamity Jane TECHNICOLOR*, flicking a whip, while Wild Bill Hickok, played by Howard Keel, stood behind her. The words *Yippeeeee! It's the Big Bonanza in Musical Extravaganza* were directly above the whip, with *WARNER BROS SKY-HIGHEST, SMILE-WIDEST WILD'N WOOIEST MUSICAL OF 'EM ALL!* at the bottom left.

One of the few facts I knew about my mom was that she loved fifties-era movie musicals, and this poster seemed to fit the bill. A quick Google query confirmed it. The film had been released in 1953 and included the hit song *Secret Love*. I thought about the locket from Reid. Was there a connection, or was it merely a coincidence?

Another Google search took me to a YouTube clip from the movie. I couldn't help but chuckle as I watched

Doris scamper along with her horse, stop at a tree, and start singing, arms spread wide before stooping down to pick up a daffodil. It got even cornier when she hopped back on her horse, and riding sidesaddle, continued to sing as she made her way back to town. The bottom line was that her secret love was not a secret any longer. I knew the Hollywood version of Calamity Jane had been considerably softened, although it had been a couple of decades since I'd done any research, and I'd forgotten most of what I'd learned. I promised myself I'd read up on the real Calamity Jane.

I could also bring the poster along with me when I visited Arabella Carpenter. It wasn't an antique, exactly, but I knew Arabella had an interest in vintage posters. She'd told me about a group of railway and ocean liner posters she'd purchased from a collector in Niagara Falls. True, this didn't fall into the travel poster category, but it wouldn't hurt to show her and see what she thought. For all I knew, this could be a reprint. In the meantime, I could send her a few photos of it, back and front, the same way I had with the locket.

I turned the poster over and saw what I now believed to be my mother's backhand slanted handwriting, albeit slightly more spidery than the examples found on the back of the photos. Had she been worried when she wrote the inscription?

For my very own Calamity Doris on her 7th birthday.
Love always,
Mom

Not "Love always Mom and Dad." Just "Love Mom." Except that my birthday wasn't until May 1st, and my mother had left on Valentine's Day. Did that mean she knew she was leaving and wanted to be sure I had a birthday gift? Or was she the sort of person who bought things when she saw them and saved them for the occasion? And why had my dad hidden it in the attic all these years, wrapped in bubble plastic? Was it because my mother hadn't signed it from him as well? Was there some sort of hidden meaning? I realized I didn't know the answer to any of those questions, and probably never would.

I looked at the vibrant colors, the vivid fifties imagery. I could imagine this poster hanging in my bedroom as a little girl. It would have made adorable wall art. It still might, come to that. I decided to give it a try. It wasn't like I had anything on the bedroom wall now, and it *was* unique.

Besides, it was a gift from my mother—the only one I had. That had to count for something.

ELEVEN

I COULD HAVE done a lot of productive, potentially case-solving things on Saturday; "could have" being the operative words. Instead, I gave myself permission to take the day off from sleuthing and carpet removal to explore the twelve-mile paved trail system that ran through the center of Marketville. According to the town's website, the trail followed the Dutch River and passed through parks and green spaces, past wetlands and historic cultural sites, and had links to trails in two surrounding towns. It sounded like a runner's paradise.

The great thing about running—besides the fact that it allows you to eat more than kale and cabbage soup—is that it clears the clutter from your mind. By the time I arrived home, I had made the decision to show the photographs I'd found to Royce. With that decision made, I felt as if I would at least accomplish something investigative. I went to work getting the lasagna—and myself—ready for Royce. I knew it wasn't a date, but it didn't hurt to put my best face forward.

DINNER WENT BETTER than I could have hoped for. Not only did Royce have a healthy appetite, he was beyond complimentary, insisting the lasagna and Caesar salad was the best he'd ever had, and showering great praise on a store-bought baguette I'd turned into bruschetta. He also showed no reluctance to sitting cross-legged on the floor while we ate, our plates and wine glasses on the coffee table.

"It's either here or at the bistro table in the kitchen, and that isn't really meant for a dinner," I said. "Besides, the smell of garlic might be a bit overwhelming in there. I know I need to find a dining room table, but I'm not sure yet how I'm going to use this space. I've been thinking of knocking down the wall between the kitchen and living room. Even if I don't do that, the kitchen is long past its best before date."

"Why don't you buy an inexpensive patio set? At least that way you'd have a table and chairs, and you'd have something to use outside as well."

"That's a great idea. Why didn't I think of that?"

"You would have eventually."

"I'm not so sure. What about the wall?"

"You could definitely knock down the wall here, and it would make a huge difference in opening up the room. Mind you, the wall between your kitchen and this room happens to be load-bearing, but there are inventive ways of using an island with pillars to get around that, which is what I did in my house. Your father had been thinking along the same lines, so I already have the measurements, plans, digital renderings, and an estimate based on the quality of finishes he wanted. I can also give you the name of a couple of other reputable contractors who can do the same thing."

"I don't need to call anyone else. I trust that my father would have done his due diligence."

"If you're sure—"

"I'm positive. When can I see the plans?"

"How about I come by Monday morning, nine o'clock? But fair warning, renovations are messy, they take time, and they can get expensive, depending on what sort of fixtures and finishes you select."

"Messy I can deal with and I've got time. As for the budget, my dad did leave me some money for renovations. Hopefully it's enough."

"We're used to working with budget restraints. As long as you understand that unless the sky's the limit, there are going to be compromises."

"Understood."

"Then it's settled. Now, enough shop talk for this evening. Let me help you clear the dishes so we can both enjoy a glass of wine."

Hunky, handy, and willing to do dishes. Now that was a winning combination. Still, I couldn't in good conscience ask a dinner guest to help me clean up. "You relax on the couch, it'll only take me a few minutes."

Another thought struck me. The photographs. "You mentioned that you grew up in Marketville. Would you mind looking at some pictures in the meantime?"

"Pictures? Like on your phone?" Royce's eyebrows knit together in a worried expression, as if I might be one of those annoying people who took hundreds of photos on their phone camera and expected you to scroll through all of them one by one.

"Not on my phone. These are real photographs. There are only four of them. They were taken with my mother and father. I was hoping that you might recognize the setting. I have to warn you, though. There's a slight catch."

"There's always a catch," Royce said, but he said it with a smile. "What's this one?"

"The pictures were taken about thirty years ago."

"You don't make things easy, do you?" Still smiling, maybe even a little bit flirtatious.

"Sorry." Smiling back.

"No apology necessary. I'm more than willing to give it a whirl. But wouldn't it be easier just to ask your mom?"

"I assumed you knew. My mother left us on Valentine's Day, 1986. She never even left a note. We never saw or heard from her again."

"I had no idea. It must have been horrible for you and your father."

"We managed."

"Do you think your father rented the house out all these years in the hopes she'd come back for him?"

I wanted Royce's help but I wasn't prepared to play twenty questions. "I don't know. He didn't really talk about her much."

"I'm sorry. Clearly I'm overstepping. Let me take a look at the photographs, see if I can recognize the setting."

I whipped into the kitchen and grabbed them from the drawer before he could change his mind.

"Thanks, Royce," I said, handing the envelope to him. "I'll leave you to it while I do the clean up. Oh, and I made a tiramisu for dessert, if you're interested."

"Tiramisu. You're a goddess. When we have coffee, a bit later though, okay? Another glass of wine first?"

"I can live with that."

I KNEW THE minute I walked back in the living room that something had changed. There was a tension in Royce's shoulders that hadn't been there before.

"Where did you find the photos?" he asked.

"In the attic." I decided not to mention *where* in the attic. "Why? Do you recognize the spot?"

Royce nodded. "I'm fairly certain these were taken

in the park next to the public school on Primrose Street a couple blocks north of here. The tree is a lot bigger now, but if you look closely at the winter photograph, in the left hand corner you can see a tiny bit of brown and yellow speckled brick in the background. That would be the school. It's an unusual brick color."

I looked at the photo closely. The snippet of brown and gold mottled brick was barely visible, but it was there. "I'll make a point of running by there tomorrow and scoping it out. Maybe it'll bring back other memories. Thanks."

"There's something else, Callie."

"What is it?"

"I think I recognize your mother."

I stared at him. "How is that even possible? You didn't live next door until ten years ago."

"True, but I grew up in Marketville. The reason I recognized the school is that I went there, kindergarten to grade eight. Now my folks spend six months a year in Arizona, and six months at a cottage in Muskoka, but we used to live a few blocks from here."

"Were your parents friends with mine?"

Royce shook his head. "I don't think so. When I met your dad a few months ago, nothing about him seemed familiar and he didn't mention knowing my family. I think he would have, don't you?"

"Probably," I said, though in truth I wasn't sure. He'd managed to keep more than that a secret from me. Then again, I couldn't imagine why he wouldn't have told Royce he knew his parents. "You said you recognized my mother. When did you meet her?"

"My mom has always been into fundraising. She still is. When I was a kid, bake sales were popular, especially when it came to supporting school initiatives. The

woman in the photos you showed me—your mother—
dropped off a huge platter of peanut butter cookies to
our house for one of those sales. I would have been about
nine or ten at the time. This was before all the peanut
allergies you hear about now."

"You can remember a woman you met once, back
from when you were nine or ten? I'm impressed."

Royce grinned. "I remember because your mom
brought me my own special cookie, three times the
size of the other cookies, and she put a smiley face on
it using chocolate chips. To a kid, merging peanut butter
with chocolate to make a giant cookie was on par with
getting a day off school without being sick."

"My mom used to make me a cookie like that for special occasions. I haven't thought about that for years."
I frowned. "But why is it that I have no recollection of
these photos being taken? Even after studying them,
nothing rings a bell."

"Sometimes we suppress memories to protect ourselves. Perhaps when you're ready to remember, you
will."

"Why would I need to protect myself?"

"I don't know."

"Do you remember the woman's name?"

"I'm sorry, I don't."

"Would you mind calling your mom? I'd like to know
if she remembers anything about my mother. Her name
was Abigail, but I'm pretty sure that she also went by
Abby."

"Consider it done."

I tried to make conversation after that, but suddenly
my head was filled with a kaleidoscope of old memories. My mother baking a cake and letting me lick the
bowl. The two of us building sandcastles at Musselman's

Lake. Me playing jumpsies in the driveway, my mother's face lighting up as I called out M-I-SS-I-SS-I-PP-I, my feet and legs navigating the carefully connected elastic bands, without thought to the fact that Mississippi was an actual place, many miles to the south, in another country.

It occurred to me that my father wasn't in these particular memories, but I wasn't ready to go there.

Royce seemed to understand, passing on my half-hearted offer of coffee, although he did accept a small serving of tiramisu, probably because he'd made a bit of a big deal about it earlier. When he finally got up to leave, promising to return Monday morning with the renovation plans, we were both more than ready to be alone with our own company.

"I'm sorry to be such a poor hostess," I said. "Being in this house, the photographs, hearing that you might have met my mother. It's starting to bring back memories long buried."

"I can only begin to imagine. Look, if you'd like, we could both pay my folks a visit, take the photographs with us. My dad travels a fair bit, but I'm pretty sure he's around next weekend."

"Are you sure?"

"I'm positive. My folks love company, especially my mom. Besides, you'd be getting anything they knew firsthand instead of filtered through me. Even if it isn't much, or my memory is faulty, there are worse ways to spend time than a weekend at Lake Rosseau."

"I'd like that," I said, although I wasn't entirely sure. What if the Ashfords didn't remember anything? Even worse, what if they told me things I didn't want to know?

"Let me set something up," Royce said, leaning over

to kiss me gently on the forehead, the soft scent of Irish Spring soap lingering. "Sweet dreams, Callie."

"Sweet dreams, Royce." I closed the door and gently touched the spot where his lips had been.

TWELVE

I GOT UP early Sunday morning after a night of tossing and turning, the odd bits of sleep I did have filled with disjointed dreams. I ate a light breakfast of oatmeal and tea, then got my running gear on and headed out, winding my way around the side streets and occasionally getting turned around. It would take some time to figure out the neighborhood. Eventually I found the public school Royce had mentioned. The distinctive brick made it easy to spot, as did the gigantic maple tree now in full bud. I stopped my GPS wristwatch and closed my eyes, trying to remember standing there.

Nothing.

I don't know what I'd been expecting, but nothing wasn't it. I plopped onto a wooden bench by a baseball diamond and surveyed my surroundings. Maybe if I sat here for a bit something would come to me. It didn't. I felt an errant tear trickle down my cheek, quickly followed by a torrent of them.

The tears took me by surprise. I've always been a bit of a loner, and after my St. Valentine's Day massacre I'd made it a rule to eschew sentimentality. Yet here I was, sitting on a schoolyard bench, crying over a woman who had probably abandoned me and whom I could barely remember. I wiped my eyes with the sleeve of my shirt, restarted my watch, and ran back to Sixteen Snapdragon Circle, wondering if I'd ever think of it as home.

I GOT BACK, made and drank a pineapple banana protein smoothie, put together a macaroni and cheese casserole for later—comfort food at its finest—and spent the remainder of the day removing the carpet in both bedrooms. It was tedious work that took a lot of muscle, moving furniture around to get at it, and taking the rolls out to the carport until next week's garbage day, but it felt good to know the job was finally done.

I wasn't sure whether to be grateful or disappointed that there were no more hidden surprises. I checked my watch. Time to pop in the mac and cheese and toss a salad.

AS TIRED AS I was physically, I couldn't seem to relax after dinner. I tried reading, watching TV, and cruising around Facebook and Pinterest. I thought about the lease agreements Leith had emailed to me. I'd no sooner poured a glass of chardonnay, grabbed a notebook, and sat down at my desk to Google Jessica Tamarand, the tenant who'd broken her lease, when the doorbell chimed.

I checked the peephole. The woman on the stoop was in her late sixties or early seventies, with soft wrinkles, over-permed gray hair in an afro-style popular three decades back, and gold-rimmed bifocals, the lines heavily etched into the glass. No progressive lenses for this one. Her thin lips were smeared with candy apple red lipstick and a shade of liner that didn't quite match. I opened the door and caught a whiff of face powder and rosewater. Both had been used more than was absolutely necessary.

"I'm sorry to be calling so late," the woman said, though it was barely seven o'clock. "It's just that I just ran into Royce when I was coming back from my evening constitutional—I like to walk around the block every night after dinner—and he told me you're not just another tenant. He told me you were Jim and Abigail's daughter." The woman smiled broadly, revealing a smear of red lipstick on her upper eyetooth. "Ella Cole. I live next door, on the left side of you. The brown brick bungalow with the hunter green shutters and the rose garden. Our house is on the Marketville Gorgeous Gardens Tour. Not that the roses are in bloom just yet. I'm an original."

"An original?"

Ella nodded. "As in an original homeowner in the Wildflowers subdivision. Picked the house from plans way back in the seventies when Marketville was just a blip on Toronto's horizon. All of twenty thousand residents back then, the mall had only forty stores. And there were none of those big box monstrosities that are sprouting up everywhere like a bad case of teenage acne."

The last thing I needed to hear was a tangent on urban sprawl. I recalled something a builder friend had told me a few years back. "Sprawl is the house built next to yours." I attempted to divert her. "An original resident? That must have been very exciting."

Ella Cole practically preened; I could almost see the tightly permed curls spring into action as her chest puffed out. "Of course, I've made some improvements since. We all have…" She looked down at the linoleum and blushed. "Well, most of us. Those of us who haven't rented out. Not that I blame your papa."

I disregarded her blathering while I took full meaning of her words. Ella Cole might know something about my mother. Maybe even my father. "Won't you come in? I was just having a glass of wine. I have red and white."

Her mouth pursed into a tight grimace, the red lipstick making it look like shriveled poppy. "You like to drink alone."

I should have been annoyed at the implication that I was some sort of fall down drunk. Instead, I found myself going into full defense mode. "Just a small glass of wine after Sunday dinner following a day of hard work. I've been stripping carpet all day." The mouth remained pursed.

A large part of me wanted to tell her to sod off, but that wasn't the way to get information, or to be neighborly. I made an effort to be conciliatory. "I can make a nice pot of herbal tea, chamomile perhaps, always good at night, and I have some chocolate chip cookies. Store bought, I'm afraid, but quite good."

"Store bought is fine," Ella said, visibly thawing, "though as I remember, your mama loved to bake."

"A passion I didn't inherit, I'm afraid, but come on in and make yourself comfortable. Kitchen or living room?"

"I always find a kitchen so much more intimate."

"Kitchen it is." I plugged in the kettle and realized I'd neglected to tell Ella my name. "Excuse my bad manners. I'm afraid I haven't properly introduced myself. Callie Barnstable."

"Of course I know who you are, Callie, although as I recall, your mama always called you Calamity."

Why didn't I remember my mother calling me Calamity? Was that the reason I insisted that everyone, including my father, call me Callie?

"I go by Callie now, Mrs. Cole," I said, forcing a smile.

"No need for formalities between neighbors. Ella will do just fine."

"Thanks, Ella. Let me get the tea and cookies then

we can chat. I'd love to hear more about my parents. That is, if you've got any stories to share."

Ella gave a smile fit for a lottery winner, and I knew I'd nailed it. This, then, was the neighborhood busybody. Probably avoided by everyone on Snapdragon Circle, if not the entire Wildflower subdivision.

In short, my new best friend.

THIRTEEN

ELLA DUNKED A chocolate chip cookie into her tea. "You mentioned stripping the carpet. I noticed the rolls at the curb on garbage day. I thought I saw Royce giving you a hand with them on Thursday evening. Did he help you with the work?"

My assumption of Ella being a neighborhood busybody was confirmed. "No, I did all the work. Royce saw me taking the rolls of carpet out and offered to help."

As if she didn't know. Probably had her window open, trying to listen in to our conversation.

"I still have a bunch more in the carport, ready for next week's pick up. I'm pleased to see how good the hardwood looks. The floors should refinish nicely."

"They will indeed. It was all the rage to put wall-to-wall carpeting in back then. We did it, too, though we got rid of it about fifteen years ago. I'm delighted to see that you're putting in some elbow grease. Does this mean you plan to stay?"

"For a while, anyway." I wasn't about to tell her about the conditions of the codicil. Ella would have it spread all over town by the next morning. It was time to steer the conversation into another direction.

"Maybe you can give me some advice on gardening, Ella, seeing as how you've done so well with yours. I've been told that nothing grows on this property but the lilac. I'd love my own vegetable patch. Nothing elaborate. Some tomatoes, cucumbers, maybe some zucchini."

"Those are all easy to grow in this area. I'd be happy to go to the garden center with you, once you've dug up the plots. I won't do any digging, but I can show you a perfectly good location. There's plenty enough light now, if you're interested in seeing it."

"You're on."

We wandered outside where Ella proceeded to point out a rectangular weed-infested area near the back of the yard, behind a storage shed that had seen better days. The rest of the yard might have been patchy, but this section was downright depressing.

"Your mama planted a vegetable garden here the last summer she lived here," Ella said. "Of course, it's been left to go to seed, but there's no reason you can't pull out the weeds and turn the soil over. Gets good sun and it's tucked out of the way, so when you're sitting on your patio, you don't have to look at zucchini and tomatoes. You'll also want some flowers. I'd suggest that you start with a couple of whiskey barrels. I've got a diagram that tells you what plants to buy so you get season-long color and contrasting heights."

"Whiskey barrels?"

Ella nodded. "Distilleries sell the whiskey barrels to garden centers, who in turn cut them in half. They make lovely rustic planters."

"Rustic. I like the idea." I swatted away the fifth mosquito in as many seconds. "Let's get back inside before we become bug food. They seem so much worse up here than in the city."

"More trees and water, less concrete. It's one reason why my late husband, Eddie, built us a screened gazebo," Ella said as we headed back indoors.

"Your late husband? Did he die recently?"

"It will be five years this August. Hit by lightning on the golf course, if you can believe that. Apparently Eddie ignored the warning horn, wanted to putt out. Well, he did that, the stubborn old fool."

"I'm sorry."

Ella waved away the sentiment with a weathered hand, although I noticed she was still wearing her wedding band.

"Do you have any other questions, Callie? I'd be happy to answer them if I can."

"I suppose you've been in this house a few times, over the years, living next door and all. Did you get to know any of the tenants?"

"A lot of people have come and gone through that front door over the years." She pursed her lips again. "Some nicer than others."

"I gather you didn't approve of all of the tenants."

"Wasn't so much about approving or not approving, it was more like some people thinking they were too good to mingle with others." Ella sniffed loudly. "Every tenant with the exception of one invited me over, not that she stayed long, good riddance. Claimed to be a tarot card reader. Last I heard she was doing readings at that new-agey place at the back of the organic whole foods store on King. I've never been in there, but I understand they sell dream catchers and crystals and beads with the evil eye, all under the guise of helping folks find peace. Parting fools with their money is more like it."

"I assume you mean Misty Rivers, the last tenant?"

"Good heavens, no. Misty is the real deal. She gets visions from the spirit world that she shares to help others."

I decided not to mention that Misty had already been

to see me with an offer of "help," or that my father had started to fall for her story. Besides, in all likelihood Ella already knew that.

"Tell me a bit about the old days, Ella."

"You mean, tell you a bit about your mama." Ella leaned forward and patted my hand. "I know, dear, that you were left without a mama when you weren't much bigger than a bud on a rose bush. Fair devastated your papa, and why not? If there was ever a man who loved his wife, it was Jimmy Barnstable. Why if your mama got so much as a cold, he'd start acting all crazy, as if she had one foot in the grave. He didn't want you to see her sick, either. He did everything he could so you wouldn't." A memory floated over me. Was that Ella's lap I was sleeping in?

Once again, Ella seemed to read my mind. "Your folks hired Eddie and me to babysit you more than once, all because your mama had a touch of the flu. I understand as a young child your papa had seen both his grandparents succumb to cancer. The memories of them dying continued to haunt him as an adult."

I nodded, finally getting it. My dad had been the same with me whenever I was sick, protective almost to the point of panic. Until now, I'd never understood why. He'd never told me about losing his grandparents, and I'd never questioned their existence or lack thereof. We simply didn't talk about the Barnstables.

"My dad never talked much about my mother. I always wondered if he truly loved her, or if he only married her because she was pregnant."

"Nonsense, dear. You get that thought right out of your head. The Jimmy Barnstable I knew would have married your mama, expecting or not. He worshipped the ground Abigail walked on." Ella shook her head. "I never did believe all those nasty rumors."

I decided to play dumb. "What sort of rumors?"

Ella blushed. "I shouldn't have said that."

"Except you did. You said there were rumors. I'd rather hear them from you, someone who knew and liked my parents, than some stranger on the street." Never mind that Ella was pretty much a stranger to me.

She bought it. "I suppose if you went to the library and read reports from the *Marketville Post* way back when you'd find out anyway."

I made a mental note to visit the library. I only hoped they maintained archives of the *Marketville Post*—and that my brain could remember all the mental notes I was filing into it.

"Go on."

"The day your mama left, your papa called the police and reported her missing. He insisted she would never have left you behind. I have to agree with his logic. From what I could see, your mama doted on you, Callie. Besides, best as we could tell, she hadn't taken anything with her. Who leaves without at least taking a suitcase full of clothes?"

I shook my head, but I was thinking: who leaves an envelope with five tarot cards and a locket under the carpet? Someone who thought they'd be gone for a while and didn't want those things found? Or someone who didn't expect to come back? What about the signed Calamity Jane poster she'd left behind for my seventh birthday, two and a half months in the future?

"What did the police do?"

"Nothing at first. Made your papa wait forty-eight hours. But eventually the officers in charge tracked her final days and hours and interviewed everyone in the neighborhood. Nobody had seen her since the morning of Valentine's Day. I remember it was a Friday, and Eddie had made reservations for dinner at the Thatcher House. It's closed down now, couldn't compete when all the chain restaurants started moving in during the nineties, but back then it was about as fine a dining spot as you'd find in Marketville. Anyway, your folks were supposed to dine with us, but given that it was a Friday and Valentine's Day, they couldn't get a sitter."

"So you didn't see her that day."

"Oh no, I did, only it was in the morning. She was walking you to school—she walked you there and back every day, no matter the weather, none of the laziness you have today where everyone drives everywhere. No wonder so many kids are fat." Ella stopped as if waiting for me to chime in. I didn't. After a few moments of silence, she started up again.

"That day you were carrying a little red purse with Valentine's Day cards in it. I know it had valentines in it, because the two of you stopped by my house and you gave me one." Ella beamed.

"Meant a lot to me, especially since Eddie and me were never blessed with kids of our own."

I tried to remember walking back and forth to school. Nothing came to mind, but maybe if I walked there and back, slowly, using the same route we did all those years ago…

"Do you happen to know the route we took, Ella? Because I'd like to remember that, and for some reason I don't."

"As a matter of fact, I do, because on a few occasions, when your mama was sick, she asked me to take you. The first time I did, I took a different turn. You were very quick to correct me." Ella giggled at the memory. "It was Snapdragon to Trillium to Coneflower. Follow Coneflower to Primrose and you'll wind up at the school. Right hand turns all the way."

I got a paper and pen and wrote that down. It was a different way than I'd run the day before.

Another thought occurred to me.

"You said my mother walked me to school and back every day. Did she pick me up that day?"

Ella shook her head. "That was the first clue that something was wrong. When your mama didn't come to pick you up, they tried calling her. Nobody answered. They called me next. I was listed as the secondary contact, seeing as your daddy worked construction and could have been anywhere. Remember, this was before cell phones. I went right over to the school and walked you home. I stayed with you until your papa got home from work."

"What did he do when he found out my mother wasn't there?"

"At first, he couldn't believe it, even after I told him we'd searched the house and backyard. He just ignored me, ran around the entire house like a madman, opening closets and calling your mama's name. Then he went outside and searched the yard. Not that there was anyplace to hide, though I suppose she could have hidden inside the shed."

"I take it there was no sign of her."

"Not a trace. It was as if she'd vanished into thin air. Your papa jumped into his pickup truck and drove around the streets like a man possessed. He called the police the minute he got home, but, like I told you before, they told him he had to wait forty-eight hours before filing a missing persons report. Maybe they thought she was off somewhere with a lover, given it was Valentine's Day."

"But my father didn't believe that?"

"I'm not sure what he believed, Callie. Only he could tell you for sure, and he isn't with us any longer. All I know is that once the police got involved, they seemed to think your mama's leaving might not have been her own idea. They must have come by the house a dozen times, asking your papa the same questions in a hundred different ways. I know, because he told my Eddie."

The same questions a hundred different ways. Easy to slip up.

Ella seemed to read my mind. "Your papa never changed his story, not once. You'd have thought that would have cleared him, but instead it made the police even more suspicious. As if he'd memorized his story instead of telling the truth."

"But why would the police think he had something to do with my mother's disappearance? What did he do to make anyone think that?"

"There was a woman from the food bank, Maggie Lonergan—or should I say Magpie Lonergan. She insinuated that your mama was having an affair. As if I wouldn't have known about it. Maybe I didn't volunteer at the food bank, but I knew your mama."

I stifled a grin. It sounded as if Maggie Lonergan and Ella Cole were rival gossips in the same small pond. I wondered if Maggie still lived in Marketville. I was about to ask when Ella continued.

"Maggie's loose lips added fuel to the fire, and she wouldn't let it go. She told anyone who would listen, and plenty of folks did. You and your papa moved to Toronto just before school started. He wanted you to have a fresh start in a new place, bless his heart."

"What about the police? Do you know what they did with the case?"

"I suspect it's what the police call a cold case. It's doubtful that anyone has looked into it for years. No reason to without a body. As for your papa, I never heard from him after he moved, that is until three months ago, when he dropped by for a visit with me. He said he was thinking of moving back in. I'll admit I was surprised, but it wasn't my place to pry."

I almost choked on my tea. It might not have been Ella's place to pry, but you could be darned sure she would have, given half a chance. I decided to stretch the truth. "Maybe he thought if he came back to Market-ville, my mother would finally come back, too."

"If that's what he believed, Callie, then he was a gosh-darned fool."

I felt my spine stiffen, heard myself blurt out the words before I had the chance to bite them back. Now that was the real Barnstable curse, the not knowing when to zip it. "I never thought of my father as a fool, Ella. Even, and I'll admit the possibility, if he had been decidedly foolish in his love for my mother. Who among us hasn't been a fool in love?"

"You misunderstood my meaning, Callie. I never meant to imply that your papa was a fool for loving your mama. What I meant was, he was a fool if he was waiting for her all these years."

"Why is that?"

"Because I believe your papa was right about one thing. Your mama would never have left you. At least not voluntarily."

"Meaning?"

"That the dead don't return, Callie. At least not in the flesh."

I stared at Ella Cole for the better part of a minute before responding. I didn't want her to suspect the real reason for my moving in. On the other hand, I had to find out what she knew.

"I always thought she'd just left us. Are you saying my mother is dead?"

Ella nodded, her gold-rimmed glasses sliding down her nose. She pushed them back up impatiently. "Darned things are always doing that. I don't know how many times I've taken them to the optometrist to get them fixed. Something about the type of hinge."

I dug my nails into my palms and tried not to show my impatience. "You were saying that you believe my mother is dead. Why is that?"

Ella nodded again. "I told the police this, though I'm not sure they ever did anything about it. Anyway, the year before that Valentine's Day, it would have been 1985, I remember it clearly because that was the year I turned forty, and back then forty meant forty, not like today where you see forty-year-olds and even some fifty-year-olds wearing their teenaged daughter's clothes, not that I'm judging, though I don't think it's becoming for someone that age to wear sweatpants with writing on their butt. Of course, that's a conversation for another day."

I nodded again, determined not to interrupt Ella's flow. If I'd learned anything from my job at the call center it was that everyone had his or her own way of telling a story. Trying to speed that up was like taking an alternate route to avoid a construction zone, only to find yourself ten miles out of your way and stuck behind a traffic accident.

"As I was saying," Ella said, "I remember because I turned forty the same day your mama turned twenty-five. Saturday, December 14th, 1985. Eddie and Jim—your papa—threw us a party, all folks from the neighborhood, we were a closely-knit bunch back then, and Eddie and Jim were best friends, despite a fifteen-year difference. Your mama and me, we got on well enough, especially since she could feed my sweet tooth with all her baking."

Ella gave a soft laugh. "I like to say I don't just have a sweet tooth, all my teeth are sweet." I gave an obligatory chuckle. It was enough to get Ella to continue.

"It was that night I first suspected your mama was scared of something, though I should have cottoned onto it sooner, what with the photographs."

I perked up considerably. "What photographs?"

Ella put one finger on the bridge of her glasses and nodded slowly. "She first mentioned it in February of that year, I think, though it might have been before. Time has blurred the edges off a lot of things. Anyway, your mama got it into her head to put together something she called 'four seasons of a happy family.' Four photographs of the three of you, all taken in the same place, one during each of the four seasons. As I recall, the first picture was taken right around Easter time."

Even if I wanted to speak—which I didn't for fear of Ella going off on a tangent—I didn't think the words would come out.

"In hindsight," Ella said, "I might have questioned why she felt the need for such a thing, but at the time, I just felt honored that she asked me."

I almost blurted out, "Why the school?" which not only would have clued Ella onto the fact that I'd found the photos, but that I'd figured out where they were taken. I sipped my tea and waited. Thankfully, I didn't have to wait too long. At this rate, Ella would still be here for breakfast.

"We decided to take the pictures in the schoolyard a couple blocks over. Your mama had planted a maple tree at the schoolyard the year before on Canada Day. It's still there, if you go and look. She was real big on Canada Day, your mama was, and it had been part of some tree-planting initiative in Marketville. The residents went around planting saplings that had been provided by the town."

I was wondering why my mother would have asked Ella to take the photographs when she answered my question.

"I liked to dabble in photography, which is why she asked me. Still do, though it's decidedly easier with digital, especially with the variety of computer software out there now. Mind you, there is a learning curve if you want to do it right, and by that I mean not just snapping madly with your phone and seeing what shakes out. Back then, you took your shot, and it wasn't until you developed it you knew whether it would turn out okay. I was a pretty good photographer if I do say so myself, and I had a decent camera. So your mama asked me, would I take the four seasons photos, and I said, sure, why not, because it never occurred to me at the time that there was anything odd about the request. Of course, you were too young to argue, and your papa, he would have done anything your mama wanted."

"So you took the four photos."

"I did. We took the first one in the spring, and we were all pleased with how well it turned out. I might not have given the whole matter another thought, but sure enough, come summer your mama asked again. By the time autumn came around, I was looking forward to her asking. I'd already planned the shoot in my head, the leaves turning that pretty shade of red-gold the way they do. The last photo, the winter one, was taken on December fourteenth, the morning of our birthdays."

Ella fidgeted with her teacup and took another cookie. "There was something different about your mama that day, something skittish and edgy, though you'd never know it from the photograph I took. At the time I put it down to nerves for that evening's birthday party. Your mama was never comfortable with a crowd, blamed it on being an only child."

I could understand that, being an only child myself. I didn't mind one-on-one, but I much preferred my own company to the company of a group of others. Even so, I didn't usually get skittish and edgy at the thought of a party. "You said 'at the time you put it down to nerves.' Do you mean that later on you thought it might have been something else?"

Ella bit her lower lip, the red lipstick now all but worn off, then gave a tentative nod. "It was when I gave her the last picture, the winter one of the three of you. She said, 'Now if something happens, Callie will have something to remember our family by.' That struck me as odd, but when I questioned her, she just laughed and said she was being overly dramatic. I wanted to pry but Eddie was always on me to mind my own business. Maybe if I had pried, your mama would be with us today."

"So you're absolutely convinced she's dead?"

"Oh, it's nothing I can prove. I do know something had put a scare into her good and proper. As to what, who, or why, I don't have the answers. I wish I did."

And I wished I knew why my dad had hidden the photos in a coffin underneath a plastic skeleton.

"I know you think my father was misguided, but he

must have believed she'd come back. Why else would he have kept the house all these years?"

"He never talked about it with you?"

"I didn't even know this house—" I stopped myself, but not in time. Ella caught on quick.

"You didn't know about this house?"

I silently chastised myself. Before long, the neighborhood would be buzzing with this latest tidbit of information. But it was too late now.

"Not until the reading of my father's will. I'll admit to being surprised."

"So you returned here." Ella studied me with shrewd eyes. "But why?"

I stayed silent, shrugged, and stared at the floor, hoping that would be the end of it. No such luck.

"Let me guess. Some clause that made you live here for a certain period of time before you inherited the property. Misty Rivers suggested as much, but I thought she was just spouting nonsense. Same as I told her thinking this house was haunted was nonsense."

"Misty Rivers told you this house was haunted?"

Ella nodded. "You see, Callie honey, she's convinced that your mama was murdered, and until her killer is caught, she won't rest."

I tried to keep a neutral expression on my face. The last thing I needed was Ella telling anyone who would listen that my father had started to believe the same thing. I also wasn't too impressed with Misty spreading that sort of gossip, making herself sound like some sort of great savior, instead of the money grubbing mercenary I suspected she was. I was about to tell Ella exactly that when her next question caught me off guard.

"What about you, Callie? What do you believe, now

that you're back here, living in this house, and rekindling old memories?"

Maybe it was the way she asked, straightforward and direct. Or maybe it was because at that very moment the furnace groaned, loud and clear. Whatever the reason, I found myself being completely honest with her for the first time since she'd stepped inside the front door. "I don't know, Ella. I guess I'm here to figure that out."

FOURTEEN

ELLA LEFT SHORTLY THEREAFTER. I felt somewhat bad about not fessing up to finding the photos; it wasn't like I'd have had to tell her about where I found them. Then again, I only had Ella's word for it that she had taken the pictures, though I wasn't sure how else she would have known about them, and I couldn't think of a reason why she'd lie. I decided I needed to think on it for a while longer. If I couldn't come up with anything, then I'd take them over to her house next week. I could always tell her I found them while going through my father's things. Which wasn't technically a lie. This house had been one of my father's things.

There was something else in what Ella said, something that niggled at the edges of my mind, but I was too tired to try to pin it down. I decided to call it a night and fell into a dreamless sleep the minute my head hit the pillow.

I WOKE UP refreshed and raring to go early Monday morning. The first thing I needed to do was phone Leith. I was put through after a brief chat with his receptionist.

"Callie," Leith said. "I got your report on Friday. It was quite sufficient. There's no need to call." It was good to know Leith didn't expect a play-by-play of every detail in my life.

"This isn't about that."

"Surely you didn't find any more skeletons?"

"No, thank heavens. I'm calling because I found a bank statement showing a safety deposit box rental. I'm pretty sure the key is on the ring you gave me. I wondered if you knew where the bank was and if you could make arrangements for me to check the contents."

"Let me look into and get back to you by the end of the day. Anything else?"

"Actually, yes. All of this has made me want to find my grandparents. Maybe it's just feeling like an orphan. Any suggestions on where I should start? I don't even know where they live, or what their names are."

"I'm afraid I don't have much to tell you. I know your mother was from Lakeside. It's a cottage community with a handful of year-round residents, roughly forty-five minutes northeast of Marketville. Your father met her one summer when he was up there camping. Unfortunately, I don't know any more than that. Your father refused to talk about them. I gather they were less than accepting of him."

That confirmed what I'd always believed, though it didn't stop me from wanting to meet them. It was a long shot, but it was possible that my mother had stayed in touch with them without my dad knowing.

"What about my dad's family?"

"Peter and Sandra Barnstable. They used to live in Toronto, but I know they moved around the time your parents got married. I'm afraid I don't know where. They didn't approve of the wedding and your father never forgave them. The man could hold a grudge." I sighed audibly, knowing it was the truth.

"You might consider hiring an information broker," Leith said. "I'll get my assistant to email you the names of a couple of reputable individuals we've used in the past. There are more than a few bandits out there."

I'd no sooner hung up, wondering how much an information broker would cost, when the sing-songy chime of the doorbell rang through the house. That would be Royce, ready to talk about renovations.

ROYCE SPENT THE better part of an hour showing me before-and-after plans on his tablet, which included knocking down a wall and adding a large central island that worked not only as a table with seating for eight, but as a room divider. I had to admit the finished product would be perfect: a cook's kitchen, an open concept layout, and the added bonus of tying in the existing hardwood to slate tile in the entry and kitchen.

"It looks fantastic," I said, "but how much will it cost?"

"That will depend on the cupboards and finishes you want, but I get a contractor's discount at all the major building centers. Why don't we go shopping one day this week and check out your options?" He checked his phone. "I'm good for Wednesday. I could pick you up around two."

I didn't want to explore how good the thought of spending time with Royce made me feel. At least not yet. Besides, kitchens sold houses and at the end of the year—or sooner—I planned to get out of Marketville and back to the anonymity of the city.

"Wednesday at two it is."

AFTER ROYCE LEFT I pulled out the folder with the printed copies of the tenancy agreements from the past five years, hoping to find a possible key holder. I started with the one submitted by Misty Rivers, since I knew where she was now. Under Employer she had written "self-employed" and under method of rental payment, she'd agreed to first and last month's rent and direct withdrawal from her bank account on the first of each month.

Misty had used two former landlords for her references. Both said she was a good tenant who always paid the rent on time. There were no other details, meaning it was unlikely Misty would have stayed in touch, let alone handed over a key to her new digs.

It was time to check out Jessica Tamarand, the woman who had broken her lease because she believed that the house was haunted. The agreement listed Jessica Tamarand's employer as Sun, Moon & Stars. I looked up the website. It advertised "a unique store setting supporting local artisans, fair trade, handcrafted and environmentally friendly products to assist in the healing journey."

Under their services they listed Holistic Healing, Psychic Readings using tarot, tea leaves, and personal objects, Energy Psychology, Chakra Balancing, and something called *Belvaspata*, which was described as "angelic healing modality of effortless and quick change, that awakens you to your true Divinity and Majesty filling your heart with Joy." A list of their practitioners gave first names only. The tarot card reader went by Randi.

Could Randi be Jessica Tamarand? Leith told me Jessica had complained about noises in the attic and gotten out of her lease. Ella said she hadn't stayed long, that she had worked at the new-agey place in the whole foods store on King. I checked the location. It fit.

Leith had believed Jessica was just looking for an early way out without paying the price, but what if some psychic ability actually made her uncomfortable in the house? I'd never been a believer but I was beginning to wonder.

What was it the Sun, Moon & Stars listing had said? I went back to the website and read it again: "Psychic Readings, Using Tarot, Tea Leaves, and Personal Objects." Tarot cards.

I needed to make an appointment with Randi.

THE BREATHY-VOICED receptionist at Sun, Moon & Stars informed me that Randi worked Tuesdays and Fridays, that readings lasted about an hour, and that Randi tended to book up quickly. However, she said, there had just been a cancellation. Could I make it tomorrow at eleven? If not, it would be another week. I took the appointment and asked if I could bring something for Randi to look at. I was assured that doing so would only assist Randi, and get me a more accurate reading, "although only God is completely accurate," the receptionist said, and chuckled softly.

FIFTEEN

SUN, MOON & STARS was tucked at the back of Nature's Way Whole & Organic Foods, an expansive store that capitalized on all things organic, from meat, fish, poultry, eggs, and vegetables, to vitamins, protein powders, natural skin care, environmentally sensitive cleaning products, and herbal remedies. There was also a dizzying array of baked goods—many made with grains I'd never even heard of—and gluten-free products, as well as a massive section devoted entirely to the vegan lifestyle. If you couldn't find what you were looking for at the Nature's Way, you were probably too picky to live.

On the opposite end of the sprawling store you had Sun, Moon & Stars, a minuscule retail space packed with a treasure trove of trinkets and textiles, most made by local artisans. Here the savvy shopper could find natural stone jewelry, healing crystals, books on the occult, and flowing cotton garments with tie-dyed patterns, shiny beads, and silk embroidery. A hand-painted ceramic holder in the shape of a lotus flower held a stick of lavender-scented incense.

A vibrant young woman wearing a flurry of multicolored scarves and what looked to be a one-piece black leotard greeted me. Judging by her voice, soft and breathy, this was the lady I'd spoken with on the phone. I found myself wanting to whisper, as if I were in a library or a place of prayer.

"Callie Barnstable. I'm here to see Randi."

"Welcome, Callie. You're right on time." She pointed to a narrow wooden staircase on the right hand side of the room. "All of our practitioners are located on the upper level. I'll buzz Randi to let her know you're on your way."

The upper level featured a hallway with seven doors, three on each side, with a public restroom at the end. A small waiting area offered a tweedy orange couch with a matching chair, vintage Salvation Army if I had to guess. The main wall was blanketed with a patchwork quilt, the patches comprised of embroidered and embellished fabric scraps in a variety of shapes, colors, and textures. It looked as if it had been a project that many hands had worked on, over many, many hours. The end result was compelling.

I was just about to take a seat when a door opened and a woman drifted out. She had long, dark hair that fell in loose waves down to her waist, cinnamon skin, eyes the color of lapis lazuli and a dancer's body, long and lithe. She wore black leggings and an oversized sweater in shades of copper. Her nails were painted gloss black, and every finger, including her thumbs, sported a silver ring, some filigreed, some plain, some with stones, some without.

There are few people in this world who radiate kindness, beauty, and charisma. Randi was the personification of all three; she could have bottled and sold her essence like some sort of magic potion. I found myself staring at her, mesmerized. She smiled, revealing a row of perfectly straight, pearl white teeth.

"Welcome to Sun, Moon & Stars, Callie. My name is Randi. I've been expecting you." Her voice had a soft, musical lilt to it, and the faintest hint of a British accent.

Maybe it was her intonation, or maybe it was just my

imagination, but I could have sworn she meant she had been expecting me *before* I'd made an appointment. But that was just crazy thinking, wasn't it? I followed her down the hall and into her room.

The space had been painted floor to ceiling in an inky midnight blue. A myriad of tiny pot lights twinkled overhead, giving the impression of being outdoors on a cloudless summer night. A gigantic candle in a tall wrought iron stand glowed softly in one corner, the scent a cross between cinnamon and vanilla. The only furnishings were a black lacquer rectangular desk, a deck of tarot cards laid out in the middle, and two chairs upholstered in a dark navy needlepoint fabric. There was a sun embroidered on the back of one, and the four phases of the moon on the back of the other. Randi sat cross-legged on the chair with the sun, her feet tucked underneath her, and gestured to the other. Several colorful bangles jangled on her right arm.

"Please be seated."

I did as I was told, forcing myself to ignore the overwhelming urge to bolt back down the staircase, back to the safety of Snapdragon Circle. What was I, a complete non-believer of all things even remotely occult, doing here? I didn't even read my horoscope in the daily newspaper.

Randi seemed to sense my discomfort, because she leaned forward and pushed the tarot cards over to one side. "Elaine says you wanted a tarot reading, but I get the sense that you are not here for that. So tell me, Callie, what it is I can do for you?"

I assumed Elaine was the receptionist/store clerk, and if so, when I made the appointment, I was sure I said I planned to bring an object. So Randi's "sense" could be nothing more than putting two plus two together.

I knew from my limited research that ten tarot cards probably represented the Celtic Cross. I only had five cards, which either meant half of a Celtic Cross, if there even was such a thing, or something entirely different. That's what I was here to find out. But before I laid out my five tarot cards, I needed to know that I could trust her, or at the very least, test her knowledge.

"Before we begin I'd like to know a bit more about tarot. Gain a bit of an understanding so I know what to expect."

"Fair enough." Randi took the deck out of the case and began to shuffle while she talked. "There are several variations of tarot cards. I personally use the Rider-Waite tarot deck, which is the most well-known. Regardless of the illustration, a true tarot deck will contain seventy-eight cards in two parts: twenty-two cards in the Major Arcana and fifty-six cards in the four suits of Minor Arcana. *Arcana* means secrets in Latin. The names of the suits vary, but the most common, and the ones used in Rider-Waite, are Wands, Cups, Swords, and Pentacles. Are you with me so far?" I nodded.

"Okay. Now the Major Arcana are also called trumps, from the Latin *trionfi* or triumph. Each of those are named and numbered with Roman Numerals, starting with 0, The Fool, through to XXI, The World." Randi flipped a couple of cards face up onto the desk— X Wheel of Fortune and XVII The Star. "You can see there's a lot of detail symbolism in the illustrations, too much to go into at the moment, but something you'll want to pay attention to if you decide to get more interested in tarot."

I nodded again. The reverence in her tone, the way she almost caressed the cards, drew me in. It was as if she was reading me a beloved bedtime story, and the imagery on the cards only solidified the feeling.

Randi flipped four more cards, face up, onto the desk, one of each suit, Wands, Cups, Swords, and Pentacles. "Each suit consists of the same structure, similar to the decks of cards you'd play euchre or bridge with: ace through ten, plus four court cards, a page, knight, queen, and king."

"So the Wands, Cups, Swords, and Pentacles are a bit like Spades, Diamonds, Hearts, and Clubs."

"More than you could imagine. In fact, our modern deck of fifty-two cards is derived from tarot cards, and the four suits correspond directly with the suits in a tarot deck. Wands are Clubs, Cups are Hearts, Swords are Spades, and Pentacles are Diamonds. We can take it one step further by associating the suits with hair and eye color."

"In what way?"

"In tarot, Cups represent people with light brown hair and a fair complexion, Wands those having blonde or red hair and blue eyes, Swords with dark brown hair and hazel, gray, or blue eyes, and Pentacles very dark people."

"So in the case of tarot, I would be represented by Swords, because I have dark brown hair and hazel eyes. My mother, who was blonde, would be represented by Wands."

"That's right. But there's more. Both decks also represent the elements, in the same way astrology does. Thus, Wands and Clubs symbolize Fire. Cups and Hearts, Water. Swords and Spades, Air. Pentacles and Diamonds, Earth. Someone born under the sign of Taurus, for example, would be represented by Pentacles in tarot, and Diamonds in our modern deck."

Did she guess I was a Taurus, or did she just pull that out of thin air? This whole visit was starting to wig me out.

"It sounds a lot more complicated than I expected."

"Tarot takes years to learn, and it's certainly never mastered. There are no absolutes. However, I've been studying tarot for most of my adult life, so I like to think I have developed insight into the cards." She smiled. "Now, why don't we turn our attention to the cards that you brought with you?"

I stared at her in stunned silence. How did she know I'd brought cards with me?

Randi laughed, a tinkling sound that reminded me of wind chimes. "No, I'm not a mind reader, if that's what you're wondering. Elaine mentioned you wanted to bring something personal, and if it was an object, or a piece of jewelry, I don't think you'd ask about, or have much interest in, tarot. That, plus, you've been fidgeting with something in your handbag all this time."

Actually I'd been toying with the idea of pulling out my cocoa butter lip balm, but I was trying to break myself of the habit, or at least get it under control.

"I did bring some tarot cards."

"I gather they are special in some way."

It was decision-making time. Did I tell her about finding them, or not? I opted for the transparency. If I wanted Randi's help, I needed to tell her everything I knew. "I believe they were left by my mother. I found them in a house I recently inherited on Snapdragon Circle."

"Sixteen Snapdragon Circle?" Randi asked.

"Yes."

"I lived there for a short time."

"I know. Or at least I suspected that you were Jessica Tamarand."

I saw by her arched eyebrows that I had managed to pique her curiosity.

"Are you police, or some sort of private detective?"

Odd that she would leap to that conclusion. I wondered why.

"No, it's just that I was going through my father's old papers, which included past rental agreements. He died recently and left me the house."

"I'm sorry to hear about your father. I only met him once, but he struck me as a very nice man, kindhearted and intelligent, but definitely conflicted over something. Likely the loss of your mother."

"You know about my mother's disappearance?"

Randi nodded. "My family moved here from India in 1986, when I was twelve years old. There was a lot of local coverage and at the time, my parents were horrified that something of that nature could happen here. They worried they had made a mistake, coming to Marketville."

I could only assume that Randi had heard all of the rumors, including the one where my mother might have been murdered. It was time to cut to the chase.

"As I was saying, I was going through my father's old papers and I came upon an old lease signed by a Jessica Tamarand. I noticed the lease had been terminated early, and that, along with some neighborly gossip about a tarot card reader who once lived there and worked here, led me to the conclusion you might have transformed yourself into Randi."

"Let me guess," Randi said, smiling. "The neighbor was none other than Ella Cole." I returned the smile and stifled a giggle.

"I can only imagine what Ella said about me. I'm afraid I bruised both her feelings and her ego rather badly when I didn't invite her in the first time she came over. I gather all the other tenants had done so. I'm afraid I don't much care for busybodies, and besides, the house had a bad aura, which only seemed to intensify when she was on the property. It was only after I moved into the house that I realized it was the same house where the woman had…disappeared."

I decided to let the commentary about Ella drop, but the bad aura bit had me a bit concerned. Randi picked up on it.

"Oh, not for you, Callie; the spirits in the house are there to protect you, not harm you. You are meant to be there, and you and only you were meant to find the envelope containing these cards, this message. Otherwise, why had nobody found them before?"

"Probably because they had been hidden under the carpet for many years. Since 1986, in fact, or possibly earlier."

"That only validates what I believe to be true," Randi said. "The carpet could have been replaced at any time. In reality, it probably should have been long ago, and yet it was not. Furthermore, it was one of the first things you did upon moving in. These are not coincidences. These are powerful forces at work."

I wasn't sure I bought into the theory, but it didn't seem polite or prudent to tell her so. "Would you like to see the cards?"

"I would."

"There are only five of them." I pulled out the paper with my mother's backward slant handwriting and handed it over, along with the five cards.

"Possibly left as a five card spread," Randi said. "It's

helpful that your mother made this list. Reading them out of order would bring an entirely different interpretation."

"Can you tell me what they mean?"

"I will tell you what I read in the cards, but whether this is the message your mother hoped to convey, that I cannot promise. Fair enough?"

I'd hoped for something a little more conclusive, but there wasn't much I could do about it. "Fair enough. Would you mind if I wrote down everything as you go? I brought a notebook."

Randi paused to consider. Clearly, this wasn't a typical request. After what seemed like an eternity, she nodded. "Normally I'd say no, simply because each time you come for a reading, the cards will change, just as our lives change and we continue to evolve. This situation is different, so I'll allow it. There will be a lot for you to remember, and besides, memory can be selective." I pulled a pen and a black Moleskin notebook from my purse.

"Let's start."

SIXTEEN

RANDI LAID THE cards out in the order of the list my mother had left for me. "There are hundreds of tarot spreads," she said, "but let's assume that your mother used this particular five-card spread to read the cards. I personally find it to be a very useful spread when trying to decide a given course of action. Card one represents the present. Card two, the past, or past influences that still have effect. Card three represents the future. The fourth card reveals possible reasons or factors behind any decisions. Card five shows the possible results from taking a given course of action." I wrote everything down in my notebook as follows:

- III: The Empress—The present
- IV: The Emperor—The past
- VI: The Lovers—The future
- The Three of Swords—The reason
- XIII: Death—Possible results

"So what does it mean?" I asked after I'd made my final notation.

Randi caressed the cards gently, then closed her eyes and began to hum. After a minute or so, she reopened her eyes and shook her head. "I could be wrong, Callie, but while these cards may represent the five card spread I mentioned, it's just too pat."

"I don't understand. What are you trying to say?"

"I think it's possible that these cards were given to your mother, or perhaps mailed to her, probably one at a time, since she has listed them in order. If they had been sent all at once, it's unlikely that she would have paid attention to the order and written it down."

I pulled out my cocoa butter lip balm. "You're saying someone sent her these as individual messages, possibly with a death threat?"

"I can't say with any certainty, and I wouldn't want to suggest a death threat without other corroborating evidence. However, I believe someone with only the most basic knowledge of tarot sent them. The fourth card, for example, doesn't seem to fit as an obstacle, but it's more than that. The cards just seem too...structured. I think the sender was someone who took the visual images, and the names of the cards, literally." Randi leaned over the cards, closed her eyes again for a brief moment, then nodded, as if answering some voice in her head.

"Yes, that's definitely the communication I'm receiving."

I resisted the temptation to roll my eyes. It was one thing to listen to some rigmarole about tarot cards, but subliminal messages from outer space were an entirely different matter.

Subliminal message aside, what if Randi was onto something? What if someone—possibly Reid, the giver of the locket—had sent or given my mother the cards? What did it all mean? Would it provide a clue to my mother's disappearance? I was mulling everything over when Randi spoke again.

"Shall we look at the cards in that way, Callie? As if someone sent them as a message?"

I looked at Randi, so soft-spoken, ethereal, sincere. "Why not?"

Randi started with The Empress. "The woman depicted in the card has flowing blonde hair. Do you know if your mother had long blonde hair?"

I thought of the four seasons photographs. "Yes, she did."

"Okay. Notice how she is wearing a crown with twelve stars. This is meant to represent the twelve signs of the zodiac, making the Empress the Queen of Heaven. In other words, she is much revered."

"The gown she's wearing, it's very loose," I said. "Is the Empress pregnant?"

Randi smiled warmly. "How very astute of you, Callie. This is subject to individual interpretation. Some people believe the Empress merely represents motherhood, while others believe she is with child. So in this case, either may be true. Was your mother pregnant when she left?"

My head flipped back so quickly I almost got whiplash. Pregnant? Did I have a sibling out there? "My father never mentioned it, and since no one has found a body, alive or otherwise, I don't see any way of finding out."

"Fair enough. Let's look at the second card, the one representing the past. The Emperor."

I took in the long, white beard and stern facial expression of a man sitting on a throne. He wore a crown and a flowing red robe. "He looks old and very…authoritative."

"Yes, it's easy to see him as someone who rules with an iron fist. It's possible the Emperor may signify a person's actual father. What was your mother's relationship like with her father, your grandfather?"

"I've never met him, so that tells you something. My understanding is that her parents disowned her when she was pregnant with me. She was seventeen." I thought about it. "Perhaps the first card signifies her pregnancy with me."

"That's certainly one possibility."

In other words, so was the possibility my mother had been pregnant when she left. "Tell me about the third card, The Lovers."

"In the Rider deck, the couple depicted is Adam and Eve standing before the tree of life and the tree of knowledge. They are not the fallen lovers we have learned about from the bible, but rather as a model of an ideal relationship." Randi pointed to the angel hovering above them. "Here the archangel Raphael unites and blesses them."

"Do you believe these lovers are my mother and father?"

Randi shook her head. "I don't. Your parents were already lovers. If I'm correct in my assumption that these cards are meant to depict the traditional five-card spread, then this card represents the future, and whoever sent the cards was Adam to your mother's Eve."

I looked at the darkness of the next card, the Three of Swords. It depicted a red heart with three steel blue swords driven through it, storm clouds overhead, rain in the background. "It looks like the lovers didn't have a happy ending."

"I find it interesting that this is also the only card from the Minor Arcana, if only because it serves to illustrate that whoever sent the cards went through the entire deck of seventy-eight with some thoroughness to select just five."

Randi's long fingers traced the swords. "In tarot, this card represents sorrow, deep sadness, and heartache. What interests me the most are the three swords.

As if the unhappiness is shared, not just by the sender and your mother, but by a third party."

"My father?"

Randi shrugged. "Perhaps yes, perhaps no. That is certainly a good guess."

It was time to address the final card, which depicted a cloaked skeleton riding a white stallion; a dead king lay beneath the horse, as if trampled. "What about the Death card?"

"The one card everyone who has a tarot reading fears, although not always with good reason. The card itself is filled with symbolism. The dead king signifies he who resists change. The bishop in the right hand bottom corner symbolizes facing death without fear. Beside him, a young woman looks away, as if suddenly aware of her own mortality, while a small child looks up, holding a flower, innocent and free from fear. There's a shining sun in center right, beyond stone gates. On the left we have a small Egyptian boat on the river. The Egyptians believed death was a transition from one state to another."

"So there are many meanings?"

"Hmm. No, not many meanings. The Death card does represent the end of something, possibly even physical death. The imagery allows us to view the same circumstance in different ways." Randi gave me a sympathetic smile. "I know you came here for answers, Callie. I don't have them."

"You told me a lot more than I expected."

"That was easy," Randi said, laughing. "You expected nothing."

I grinned. I had to admit that she had me there. "Well, thank you anyway, for your time and your expertise. I suppose my next step is to find out who sent the cards, though I don't have any idea how I'm going to be able to do that."

Randi turned serious, her eyes filled with concern. "You have a long journey ahead of you, and you won't be able to make it alone. Along the way there will be people you can trust, and those you can't. Sometimes it's difficult to tell the difference. Sometimes people we initially don't like become our best allies. Sometimes our best allies turn out to be enemies."

I thought about the people I'd met so far. Misty Rivers. Ella Cole. Royce Ashford. I knew that I didn't like or trust Misty. Ella was a gossip, but there was something about her that I found endearing. Besides, surely she would be helpful if handled with caution. As much as I hated to admit it, I really wanted to be able to trust Royce. But could I?

I looked into Randi's lapis lazuli eyes, bit my bottom lip, and nodded. "I'll be careful." Randi didn't look convinced. "May I recommend something?" I nodded.

"The store sells smudge sticks made of dried white sage. I recommend you purchase one and smudge Sixteen Snapdragon Circle to cleanse the house of any negativity. It will go a long way to protecting you while you live there."

I thought about the coffin and the skeleton in the attic. Cleansing the house of any negativity sounded like a fine idea, though I wasn't convinced something called a smudge stick was the answer. "I've never heard of a smudge stick before."

"Smudging is a First Nations tradition. I always recommend a candle flame to light the smudge stick, since it may take a little time to get the stick smoking. Once the stick is alight with flame, blow it out so that the smudge stick is smoldering, not burning. Then you will go throughout the house, room by room, waving the smudge stick and chanting something along the lines of, 'I am removing all negative energy and replacing it with positive energy.' Be sure to hold the smudge stick over a fireproof container to keep the ashes from falling on the floor. Most importantly, smudging must be done with care and the utmost reverence. Consider your intention carefully before you smudge and hold it clearly in your mind while you perform the ritual. When you are finished, bury the smudge stick on the property."

I left Randi with a promise to smudge Sixteen Snapdragon Circle, made my way down to Sun, Moon & Stars, and handed the breathy-voiced clerk ten dollars for what looked to be nothing more than a bunch of twigs wrapped in twine.

Skeletons and coffins. Tarot cards and twigs. Seriously, Dad, whatever did you get me into?

SEVENTEEN

THE SMUDGING RITUAL took about thirty minutes and left the house with a faint odor reminiscent of marijuana. Not that I'd ever been into pot, outside of a couple of tries in high school, but the sweet smell, that I remembered. I opened all the windows to air the place out, knowing Royce would be over within the hour for our shopping trip. I didn't want him to get the wrong impression, and I wasn't sure I wanted to explain smudging.

As always, he was prompt, ringing my doorbell at two o'clock Wednesday afternoon. He'd even managed to arrange for the roofing company to come on Friday.

The excursion dissipated any lingering doubts I might have had about him. Wherever we went, everyone seemed to know and like him. Our last stop was a big box retailer with an extensive selection of kitchen and bathroom cabinets and countertops, including several custom options. It was clear the women who came to help us had a major league crush on him. He seemed oblivious to it all, which made me ratchet up my "don't fall for this guy" armor all the more. The last thing either of us needed was a fling gone sour with the next-door neighbor.

Even so, I couldn't help but get a warm feeling in my stomach when Royce put his hand on my shoulder as he led me to a display of cabinets. He still had his hand on my shoulder when an attractive woman with shoulder length blonde hair, highlighted to perfection, sashayed toward us in black stilettos. At first glance, she appeared to be in her early thirties, though closer inspection suggested a well-maintained decade older. Judging by her killer body, artfully squeezed into curve hugging jeans and a cleavage-revealing gray sweater that brought out the dusky charcoal of her eyes, she worked out hard and often. I knew I was being catty, but I couldn't help but wonder on what or whom.

"Why, Royce Ashford, fancy meeting you here," she said, her voice sweet as maple syrup. "And whom do we have here? A new girlfriend you've been keeping a secret?"

"Chantelle," Royce said, his tone neutral. "This here is Callie Barnstable, Jim's daughter. She's moved into Sixteen Snapdragon Circle." Royce turned to face me. "Callie, meet Chantelle Marchand-Thomas. Chantelle lives across the street, at number eleven."

"Just Marchand now, Royce, remember?" Chantelle said, tapping him playfully on the chest. I could imagine her nails scratching the surface of his bare chest, trying to raise droplets of blood.

"Sorry. I forgot," Royce said.

"I dropped the Thomas when my husband walked out," Chantelle said, looking at me. "No point reminding myself of Lance the loser every day going forward." She proceeded to size me up from top to bottom, as if conducting some sort of random test. I wasn't sure if I passed or failed, but she finally summoned up a saccharine smile. "It's so nice to meet you, Callie, although I'm sure the circumstances could have been better. I understand your father recently passed, some sort of tragic accident. I gather he was some sort of…laborer."

"He was a sheet metal worker. It's a skilled trade."

"I'm sure it is, Callie," Chantelle said, her tone condescending. "By the way, on the subject of skilled trades, I see you've already put our neighborhood handyman to work. I do hope you don't monopolize all of his time. We single women need to learn to share." She gave me another swift up and down glance. "At least, I'm assuming you're single."

"Guilty as charged, and no worries from my end, Chantelle. I wouldn't dream of taking advantage of Royce's good nature just because I'm single." I favored her with a saccharine smile of my own. "I always find women who play that helpless card a bit sad, don't you? There's something about being needy that just screams pathetic."

Chantelle turned an unbecoming shade of crimson, looked at her cell phone as if it were a lifeline, then murmured something about an important appointment.

"I think the ice princess may have met her match," Royce said with a grin as we watched her strut down the aisle and out of sight.

"I probably should have been nicer to her. After all, she lives across the street from me—and she said her husband just walked out on her. That can't have been easy."

"Lance left a year ago. From what he told me, they'd been having problems for a couple of years. Besides, she goaded you. You know it, I know it, and Chantelle knows it."

"Maybe so, but she also has a thing for you."

Royce burst out laughing. "Me and Chantelle? I'll admit that she's lovely to look at, but I'd rather take my chances swimming with sharks. Besides, I don't go for the high maintenance type, and according to Lance,

Chantelle is decidedly high maintenance. Not to mention that Lance is my friend. He may have left Chantelle, but I don't think he'd be too keen on me dating her." I could see his point.

THE REST OF the shopping was quick and uneventful, at least from a meeting nasty neighbors perspective. We did, however, manage to custom-order cabinets and an island—complete with a cooktop, sink, and built-in wine refrigerator—as well as granite countertops.

I'll admit to wincing more than a little when the cashier rang up my deposit and I had to hand over my credit card. Even with Royce's contractor's discount, the overall total stung.

We loaded up his pickup with the non-custom items—sink, drawer pulls and the like—and drove back to Snapdragon Circle. We were just about to pull into the driveway when Royce threw a curve ball. I should have been expecting it, but I'd managed to put it out of my mind.

"My folks have invited us to their place in Muskoka next weekend. Are you up for it? There's plenty of space. You'd get your own room and everything. When I told my mom about the photographs, she said she simply had to meet you. We can drive up Saturday morning, head back on Sunday morning before the crazy traffic starts up. Reminisce, swim, take a tour of the area by boat. You'll be amazed at the opulence of some of the properties up there. Places owned by celebrities and professional athletes and corporate bigwigs. Some of those summer homes, the taxes alone would bankrupt me."

A weekend away sounded like fun, and being with Royce had definite appeal. Was I up for what I might learn? I wasn't sure, but I knew that I needed to find out.

"Sure, I guess. I mean, yes, it sounds great."

Royce leaned over and undid my seatbelt. Then he pushed a strand of my ever-escaping hair back behind my ears. "It will be okay, Callie. You need to find out the truth, right? Or at least try to."

That was the moment I realized Royce had heard the same rumors as everyone else. That he knew, or at least suspected, the real reason I was here. I wanted to call him on it, ask him why he didn't say something earlier. What his game was, if he even had a game.

Then I looked into those warm brown eyes, so solemn, so sincere—and silently cursed. My "don't fall for this guy" armor was fading fast.

And there wasn't a damn thing I could do about it.

EIGHTEEN

I ARRIVED HOME to find an email reply from Leith saying that he'd sent me the safety deposit authorization by courier. It arrived late in the day, allowing me to get everything organized for the next morning. I found myself almost too excited to sleep. What would I find in that safety deposit box?

But sleep I did, a dream-filled night of tarot cards and sweet sage twigs. When the alarm rang at seven a.m., I was more than ready to get up and get back to reality. I glanced outside to see a hard, driving rain, the kind an old friend from Portsmouth, New Hampshire, had called "a Canadian car wash" because of its intensity, not the sort of fine, misty rains I imagined you'd get in Seattle or San Francisco. When we got rain, we got rain. Unrepentant torrents of it.

I sighed. Any taming of my already unruly curly brown hair would be futile. Even safely secured in a ponytail or braid was no guarantee of compliance. I don't care how much people with straight hair complain about not being able to hold a curl; they had no idea how lucky they were. Straight and flat always beat fuzzy and frizzy. I was just about to head out to the bank when the doorbell chimed its sing-songy tune. I glanced out my new peephole to see Chantelle standing there underneath a black and white polka dot umbrella. I opened the door, curious to find out what impulse could have brought her here.

"Chantelle, this is a surprise. Come on in before you drown."

She ventured into the hallway, careful to shake out her umbrella before doing so. I noticed she'd swapped the stilettos for a pair of sneakers, and the tight-fitting sweater and jeans for black yoga pants and a matching hoodie. She pulled the hood off her head and shook out a cascade of carefully highlighted blonde hair, combing it with her fingers. I was forced to admit that even in yoga wear, and without a scrap of makeup, she was stunning. She also had straight hair. I tried not to hate her.

"I came over to apologize for being such a pill at the store." She gave a rueful smile and an apologetic shrug. "I'm afraid I haven't been doing newly divorced very well. It seems to have brought out the bitch in me. I also admit to having a sophomoric crush on Royce. Not that he's shown the slightest bit of interest in me, despite my rather clumsy attempts to get his attention. So when I saw him with you, his hand on your shoulder, looking all chummy, well, something in me just snapped. Not my finest moment."

I had to admire her honesty, and heaven knows it would be nice to have a female friend that was closer to my own age than Ella Cole. Besides, you never knew what she might or might not know that could potentially help me. Maybe Chantelle was also a local.

"It wasn't my finest moment either. I say we accept one another's apologies and start over."

"I'd like that." She extended her hand. "Chantelle Marchand, your across the street neighbor."

I took her hand and shook it lightly. "Callie Barnstable. New homeowner. I was just on my way to the bank, but that can wait. Come on in. I can make you something hot to drink." I didn't bother offering cookies. By the looks of her figure, Chantelle didn't eat them. If she did eat them and still managed to keep that figure, I didn't want to know about it.

"Are you sure? Do you have an appointment? Because I can take a rain check." She chuckled. "No pun intended."

"No appointment. I was just going to check out my dad's safety deposit box."

Chantelle followed me into the kitchen and pulled up a seat while I put on the kettle. "A safety deposit box. Do you have any idea what's in there?" She blushed. "I'm sorry, that was incredibly nosy of me. Forget I asked."

"Really, it's fine. In answer to your question, I have no idea. I guess I'll find out."

"You must be dying of curiosity. I know I would be."

I laughed. "Yeah, I kind of am, but I still have time for a cup of tea or coffee with a neighbor."

"I'd love a cup of tea."

"Earl Grey, Black, Green, or Vanilla Rooibos?"

"Green."

I nodded and set about making the tea.

"I gather you're planning on doing some renovations," Chantelle said as I poured the tea into oversized mugs.

"I've hired Royce's company to do the kitchen renovation. He's going to take down this wall and open up the space. It will be messy, but I think it will pay dividends if I decide to sell in a year's time. Heaven knows I couldn't have sold it for a decent price the way it was. I've already managed to strip out the ugly carpet."

Chantelle raised her eyebrows. "You're thinking of selling?"

"I might. I'm not sure yet. That's why I'm giving it a year." Not technically true, but true enough. "There's just so much to do. I was planning to buy paint for the bedrooms after the bank. If I break it down into chewable chunks, it's not quite so overwhelming."

"Do you want help?"

"Help buying paint?"

"Sure, if you want, but I meant help painting. Since Lance moved out I find myself with too much time on my hands and nothing to fill it with. I'm a pretty good painter, if I do say so myself." She grinned. "I'm also very good at spending other people's money if you want help buying furniture or anything else, come to that. Lance can attest to my shopping prowess." The grin turned to a frown. "Seriously, I know Royce thinks I'm high maintenance, but I'm not. Not really. I grew up as the fifth kid in a six-kid family. My clothes were a mix of stuff from my older brother and three older sisters, which was good news for my younger sister. By the time I was through with the clothes, they had pretty much reached their life expectancy. So she got all new stuff, from toys to tank tops."

"I'm an only child, so I can't begin to imagine living in a house with eight people, let alone wearing hand-me-downs. Not that my father was up-to-the-minute on the latest fashions, and shopping for clothes was way down the list of his priorities. I'm afraid he transferred that lack of enthusiasm to me. I can understand, though, how you'd want your own things."

"Oh yeah. My main goal growing up was to own clothes that nobody else had ever worn, read books that nobody else had ever read, and sleep on a mattress that nobody else had ever slept in. I don't think that makes me high maintenance. Besides, I'm a phenomenal bargain shopper. I have to be, especially since divorcing Lance. I wanted to stay in the house, and that meant buying him out." Chantelle laughed. "Listen to me, telling you my life story, when all I wanted to do is offer to help you paint."

I wondered if Chantelle worked. I also wondered if there was a catch, and chided myself on being a cynic. Why not embrace her kindness instead of assuming she had an ulterior motive? I remembered what Randi had said. Sometimes people we initially don't like become our best allies. Sometimes our best allies turn out to be enemies. Maybe Chantelle would become an ally.

"I've only ever rented, and the painting was done by the landlord. I could use someone to show me the way. If you're absolutely sure you don't mind, I'm not about to turn you down."

"Are you kidding? You'd be doing me a favor. My genealogy work is flexible. We'll just have to work around my schedule at the gym." She must have caught my look, because she tilted her head back and giggled like a schoolgirl. "No, I'm not a gym rat. I teach classes—yoga, Pilates, weight pump, and spinning—but the hours are scattered, depending on the day. I usually have some mornings, some afternoons, even the occasional weekend shift if someone needs a sub."

That would explain her killer body. "I've been thinking of joining a gym. I belonged to one in Toronto, and I'm already missing it. It would also be a way to meet new people."

"I'll arrange for you to get a free monthly pass. If you decide to join, I can also get you a bit of a discount. Also, if you're planning on buying any furniture, I can drive. I got Lance's pickup truck as part of our separation agreement." Chantelle gave a sad smile. "It was harder for him to part with the damn truck than it was to walk out on our ten-year marriage."

IT WASN'T UNTIL after Chantelle left that I realized she'd said something about genealogy work. Perhaps she could help me trace my grandparents. I still hadn't done anything about contacting an information broker. Maybe now I wouldn't have to. I'd have to trust Chantelle, of course, but then I'd have to trust anyone I hired. I also found myself ridiculously pleased at the possibility of making a female friend. It had been a long time since I'd been close with anyone; a few co-workers to go to the theater or movies with, but no one I felt the desire to confide in. When it came to true confessions, I was more about getting them than giving them.

I made my way to the bank, thankful it had finally stopped raining, and grateful for the GPS in my car. I was the kind of person who could get lost after three spins in their backyard, and so far, I hadn't completely gotten a handle on Marketville. Small as it was in comparison to Toronto, at least Toronto bordered on Lake Ontario to the south. Then there was the CN Tower, also to the south, and which, at 1,815 feet, was visible from a fair distance if you were in most parts of the city proper. The landmark wasn't a guarantee I'd find my way around, but it did act as a bit of a compass. Not that a compass would do me much good. Don't tell me north and south. Tell me left at the mall, right at the convenience store just past the bridge, and left into the strip mall with the Chinese take-out. Which, as it turned out, was pretty much the way to the bank.

The lineup at the bank was about ten deep, despite the presence of four ATMs outside of the main lobby. I took my place in line behind a rain-sogged construction worker staring down at his mud encrusted work boots and looked around. It was pretty much like any other bank in any other town or city. A row of teller's cages, an information desk, some visitor chairs, a few glass-walled offices for managers, loan officers, and the like.

An annoying plus-sized woman in gold leggings and a leopard print tunic was having a loud and animated conversation with someone on the other end of her phone. She didn't hang up, even when a teller became available. I wondered if the woman knew how rude she was being, and realized that even if she did, she probably wouldn't care. She was still chattering away when she left, something about a backyard barbecue and an inconsiderate sister-in-law. I grinned at the irony of it and sidled up to take her spot at the teller's cue.

The teller, a twenty-something guy with dark wavy hair, dimples, and thick-rimmed glasses, reviewed my paperwork carefully then said he'd have to check with a manager. I could feel the stares of the people in line, wondering how long it would take. I empathized. I read once that we spend one-third of our lives sleeping. I was starting to think the same thing held true of line-ups. I turned around to give them an apologetic smile and couldn't believe it when I saw Misty Rivers at the end of the line. Coincidence? Maybe. Or maybe she followed me. But for what purpose? I nodded in her general direction. She nodded back, but didn't say anything. I was probably being paranoid.

After what seemed like forever but was probably all of a couple of minutes, the teller came back and escorted me to a secure area behind a steel door, where I was faced with several rows of safety deposit boxes. The teller used his key then told me my key would open the box.

"Ring the bell when you're done and I'll come and get you," he said.

I nodded and opened the box with trembling hands.

NINETEEN

IF I THOUGHT the contents of the safety deposit box would answer all of my questions, I was sadly mistaken. There were a few old coins, possibly of some value, and a couple hundred dollars in U.S. cash, a mix of fives, tens, and twenties.

There was also an envelope. I recognized my father's spidery handwriting scrawled in black ink across the front. "To be opened by Calamity Doris Barnstable in the event of my death." Seeing those words felt like a punch to the gut, because it meant my dad knew he might die. The man I knew—or thought I knew—hadn't given me the slightest indication he was worried.

I thought about taking the letter back to Sixteen Snapdragon Circle, but I'd waited so long already. Waiting another thirty minutes just didn't seem like an option. I tore the envelope open.

The letter was dated a month before my father's death. I stared for a minute at the familiar scrawl and forced back the tears that were threatening to fall. Then I started reading.

Dear Calamity,
Yes, I know you hate being called Calamity, but I figure if I'm dead, you'll give me a pass. If you're reading this, then I suppose I am. I'm also hoping that you'll forgive me for the Marketville codicil in the will.

Of course, I knew there was a chance you'd just wait out the year and let Misty Rivers take over the investigation, and maybe that's what I should have insisted on, especially if I wanted to protect you from any possible hurt or harm. The thing is, I've been trying to protect you from knowing the truth for so many years. I was wrong. You had a right to know, maybe not when you were six, but certainly when you were old enough to understand. Instead, I allowed the years to go by, never talking about your mother. That was as unfair to her memory as it was to you.

Here's what I know: Your mother loved you. She also loved me, although I admit we had our share of ups and downs. What marriage doesn't? Especially with two people who were nothing more than children themselves when they brought you into the world. I do not believe, however, and never have, that your mother left us voluntarily. Something, or someone, forced her to go. For many years, I thought she'd come back. It's the reason I kept the house at 16 Snapdragon Circle. How else would she find us, if not for that house? This was a time well before social media and the internet.

The years ticked by, and after a while even I started to give up hope. Leith Hampton, old, dear friend that he is for all his pompous ways and multiple marriages, begged me to give up the search years before, after a private investigator, someone I paid a great deal of money to, found out nothing. For a long time, I heeded that advice. After all, the investigator had come highly recommended by an old friend, a man I trusted implicitly.

Things changed when Misty Rivers rented the house. She told me the house was not haunted, but possessed by your mother's spirit. I know it sounds farfetched, but another renter had insinuated much the same thing.

Misty was convinced your mother had been murdered, and she wanted to help me seek out the truth. I'll admit I was skeptical at first. I'm not a believer in spirits or psychics, but I've never been able to reconcile your mother's disappearance. I decided to put my trust in her.

We had barely scratched the surface when I was almost killed on my lunch break. The job was a new condo development with more than a few complications, and construction was well behind schedule. In an effort to save time, each day one of the workers would take everyone's order and phone it in to a local restaurant and then pick up the food. That day happened to be my day. I was crossing Yonge Street to get to the sub shop when one of our construction company's vans ran the red light. If it hadn't been for another pedestrian, an elderly man who managed to pull me back with his cane at the last possible second, I would never have had the opportunity to write this letter.

About a week later, another incident occurred, this time as I was leaving the job site. I'd already taken off my hard hat and was just outside the building when a rivet gun fell from thirty floors up, missing my head by less than an inch. If that rivet gun had connected, death would have been instantaneous.

I stopped reading at that point and closed my eyes. Two near misses close to his work. Followed by an unfortunate occupational accident. Was it merely coincidence, evidence of a job site with substandard safety procedures, or was it deliberate?

I was just about to start reading again when the teller came back in to make sure everything was fine. I assured him it was and told him I was ready to leave. I closed the safety deposit box, leaving the coins and cash, folded the letter back into its envelope, and tucked it inside my purse. It was time to go home. And by home I meant Snapdragon Circle.

I MADE A cup of Earl Grey and sat down at the bistro table ready to read on. After a quick scan, I picked up where I left off.

I wish I had more information to share with you. What I can tell you is that the two incidents happened after I'd made the decision to move back to Marketville and look into your mother's disappearance. Misty came up with a plan to hold a séance. I was reluctant at first, but she can be very persuasive. At any rate, I bought a papier-mâché coffin at a theater supply store and ordered a skeleton from a medical supply catalogue.

Misty suggested including some photographs of our family so I took four, which were taken the previous year, and placed them under the pillow. Writing it down makes me realize just how ridiculous it sounds, but I was at the point where I was willing to try just about anything. I even imagined inviting suspects over to the house during the séance and watching their faces. Of course, first I needed to find the suspects.

That explained the skeleton in the attic. I wondered when he was planning to tell me. The next sentence answered my question.

I was planning to tell you once I'd moved. I wasn't entirely sure of how you'd react, and to be honest, I didn't know how to tell you my reasons for doing so. I only hope you haven't been to the attic yet. I can't imagine what you'd think if you found the coffin up there without this explanation. I told very few people about my plans for moving back to Marketville. Leith knew, of course, and Misty Rivers. The next-door neighbors Ella Cole and Royce Ashford. I can't imagine any of them attempting to harm me.

I did find the time to visit the Marketville Library to view the newspaper clippings from the time of your mother's disappearance. Their records are patchy at best, but they did refer me to the Regional Reference Library, which apparently has a far more extensive archive. At the time of this writing, I have not made it there.

Should you decide to do so, I'm going to warn you that you're going to read things about me that you won't want to know. While I was never held in custody, everyone in town, the officer in charge included, seemed to suspect me of wrongdoing, believing that I killed your mother and hid the body. I cooperated with the police, but I also made the decision to move us to Toronto for a fresh start. I didn't want you to have to spend your childhood dodging rumors.

For all I know, I'm still a suspect. Certainly the case has never been solved. But believe me,

Calamity, when I say that I did not do anything
to harm your mother. I only ever wanted to find
out where she went, and why. It is my belief that
if you find out who wanted me dead, you will also
find out what happened to my beloved Abigail. I
know it's a risk, and I beg you to be careful, but
I also hope you find out the truth. Perhaps then,
your mother's spirit will be set free.

 With all my love,
 Dad

I reread the letter twice more. Then I poured myself
a large glass of white wine and ordered a cheese pizza
with hot peppers and extra tomato sauce. It was time
for comfort food and a plan.

I PULLED ONE of the bistro chairs onto the front porch and
was sitting there, munching on pizza and sipping wine,
when Chantelle dropped by on her way home from work
at the gym. I had been so wigged out by the letter that I
never did get the paint. I had, in fact, forgotten all about
it, and told her so. I was somewhat embarrassed by the
admission. After all, she'd volunteered to help me paint
and I couldn't even manage to get the supplies.

 Chantelle waved off my apology and asked me if anything was wrong. I suppose my sitting outside drinking
wine and eating pizza was a signal. Or maybe it was the
stunned look on my sauce-smeared face.

 "Nothing wrong. I just received a letter and the contents were a bit upsetting." I found my manners. "Can I
get you a glass of wine? I probably shouldn't be outside
drinking alone. Ella Cole will have a field day."

 "If she's talking about you, she's leaving the rest of
us alone," Chantelle said, laughing. "But, sure, I'd love

a glass of wine and a slice of pizza if you're offering.
I just did three one-hour workouts and I could eat the
arm off a bear. Are those hot peppers I see?"

I nodded. "Plus extra sauce. Messy, but good."

Chantelle followed me inside and brought out the
second bistro chair while I poured the wine and put a
slice of pizza on a plate. Then we made our way back
out to the porch.

"This front porch is the nicest thing about this
house," I said, not quite sure what else to say. "I should
get a couple of wicker chairs or something, make it look
more inviting."

"That's a good idea. But the rest of the house will be
just as nice or nicer once you get at it."

"I'm sorry, again, about not getting the paint. I'll try
to go tomorrow." Then I thought about going to the Regional Reference Library. "Or maybe Saturday."

"If you can wait until Sunday, I can go with you. It's
my day off. We can pick out paint. Maybe even get a
couple of wicker chairs. I told you, I love to shop. I've
also got a good eye for décor. What color is your bedspread?"

"I could actually use a new one. The one I have is
as old as the hills. And I'd love to take you up on your
offer of helping me shop. It's not one of my strong suits."

"Perfect. How's eleven o'clock? We can do some
shopping, maybe even grab an early dinner if you have
the time."

Not cooking Sunday dinner for one sounded good
to me. "You're on."

I wondered if Chantelle would ask me about the letter, but she didn't. I found myself oddly disappointed;
I really needed a confidante.

Could I trust her?

"How long have you lived on Snapdragon?"

If the question seemed out of the blue, Chantelle didn't seem to notice.

"It will be ten years come October. Lance and I bought the house when we got married." She gave a rueful smile. "Happier times."

"Are you from around here originally?"

"Hell, no. Neither is Lance. We're both from Ottawa, but Lance got a job in Toronto, and we couldn't afford anything there. Even Marketville was barely in our price range. At first I hated it here, but I've grown to like it. I still miss Ottawa, but this is home now."

"Did you ever meet my dad?"

She shook her head. "I saw him come by a couple of times, but I never spoke to him. I think Royce knew him though. Why? What's with the twenty questions?"

"I'm sorry. I'm being insufferable."

"No, no you're not. It's just that I get the feeling I'm being interviewed for something." She studied me through narrowed eyes and then nodded. "This is about the letter, isn't it? You want to tell me about the letter, but you don't know whether or not you should trust me."

I didn't realize I'd been so transparent. Or maybe Chantelle was just really perceptive.

"I want to tell someone about the letter," I said. "I'm just not ready to do that yet."

"When you're ready to talk about it, I'll be ready to listen."

We sat in silence after that, sipping our wine and munching on pizza. I wanted to ask her about her genealogy work, but now didn't seem like the time to do that. After fifteen minutes of companionable silence,

Chantelle promised to return on Sunday and made her way across the street.

I heard a window close at the house next door.

Ella Cole had gotten an earful.

TWENTY

I WOKE UP to the sound of footsteps clomping around overhead. It only took me a minute to remember that Royce had arranged for the roof to be done that day, but I'll admit in that minute I was pretty much terrified. Once my heart stopped pounding, I got out of bed and got ready to face the day.

The first thing I did after breakfast and a quick chat with the roofers was to prepare my weekly report to Leith.

To: Leith Hampton
From: Callie Barnstable
Subject: Friday Report Number 2

Met two more neighbors, Ella Cole and Chantelle Marchand. Ella and her late husband, Eddie, were friends with my parents. Ella provided some history into my mother's disappearance, specifically that my mother had walked me to school the morning of February 14, 1986, and was never seen again. Ella believes the police suspected my father of foul play, but could find no evidence. I believe Ella may have more information, and will attempt to befriend her. Chantelle does not appear to have any connection to the past. Found a safety deposit key, as you know, and went to the bank. The safety deposit box held a few coins and some U.S. cash.

Finally, I tracked down the second tenant, Jessica Tamarand. Jessica is now Randi, a tarot card reader at Sun, Moon & Stars, a new-age shop in Marketville. I met with her on Tuesday. She recalls my mother's disappearance because her family had just moved into town, and it was big news. However, she was just a teenager and had no information to offer.

I was omitting some of the facts in my report to Leith, in this case the found tarot cards and the letter from my father, but I reasoned that both were private communications. I would share in due course, once I knew where all the pieces fit. Satisfied I'd given Leith enough to comply with the terms of the codicil, I hit Send and then logged off. It was time to go to the Regional Reference Library. I just hoped no one fell through the roof into the attic. I'd have a hard time explaining that coffin.

The library was south of Marketville. A sprawling, four-story building, the library served the whole of Cedar County. It boasted the largest collection of books, magazines, digital editions, and archives in the region. I signed up for a library card at registration then made my way to the information desk on the main floor, trying to keep my heels from clicking on the tiled floors. "Where might I find the newspaper archives?"

"From what year?" the information clerk asked.

"Nineteen eighty-six."

"That would be on the third floor. You'll have to ask Shirley to help you. She's head of Archives. I'm pretty sure those records are still on microfiche."

I had absolutely no idea what microfiche was, but I nodded anyway. I took the staircase, a winding af-

fair with glass walls and wrought iron railings. Along
the perimeter there were dozens of rows of magazines,
shelves upon shelves of books, and a bunch of black
metal filing cabinets. In the center of the room there
were several long tables with chairs. Some of the tables
held computers, many of the monitors large and out-of-
date. Two of the tables held something that looked like
an overhead projector. There were a couple of people
reading magazines, and another couple on computers,
but no one seemed interested in the projectors.

The librarian in charge sat behind a counter near the
back of the room. She was busy tapping away on her
computer when I approached her. She looked up and slid
a pair of black-framed reading glasses onto her forehead.
I assumed this was Shirley, Head of Archives.

"May I help you?"

"The woman at the information desk on the main
floor told me someone named Shirley could help me
access the *Marketville Post* newspaper archives. From
1986." I handed her my library card. She glanced at it
briefly, scanned it into a computer, and handed it back.

"I'm Shirley," she said, and pointed to a name plate
on the desk. "Those records will be on microfiche."

"I'm not sure what that is."

She grinned. "No, I suppose you'd be too young to
remember when microfiche was the next big thing. You
probably barely remember the fax machine, let alone
telex."

The bank still used faxes on occasion. But telex?
What the heck was a telex? I suppose the confused look
on my face confirmed her guess.

"Never mind," Shirley said with a smile. "It has nothing to do with your request. I'm just showing my age.
Basically, microfiche is a way of storing many docu-

ments in a small space. The film is an index-sized card, which you insert into a microfiche reader—those machines that look like an overhead projector. The reader blows up the image and displays it on screen. Obsolete technology now, of course, but it was quite innovative at the time."

"Is it difficult to use?" The machines looked like something out of the last century. Which, of course, they were.

"Not at all. We even have a printer if you want to print a copy, and there's a charge of ten cents a page, plus one dollar for the file folder to keep them in. Now, let's find the section you're looking for and I'll give you a quick lesson."

The microfiche storage for the 1980s took up several drawers in a black metal filing cabinet.

"They're all sorted by the date and name of the publication," Shirley said, pointing at the index labels. "Do you know the name of the publication? Or the exact date?"

I had decided to start with the *Marketville Post*, February 13, 1986, the day before my mother "disappeared." It was a long shot that there would be anything in there, but since the *Post* was only published on Thursdays, it couldn't hurt. Besides, maybe something in that paper had triggered whatever happened to my mother.

Shirley pulled the microfiche, duly indexed under name and date, and instructed me not to re-file the cards, noting that, "If they get out of order, it will be hopeless for the next person." I promised, although it amused me to think that I couldn't be trusted to file by name and date.

Once we had the rules sorted out, Shirley showed me how to use the reader. It was all pretty simple, though part of me empathized with whoever had taken on the tedious task of filming all the back issues. I'd been asked to scan and convert a series of articles on fraud into PDF format for the bank's newsletter, and it had been mind-numbingly boring.

A quick read through didn't offer any immediate clues, but it did provide a glimpse into a much smaller town than Marketville was today. There were want ads and obituaries, even some birthday greetings and wedding announcements, but mostly there were lots of photographs of local residents doing local things. Kids bundled in snowsuits tobogganing, their parents looking on with frozen smiles. Acne-ridden adolescents dancing at the Sadie Hawkins school dance, a couple of teachers acting as chaperones standing in the corner trying, somewhat unsuccessfully, not to look bored. A two-page spread on Marketville's Rep hockey team, complete with a play-by-play report of recent games.

I studied each and every photo, reading the names. None of them rang any bells. It did make me realize, however, that my mother's tree planting on Canada Day in 1984 would likely have been covered. Time to back-track. I put the February 13, 1986 fiche into the box supplied by the librarian, and went back to the files. My choices were June 28 or July 5. I went with July 5, since the tree planting would have been on July 1st.

I wasn't disappointed. There on the front page was a picture of my mother, her long, blonde hair tied back into a ponytail, a smear of dark earth on her smiling face. She was wearing gardening gloves, denim shorts, a red tee shirt sporting a white maple leaf inside a shovel, and hiking boots. The caption read: Local resident Abigail Barnstable leads the Marketville Canada Day tree planting initiative at Marketville P.S.

There was a brief story written by a G.G. Pietrangelo to go along with the photo, with a couple of quotes from my mother on the importance of volunteering and community. From what I could gather, there were similar tree planting ceremonies around the town, all organized by my mother. The article ended with *More photos on page 8*.

I started up the printer. As promised, page eight had a collage of photographs, also credited to G.G. Pietrangelo. Unfortunately none had captions. I made a note of the name, though I wasn't sure what I would ask or tell him or her, even if I was able to track them down all these years later. Then I studied the photos more closely. The images were grainy, the quality of the reproduction less than perfect, but I could still make out the faces. In a group photo of ten smiling volunteers, all wearing the same red maple leaf tee shirts, my father was standing in the front row, next to my mother. He looked relaxed and happy. They both did. But there was one other face that stared out at me. A man's face. A man with fair hair, serious brown eyes, and a chiseled chin tilted ever so slightly upwards. It was the man from the locket—Reid, according to its inscription—standing in the back row, and he was positioned directly behind my mother.

Once again I was struck by a feeling of familiarity. Had I met this man, and if so, when? Whether I had or not, it was obvious that my father also knew him. Could they have been friends?

Was the affair going on by Canada Day, 1984? Was Reid one of the "downs" in the "ups and downs" my father mentioned in his letter to me? Perhaps it was, and my mother had tried to end it. That could explain the photos taken in 1985 in front of the maple tree she had planted in 1984. My parents had been happy that day, I was sure of it.

The locket was dated January 14, 1986. Ella Cole had said my mother had been visibly upset on her birthday in December 1985. Maybe the affair had started back up. Or maybe Reid wouldn't let it go. I thought about the tarot cards. Randi believed they were meant to send a literal message. Could Reid have sent them? If not him, then who?

I massaged my temples. There were so many questions left unanswered, so many possibilities. I picked up my printed copies and put them in the file folder Shirley had provided. I removed the microfiche and put it in the bin. I knew I should go through the rest of 1984, all of 1985, and then onto 1986. The thought of doing it alone was daunting, not to mention time consuming. I sighed and went back to the file cabinet.

THE REST OF the 1984 issues of *Marketville Post* turned out to be a bust. I leaned back in my chair and attempted to unkink my neck and back. I'd been hunched over the microfiche viewer for the better part of the morning, and I was stiff, sore, and hungry. I needed a break before I could tackle 1985. I'd already decided that 1986 would wait until after I returned from the Ashfords' cottage. Reading about my father as a murder suspect needed fresh eyes and a strong stomach. I told Shirley I'd be back in an hour, paid for my copies and the file folder, and headed back down the winding staircase.

There was a small café on the main floor of the library that served muffins, cookies, bagels, and some pre-made tuna and egg salad sandwiches, as well as an assortment of teas and coffees. I ordered a large peppermint tea and a toasted sesame bagel with plain light cream cheese—I never trust those pre-made sandwiches—and took a seat at a small round table. I pulled out my cocoa butter lip balm and took comfort in the ritual.

I studied the newspaper article and photos while I ate my bagel and sipped on my tea. No one else looked remotely familiar. I contemplated asking Royce if he recognized anyone, but in 1984 he would have been eight years old. It was a long shot at best, and I'd have to admit to him that I'd been digging around old records. Wanting to find out more about my mother and doing serious research were two different things. I didn't want him to think I was obsessed with it, and I wasn't ready to tell him about the codicil.

I could also ask Ella Cole if she knew who any of the people were, though I hated to think what sort of gossip she'd spread if I did so. Maybe if I approached it as a quest to find out more about my past, versus trying to solve a mystery. I decided to give it some thought. Bagel done, I went back upstairs to the third floor, ready to tackle 1985.

FOR A WHILE 1985 wasn't looking any more promising than the latter half of 1984. It wasn't until I reached May 15 that I found another photograph of my mother. Once again, she'd made the front page, this time surrounded by tins of tomatoes. The article lauded her volunteering efforts, this time for spearheading the first local food bank.

"Hunger isn't limited to big cities like Toronto. In Marketville there are many families barely scraping by," she was quoted as saying. "Everyone can help by bringing a non-perishable food item to the town's Canada Day celebration on July 1st. Peanut butter, tinned fish, canned beans, vegetables and soup, baby formula, cereal, and juice in Tetra Paks are especially needed. Let's fill up our food bank shelves!"

I found myself tearing up. My mother might have had an affair. Truth be told, she probably had, but she was a good person.

She cared.

I went through the rest of the paper. Nothing else stood out. A few more weeks without anything of interest, until, finally the July fourth issue. This time the front page had a photograph of the Canada Day fireworks. The caption read:

Canada Day celebrations ended with fireworks at the Town Hall. The all-day event included face painting for kids, a food drive for the new Marketville Food Bank, and an artisan fair with farmer's market. More photos on pages 15 and 16.

I flipped through the next fourteen pages—nothing—and stopped at page 15/16, the paper's center spread. My mother was in one of the photos, surrounded by stacks of nonperishable food, my father by her side. There were no photos of Reid. Which didn't necessarily mean he wasn't there.

I printed off the page, took out the microfiche, and went back to the files. By the time I reached the December 12th issue, I was pretty much bleary-eyed, and my neck and back were begging for relief, but the reward was seeing my mother back on the front page, this time promoting a holiday food drive. Maybe it was my imagination, but she looked thinner in this shot, the smile strained. I scanned the article:

"I know there are many charities and good causes reaching into our pocketbooks at this time of year, not to mention our own families, but we're hoping that those who can afford it will drop off a non-perishable food item at the fire hall or at the food bank," said Abigail Barnstable. "We're heading into winter, a time when people tend to hunker down indoors. Let's try and stock our shelves!"

Although my mother was in the foreground, there were four other volunteers in the photograph. A man with a close-cropped beard, a small crescent-shaped scar above his left eyebrow, and two women, one mousy brown and curvy, one red-haired and lean. The curvy one looked vaguely familiar. Then there was Reid. Definitely Reid.

I tried to place the curvy woman. There was something in the way she held herself, but it was more than that. It was the eyes, jet black and shrewd.

Then I had it. She was thirty-plus years younger, and at least that many pounds lighter. Her mousy brown hair was in a permed eighties Afro instead of a fluffy platinum blonde. But without a doubt, the woman was Misty Rivers.

The realization that Misty knew my mother, but hadn't shared that information with my father, brought about more questions than answers. What did Misty Rivers really know? Why had she rented the house on Snapdragon Circle—and was Leith aware of her past connection? Was she hoping to find out the truth? Or was she trying to stop it from ever seeing the light of day?

Randi had warned me to be careful. I had a feeling that went double when it came to Misty Rivers.

TWENTY-ONE

I DECIDED TO finish all of my microfiche research before contacting Misty. It was possible that I might discover some additional information to prepare me for that inevitability. It meant going over the records from March 1979—the month and year my parents moved into town—until December 1986. My father had moved to Toronto in September, but it wouldn't hurt to check an extra couple of months. The tediousness of the task ahead was overwhelming. The *Post* was published fifty-two times a year, which meant that I had four hundred-plus issues to go through.

I was about to backtrack to 1979—a delay tactic, I admit, since I wasn't quite ready to read about my mother's disappearance—when it occurred to me that the bearded man in the food bank photo might have also been in the 1984 Canada Day tree planting photo. I pulled the printout out of the folder and scanned the collage of photos for his image. There he was, standing in the back row. Definitely the same man; the scar was a dead giveaway. Who he was remained a mystery.

I put the microfiche in the bin, got up, stretched, and knew I didn't have another microfiche review in me. Tomorrow was another day.

SHIRLEY, THE HEAD archives librarian, was on duty again. She smiled when she saw me and gave me a little wave. I smiled back, wondering if I might enlist her help. I meandered over. "Shirley, I'm not sure if it's against the rules, but I wondered if you could assist me with my research? I need to go back to 1979 through to the end of 1986. I've tackled 1984 and 1985, but at the pace I'm going, I'll need to take up residence here. I could use some company."

Shirley pressed her lips together and looked around the library. There were a handful of people on computers, but everyone seemed settled in. After a couple of minutes of reflection, she said, "I'm going on break in ten minutes. Meet me in the café, and you can tell me what you're looking for. Then I'll decide."

The café was busier today than Friday, but we managed to find a table for two. I bought Shirley a decaf coffee, double sugar, and myself an Earl Grey tea. When I told her I was looking for any reference to my mother, Abigail or Abby Barnstable, or my father, James or Jim Barnstable, the emotion in my voice surprised me.

"Why are you looking for them?"

A simple question and one that deserved a truthful answer, especially if I was asking for help. "My mother disappeared when I was six years old. On Valentine's Day, 1986. I believe there was some suspicion pointed at my father, although nothing was ever proven and he maintained his innocence. He passed away a couple of months ago in an occupational accident. I inherited his house in Marketville and moved here last week. Maybe it's pointless, but I'd like to find out why, or at the very least, find out more about my mother. Not just her disappearance, but also anything else I can find. I'm afraid my memories of her are vague at best."

"You poor lamb," Shirley said. "I actually remember something about the case, although I'm foggy on the details. It was big news at the time." She leaned back in her seat and closed her eyes for a moment. "I'm sure we had a Missing Person poster on our wall downstairs. I seem to remember a reward being offered. It's probably long gone, but who knows? Maybe someone put it in our basement archives. Stranger things have found their way into storage."

I wasn't sure what a Missing Person, Reward Offered poster would do to help me, but I was willing to explore every avenue. "Do you think I could check the basement archives?"

"Hmm? Oh no, that would be staff only, but I'd be happy to look for you." Shirley looked down at her light gray pants and white blouse. "Well, maybe not today, dressed like this, but I promise to do so one day next week."

"Thank you." I didn't want to push my luck but... "Do you think you'd be able to help me with the research?"

"That's a gray area. Technically, I'm only supposed to guide you to the archives."

"I understand," I said, trying to keep the disappointment out of my voice.

"I'm not saying I won't help you, Calamity. I'm saying I'm not supposed to." Shirley smiled. "I'm retiring at the end of the month after thirty years. What are they going to do, fire me?" I didn't correct her on the Calamity.

"So you'll help me?"

"I will." Shirley glanced at her watch. "My break's just about done, better head on back."

Just the thought of getting some help was enough to invigorate me. I thanked Shirley and sprinted up the stairs, taking them two at a time.

SHIRLEY WAS TRUE to her word. She found a student volunteer to man the desk then positioned herself at the microfiche reader next to me.

"These are the people I'd like to find out more about," I said, showing her my print copies and pointing out a young Misty Rivers, my mother, father, Reid, and the unknown man with a beard and a scar. "If you see them in any other photographs, let me know."

Shirley agreed to tackle the early years—1979 through 1983—while I'd start with 1986, which would have more on my mother's disappearance.

We worked side by side, each of us focused on the task at hand. I glanced over at her every so often, only to get a shake of her head. She was working on 1979 and had yet to find a thing. Since my mother would have been pregnant with me at the time, I wasn't surprised. Moving to a new place, newly married, expecting a child. Volunteering would be way down the list of priorities.

Except I wasn't having any more luck in 1986. January was bereft of even a mere mention of my mother, as were the first couple of weeks of February. It wasn't until Thursday, February twentieth that I saw the first story in the *Marketville Post*. Which made sense, since Valentine's Day would have been the Friday before and the paper only printed once a week. The story made page one, though the details were sketchy at best. The Canada Day tree-planting photograph of my mother had been cropped and enlarged to show more of her face, but I could see it was the same picture. It read:

Popular Marketville Volunteer Goes Missing

Abigail Barnstable, well known in Marketville for her work with the food bank and other volunteer initiatives, was last seen on Friday, February 14. Her husband, James (Jim) Barnstable is offering a reward for any information that might lead to finding her whereabouts.

Abigail and Jim have one child, a daughter, Callie, aged six.

"Abigail would never have voluntarily left our daughter," said Jim Barnstable. "I'm worried that she may have been a victim of foul play, possibly kidnapping." According to the Marketville Police, no ransom note has been delivered. Any information should be directed to Detective Rutger Ramsay at 555-853-5763, ext. 241.

I printed off the page and highlighted Detective Ramsay's name and number. Then I slid the printout over to Shirley and pointed to his name. She scanned it quickly, scrunched her face up in concentration, and then shook her head, mouthing the words, "Sorry."

I wasn't discouraged. There was no reason a librarian would know a police officer. He was probably retired by now, but it was still a clue. I would call Constable Arbutus and see if she knew him.

The following Thursday's paper offered more coverage under the headline, Marketville Mother Remains Missing. This time the paper ran another photo, likely supplied by my father. Her blonde hair hung around her face in loose waves, brushing the tops of her shoulders. A faint smile played at the corners of her mouth. I was struck by how much she resembled the woman on the tarot card of The Empress.

In addition to my father, there were interviews with Detective Ramsay, Ella Cole and her husband, Eddie, and Maggie Lonergan, the woman Ella accused of being a busybody that fueled the flames of suspicion against my father. I printed a copy and reread the story, highlighting and making notes along the way.

Two weeks after her disappearance on Valentine's Day, popular Marketville food bank organizer and volunteer Abigail Barnstable remains missing. Despite concentrated efforts by the Marketville Police, led by Detective Rutger Ramsay, there are no leads, and no evidence of foul play. However, Abigail's husband, James (Jim) Barnstable, insists the couple's marriage was solid, and that his wife would never willingly leave their daughter.

"Abigail and I have a good marriage," said Barnstable. "Sure we've had our ups and downs. What married couple doesn't? But we love each other, and we love our daughter. Abigail would never walk away and leave the two of us without so much as a note. I implore anyone with any information, however slight, to contact the police. Please. I'm offering a $3,000 reward. I'd offer more, but it's all I have to give."

I wondered how much three thousand dollars could buy in 1986 and made a note to find out. I also noticed my father had used the present tense. "We love each other," not "We loved each other." I kept reading.

Abigail Barnstable was last seen walking her six-year-old daughter, Callie, to school. Both Callie's teacher and principal have confirmed that Callie was in school that day, but that her mother did not come to pick her up, as was her daily custom.

"They had to call her emergency contact, a neighbor," said a spokesman for the school. The school declined further comment, citing parent-teacher confidentiality. *The Marketville Post* has since learned that the neighbor in question was Ella Cole. In an exclusive interview to the *Post*, Mrs. Cole said that Abigail and her daughter had stopped by her house earlier that morning to give her a Valentine handmade by Callie. It was the last time she saw Abigail Barnstable.

"Naturally I left the minute I got the call from the school," said Cole. "I immediately went and picked the poor child up. Then I stayed with her until Jimmy [James Barnstable] got home from work. He was frantic with worry. We both searched the house and the yard then Jimmy drove around the neighborhood. Maybe he thought she'd gotten lost on a walk or something. But he never found her. It was as if Abigail Barnstable had vanished into thin air."

Maggie Lonergan disagrees with Mrs. Cole, believing the Barnstable marriage wasn't always a happy one. When asked to elaborate, Lonergan said she had told the police what she knew, and would trust them to find out the truth. "I don't want to be considered a gossip," said Lonergan.

Of course not, I thought. Easy not to be labeled "a gossip" after the damage was done. I wondered if the unidentified woman in the food bank photograph was Maggie Lonergan. The odds were in her favor, and it would eliminate one more loose end, but either way I needed to find Maggie and talk to her. I went back to the article.

Detective Ramsay noted that all of Abigail's personal belongings appeared to be intact. "We have no way of knowing one hundred percent," said Ramsay, "but Mr. Barnstable tells us that he has done a thorough inventory. To the best of his knowledge, nothing is missing."

There it was. The first hint of suspicion. *We have no way of knowing one hundred percent. Mr. Barnstable tells us.*

The article went on to sum up more of the same, including some references to past articles on my mother's volunteer efforts. I placed the print copy inside the file folder and leaned back in my chair, trying to ease the tightness in my back and neck. I looked over at the growing pile of microfiche in Shirley's bin. She caught my look and shook her head. Nothing.

I got up to fetch the microfiche for March's *Marketville Post*. The next month's coverage proved to be a rehash of the previous reports, with the story relegated to page three and then to page six, and finally disappearing altogether until mid-August when the headline Husband of Missing Marketville Woman Leaving Town appeared with a story by G.G. Pietrangelo. No photo this time. Despite the scurrilous headline, the story itself was pretty bland:

James Barnstable and his six-year-old daughter, Callie, are leaving Marketville to start a new life. Barnstable's wife, Abigail, a popular food bank volunteer, disappeared last February.

Police say the investigation is still active. There are no leads at this time.

"It isn't the same here, now that Abigail is gone,

and I don't want Callie to be the subject of pity or gossip at her school," an emotional Barnstable told the *Post* in an exclusive interview. "As much as we have loved this town, it's time to move some-place where nobody knows us."

I was printing off the story when Shirley nudged me. "I'm pretty much done," she whispered, "and this is all I found."

She handed me a microfiche from December 15, 1983. Marketville Volunteers Recognized at Awards Dinner. Once again the byline and photo credit went to G.G. Pietrangelo. The photograph showed several men and women of varying ages, lined up in four neat rows. My mother was in the second row. The man I now recognized as Reid was in the back row. I didn't see Misty Rivers or the bearded man, although I did see the woman I suspected was Maggie Lonergan. The caption read, *Terrance Thatcher Plays Host to Local Volunteers.* No names, which meant I had no idea which of the men in the photo was Terrance Thatcher.

The story was brief, basically a recap of various vol-unteer initiatives in town, everything from a Friends of the Library to the food bank to cleaning up the neigh-borhood parks. It was summed up with a thank-you to the local restaurant, the Thatcher House, and its owner, Terrance "Terry" Thatcher, who had graciously hosted the awards dinner.

"As a local business, I appreciate all the volun-teers do to make this town great," said Thatcher.

I remembered Ella Cole telling me about the restau-rant, that it had since closed down because of the influx of chains, but Terrance "Terry" Thatcher might still be around. I printed the story and tucked it in the file. It had grown a bit thicker since the morning, but I couldn't say it provided me with much more information than I'd had in the beginning. Still it was better than nothing.

I uncurled my stiff back and neck from my seat and thanked Shirley for her time and help. She followed me out to the hallway and promised to look for the reward poster in the basement archives as soon as she got a chance.

"I'll try to do the *Sun* and *Star* as well," she said. "At least for February and March 1986. It's doubtful they have anything more than the *Marketville Post* has, but you never know."

"I can't thank you enough."

"Nonsense. For the first time in years, I actually felt like I was doing what I've been paid to do."

TWENTY-TWO

AFTER A DAY of being hunched over a microfiche reader, I was more than ready to take a break from research and investigation. My Sunday morning ritual had long included a breakfast of poached eggs on rye toast and a thorough reading of the *Toronto Sun* with a focus on the Entertainment section. I especially enjoyed Liz Braun's tongue-in-cheek, and often hysterically caustic, look at celebrity life.

I slipped on a pair of fuzzy pink slippers and padded my way to the bottom of the driveway to pick up my copy of the paper. In Toronto, there had been newspaper boxes in front of the condo, but in Marketville the only choice was a trek to the local convenience store or home delivery, which meant someone in a minivan tossing out plastic-wrapped papers wherever they happened to land.

I bent over to grab the paper and caught Ella Cole in my peripheral vision. Given the bulk of her newspaper, she was a *Toronto Star* subscriber. I always took the *Saturday Star*, which included a section with *New York Times* book reviews. I also enjoyed Peter Howell's insightful film reviews and Jack Batten's *Whodunit* reviews of recent mystery novels.

I nodded at Ella, taking in the fluffy yellow bathrobe and matching flip-flops. She took it as an invitation to start up a conversation.

"The new roof looks good, Callie."

I glanced up at it and nodded in agreement. It was a major improvement and thankfully they'd been all but done by the time I'd returned home from the library, with no one falling into the attic. I'd had to swallow hard when it came time to pay the invoice. Roofs were expensive. "I think they did a good job."

"If Royce recommended them, they're solid. Such a nice young man, always so polite when I run into him on my evening constitutional. Any plans for today besides reading the paper?"

As if she hadn't been eavesdropping the other night. "I'm going shopping with Chantelle across the street."

"Well, you have a good time, dear, and don't forget to let me know when you're ready to tackle that garden."

The promise extracted, I made my way back into the house, just as Royce was coming out of his to collect his papers. From the looks of it, he subscribed to the *Sun* and the *Star*.

"What can I say, I'm a newspaper junkie," he said with a grin. "I also get the *Globe and Mail* through the week and the *New York Times* online. It's amazing how different the same story can be when told from other points of view."

The same story told from different points of view. Why hadn't I thought of that?

THANKFULLY, SHOPPING WITH Chantelle was both educational and enjoyable. Educational because it turned out she had a keen eye for a bargain and wasn't afraid to haggle for more. Enjoyable because she genuinely seemed to be having fun, and her enthusiasm was contagious.

That being said, being around Chantelle was somewhat humbling to the ego. I'm no beauty queen, but I've always considered myself relatively attractive in a girl-next-door sort of way. With Chantelle in the picture, I became invisible. Men just seemed to gravitate towards her, not that I could blame them. I wondered why Royce hadn't fallen victim to her very obvious charms. What did he know that I didn't?

We wound up going to more than a dozen stores, and my credit card got a vigorous workout with the purchase of a queen-sized mattress and box spring for the master bedroom—"Think long term and think positive," Chantelle said when I suggested buying the less expensive double—along with a headboard with an attached nightstand which was, according to Chantelle, "Perfect for smaller spaces." She even talked me into splurging for new sheets, a comforter in shades of turquoise and cream, along with several ornamental throw pillows, and matching lamps.

"I can't believe you were planning to pick out paint without knowing your color scheme," Chantelle said when we finally stopped for coffee. She flashed me a sly grin. "Besides, you never know when you'll need to impress an overnight guest."

I cursed myself for immediately thinking of Royce and blushed. Maybe it was also time to upgrade my lingerie. My underwear was nice comfortable cotton—entirely sensible but far from sexy. I also tended to sleep in oversized cotton tee shirts, most of them from running events.

IF I THOUGHT I could stop spending money after a quick lunch—my treat, naturally—I was sorely mistaken. Still, when Chantelle insisted the small bedroom would make a perfect office, I had to admit it made sense. I dragged my tired butt out of the diner, ready to check

out a discount office supply store that sold new and secondhand furniture.

We found a gently used desk in cherry laminate that
came with bookshelf hutch and two file drawers, perfect
for my needs and reasonably priced. I fell in love with
a brand new comfy black leather swivel chair with an
adjustable back, but balked at the price, which was three
times the cost of the desk. Somehow Chantelle managed
to talk the sales manager—a rather anemic-looking man
in his mid-thirties—into knocking the price down by
thirty percent if we took the floor model. I wondered if I
could have negotiated the same deal, without Chantelle,
and somehow doubted it. There was something about
her that just made you want to do what she asked. At
least when she was being charming. I thought back to
our initial encounter at the store. There was definitely
a darker side lurking behind that charismatically persuasive exterior.

THAT DARK SIDE showed up a whole lot sooner than I
would've liked to see it. After we loaded up Chantelle's
pickup and dropped everything off at Sixteen Snapdragon, we decided to treat ourselves to dinner after
a day well spent, pun fully intended. Chantelle suggested Benvenuto, a local Italian restaurant known for
its oven-baked pizza, fresh garden salads, and authen-
tic hot table. "They make the most incredible rapini
and artichoke pizza," she enthused, "and I know you
like pizza."

I did, and rapini and artichoke sounded good to me.
Unusual, perhaps, but certainly worth a try.

The trouble started when we were waiting to be
served, and the couple at the front of the line selected
the last two rapini and artichoke slices. It wasn't as if

Benvenuto didn't have any other choices. There were at least ten other pizzas with a variety of toppings ready to go, including one that looked more like a pie stuffed with rapini and mozzarella.

I think Chantelle would have been able to let it go. Except one half of the couple was an absolutely gorgeous young woman—porcelain skin, waist-length black hair, jade green eyes, legs that went up to her ears. She appeared to be in her early twenties, although the way girls seemed to mature these days, she could have been younger. Judging by her wandering fingers and her incessant, fluttering kisses on his face and neck, she was clearly into her equally attractive, but considerably older, male companion.

"Babysitting, Lance?" Chantelle asked. Her voice had taken on that maple syrup quality I'd noticed in the renovation center.

So this was Lance Thomas, Chantelle's ex.

Lance turned, as if noticing her for the first time, although I suspected from his rapini-artichoke pizza order—Chantelle's favorite by her own admission—that he'd spotted her earlier. Whether that was true or not, from the annoyed expression on his face, he was far from pleased with the chance encounter.

"Chantelle. I didn't realize you still came here."

"There are some things you couldn't screw me out of in the divorce. Where I choose to dine is one of them."

"I see you've found a new puppet to string along." Lance looked at me as if I was an unsuspecting mouse that the cat had dragged in. "A quick warning, lady. Chantelle has a way of cutting off those strings when you stop serving her purpose."

Folks around us started to avert their eyes and shuffle their feet. One woman took out her phone, probably to videotape and post the encounter online. Part of me wanted to disappear. Part of me wondered what purpose I might be serving. The biggest part of me was seriously annoyed at being referred to as a puppet. I also really resented being called "lady."

"The name's Callie, not lady, and I think I'm quite old enough to take care of myself."

"Unlike the adolescent pawing all over you," Chantelle chimed in.

Lance gave her a withering glance. "You have no idea who you're associating with, Callie. Chantelle does nothing that doesn't benefit her in some way, and I do mean nothing. Why should you be any different than the rest of us mere mortals? It took me almost a decade to see through Chantelle's tricks. Trust me, your time will come. Everybody's does." With that he put his arm around his date's waist and steered her out of the restaurant.

"I guess they won't be wanting their salad and pizza," the cashier said with a shrug. She gestured to the two plates waiting at the pickup counter. "Are you two interested? It's on the house."

"Free pizza and salad," Chantelle said. "Always tastes better than eating crow."

"Great, I'll pop it in the oven for a quick warm-up. Won't be a minute."

"No need on my account," Chantelle said. "Revenge is a dish best served cold."

We ate our lukewarm pizza and salad and made weak attempts to recapture the earlier magic of the day, but we never quite managed to recover the illusion. Our excursion ended on a clumsy note, both of us making vague promises to get together soon. Any thought of confiding in her or asking about her genealogy work was put on hold.

Later on, lying in bed, I replayed the restaurant scene over and over again in my mind. Was Lance right, was Chantelle just playing me? If so, for what purpose?

TWENTY-THREE

MY PLAN FOR Monday morning was to pay the attic another visit with the hope of finding something to help
me with my investigation, a diary, perhaps, or letters
and photographs.

There might also be another find—beyond the locket
and the Calamity Jane movie poster—to take to Arabella Carpenter.

I steeled myself for the claustrophobic atmosphere of
the attic and pushed my way up through the entry in the
closet. The first thing I saw when I popped my head in
was the coffin. Even knowing my father had put it there
didn't make it any less creepy. I thought about hosting a
séance and shivered in the too-warm space. I surveyed a
large steamer trunk and a smaller blue trunk with brass
trim. It would have been nice to take them both into the
living room, but I knew I didn't have the strength to do
so on my own, and this was one thing I didn't want to
ask for help with. At least not yet.

I decided to start with the large steamer trunk. It
looked as if it was made of leather and strips of some
sort of hardwood. I found the correct key from the oversized brass ring and opened the trunk to find creamy
satin lining and a whole bunch of clothes. Clearly, my
dad had taken whatever things had been in my mother's
closet and stored them here, thinking she might return.

I rummaged through the pile gently, pulling the contents out piece by piece. It wasn't a huge wardrobe,

but all the basics were covered. Jeans. Tee shirts. Sundresses, shorts, and skirts. A couple of blouses and blazers. A plain black jersey knit dress, the sort that could take you to dinner or the theater. Nothing resonated with me, though a sweatshirt from John Cougar Mellencamp's 1985 *Scarecrow* tour made me smile. My dad had been a huge fan of Mellencamp until the end.

It wasn't until I came across a pair of pink and black striped body suits, the stripes on the upward diagonal, that I felt tears threaten. One suit looked to be about a woman's size eight; the other was clearly made for a young child. A pair of black knitted legwarmers, a woman's and a child's, were pinned to each body suit, as were black leotards.

The sight of them brought back memories I didn't even know I had. Me and my mother, trying out a series of aerobic moves to a Jane Fonda workout video, falling down on the floor in a crumpled heap, hysterical with giggly-girl laughter.

I wondered if a woman who practiced video aerobics alongside her six-year-old daughter—in matching spandex outfits, no less—would abandon her child without so much as a word. A daughter she walked to and from school on a daily basis. I put the outfits aside and looked through the rest of the trunk's contents. Nothing stood out; nothing brought back any other memories. I put everything back as it was and tried very hard not to cry.

I opened the blue trunk next. Inside was an off-white wedding dress with an empire waist, white strappy sandals with tiny rhinestones, a beaded white purse, a blue garter, and a tiny blue-and-gold enameled case. Inside the blue velvet-lined case were a pearl necklace and a pair of matching pearl stud earrings. The purse was empty, save for a silver dollar from 1979, the year my parents were married.

So these were my mother's wedding things. I pulled out a thin white cardboard box and lifted the lid to find a photo album. I set it aside for the moment and continued my search.

There wasn't much else. A round blue-and-gold enameled jewelry box; a larger version of the one used to keep the wedding pearls. I opened the jewelry box to find a silver chain with a Sagittarius horoscope charm, a pair of silver hoop earrings, and five thin silver bangles in assorted filigreed patterns. No rings.

Was this all the jewelry my mother had owned? Or had she taken some of her favorite pieces with her? It didn't seem like much, although according to my father, nothing had been missing. It made sense that she'd be wearing her wedding ring.

I opened the photo album next and did a quick scan before starting back at the first page. There were precious few photographs inside, but each one was neatly labeled underneath. I couldn't help but notice the four blank spaces where the four seasons of a happy family had once been.

The first three pages of the album were dedicated to my parents' wedding day. My father looked incredibly young but undeniably happy, his wavy brown hair styled into an unfortunate mullet. He wore a steel blue brushed corduroy suit, a white shirt, and a light blue and white striped tie. I shuddered at the fashion.

My mother wore the off-white empire-waist dress I had found in the trunk, along with the white strappy sandals with tiny rhinestones. Her blonde hair had been fashioned into an elaborate updo, highlighting her long, slender neck, the pearl necklace, and the matching pearl stud earrings. There was no sign of the beaded purse. She held a lace-wrapped bouquet of baby's breath and lavender in front of her stomach, presumably to hide her baby bump.

If my father looked young, my mother looked positively like a high school senior, but her smile was radiant. There were about a dozen photos in all, and based on the backdrop they'd been shot in a studio. There wasn't a single picture with anyone else. I pulled one photograph out of its plastic sleeve to find Your Time to Shine Photography stamped in gold on the back. No photographer's name. I could do a Google search of the company, but the odds that they were still in business were remote. The digital age had destroyed the careers of many.

After the wedding pictures, the next photos were of me as a baby in a variety of poses. Inside a playpen wearing nothing more than a diaper, splashing in a green plastic wading pool in the shape of a turtle, hugging a gigantic stuffed panda bear with bright black button eyes. I felt a twinge deep in my belly. I could remember dragging that panda everywhere with me. I must have had it for years, though when and where the panda went was now a mystery. I suppose at some point I just lost interest and my father donated it to charity or tossed it in the trash. The thought of either made me more than a little bit sad.

There was a photo of me and my mother baking in the yellow and brown kitchen, or rather, she was cutting out cookies into star-shapes, while I was licking a wooden spoon, a dab of flour on my left cheek. I was wearing the red and white apron, the one with the tiny heart-shaped pockets.

The next page held a couple more photos of me, this

time with my father building a sand castle on the beach, another with him standing next to me on my tricycle. I wished I could remember those events.

Instead of being placed in chronological order in the album, there was an entire section devoted to my birthday photos, each one showing me all dressed up in a frilly dress with ribbons or another sort of "tamer" in my curl-crazed hair, while I attempted to blow out the pink and white number candle on a cake frosted with chocolate icing. The birthday photos stopped at six. My father had never been much on taking pictures, but even if he had this album had been stored inside this attic for years.

There was another section of photos taken with department store Santas. In year one, I was nearing eight months old, and my mom held me tight while standing next to Santa. In years two and three, I sat perched on Santa's knee, with a terrified look on my face as though I was desperately trying not to cry. The next three years I looked decidedly happier, with a wide smile and a confident jut of the chin. Perhaps I'd figured out by then that a visit with Santa meant presents.

One thing stood out above all. Despite the care taken with the album, the sections carefully laid out, there wasn't one photograph of the three of us as a family. Was that why my mother had asked Ella to take the four season series? Was she worried I'd look back at these photos and think we weren't happy? That we weren't a family? I closed the album, knowing it was just another question that I couldn't answer.

The final find was a white envelope stamped in red: CERTIFICATE OF MARRIAGE/CERTIFICAT DE MARIAGE. I opened it up and unfolded the paper. At the top left, PROVINCE OF ONTARIO. Ontario's official seal in the center. PROVINCE DE L'ONTARIO at the top right. I skipped the rest of the French, since only the English side had been completed.

```
I do hereby authorize and grant this license
for the authorization of marriage between
James David Barnstable of 16 Snapdragon
Circle, Marketville and Abigail Alison Os-
goode of 127 Moore Gate Manor, Lakeside.
```

The license was signed and dated December 1, 1978 by the issuer of marriage licenses in Marketville. The Certificate of Marriage followed, signed and dated December 8, 1978, with the ceremony at Marketville Town Hall. There were two witness signatures. The first was from a Dwayne Shuter of Toronto. The second was from the Justice of the Peace who performed the ceremony.

Dwayne Shuter.

I couldn't recall my dad ever mentioning him, yet he must have meant enough to my parents to witness their civil service ceremony. Maybe he had been a friend of my mother's. I would do my best to find him and see what he remembered. The marriage certificate also revealed other information. If my math was correct, my mother had been about four months pregnant when she married my dad, and he was already the owner of the house on Snapdragon Circle.

I closed the trunk, taking the album and marriage certificate. I now had a lead in Dwayne Shuter. I also knew my mother's maiden name was Osgoode, that she had lived at 127 Moore Gate Manor in Lakeside. For the first time, I felt the faintest flush of optimism. Maybe, with a bit more time and effort, I could actually solve this mystery.

TWENTY-FOUR

A QUICK GOOGLE search brought up a LinkedIn account for Dwayne Shuter. I swallowed the bile coming up in my throat. It wasn't just that Dwayne's occupation was listed as Site Supervisor, Southern Ontario Construction, the company my father had worked for when he died. It wasn't that he seemed to have moved from city to city, going west then east, before finally settling back in Toronto a year before. It wasn't even because his very first employer was listed as Osgoode Construction in Lakeside. Osgoode, as in my mother's maiden name. Lakeside, where she grew up.

No, none of that is what made me want to throw up.

It was his picture. The beard was gone, and he was older now, with a few more lines and a lot more gray in a lot less hair. But he was undeniably the unidentified man in the food bank photo. The man with the scar over his left eye. The man with my mother and Reid. What the hell did it mean?

MY FIRST CALL was to Leith Hampton. He was in court, the receptionist informed me, but she'd ask him to call me when he returned to the office. I called the Southern Ontario Construction Company next, hoping to get connected to Dwayne Shuter. After a long and tedious series of prompts, I finally got the option to leave a message. I did so, leaving my name and telephone number, but no reason for the call. Then I called the Cedar County Police and asked for Detective Rutger Ramsay. I was told there was no such officer on active duty. Determined to find out where he might be now, I called the number on Constable Arbutus' business card. I hung up when I got her recorded message.

Frustrated, I started to pace.

A cup of tea and two chocolate chip cookies later, I recalled something Royce had said about the reason for getting four newspapers. That it was interesting to read the same story from different points of view. That's exactly what I had to do now. Somewhere in between it all might be the truth. It was time to get organized, starting with making a bullet point list of everyone mentioned or photographed in the newspaper reports. I grabbed a pen and paper and started writing.

- Detective Rutger Ramsay
- Maggie Lonergan
- Ella Cole
- Misty Rivers
- Dwayne Shuter
- Reid, last name unknown
- My elementary school principal and teacher, neither one named
- G.G. Pietrangelo, writer and photographer, gender unknown
- Terry Thatcher, owner of the Thatcher House

I looked over the list. It wasn't a lot, but it was something. I was starting to feel a bit more confident in my amateur sleuthing abilities. Maybe I'd missed my calling. I looked back over my list.

Ella Cole lived next door, and she loved to talk. I'd start with her.

I LEFT MY cell phone at home—if I wanted to talk to Ella, I didn't need the distraction, and she struck me as the sort of person who wouldn't take kindly to the interruption—took my folder of printouts from the library, and headed next door. Ella answered the doorbell in less than a minute.

"Why, Callie, what a nice surprise." Ella glanced down at the folder in my hand. "You've brought something to show me?" I nodded.

"Come on in."

I followed her into a spotless, contemporary kitchen that opened into an equally spotless living area. White cupboards with ebony beading. Gold-flecked black granite countertops. Harvest wheat walls with sparkling white trim. Stainless steel appliances. It struck me that her kitchen was more modern than she was.

Ella gestured to a kidney-shaped island and invited me to take a seat.

I hopped up onto a chrome and black leather barstool and attempted to make myself comfortable.

"Can I get you something? Tea? Coffee? I just made a nice streusel cake with almonds."

"Tea would be great. Black, no sugar."

"No cake?"

I don't really care for streusel cakes. They always seem dry as dust to me, but Ella looked so disappointed I agreed to a small slice. While she bustled about getting everything ready, I filled her in on my trips to the Regional Reference Library. I left Shirley out of it. I didn't want to get her into any sort of trouble.

"Maybe it's crazy to want to read about it," I said, "but ever since you told me what you knew, it's been festering inside of me. I needed to know more."

Ella set the tea and cake plates on the table and sat down across from me. "Did you find out more?"

"Not really, at least, not from a 'what happened' standpoint. You probably told me as much or more about the events, before and after, than the news stories did. But I printed them off, and I wonder if you'd look at them with me."

"I know I answered your questions on Sunday evening, Callie, but I have to tell you that I'm wondering if I said more than I should have. Eddie used to say I talked too much, and I'm afraid he might have been right. It's not always a good idea to dredge up the past." Ella leaned over and covered my hand with her own. "What if you find out something you don't want to know? Stir up past troubles that might be best left buried."

I removed my hand from hers. "You're implying that I might find out my father was guilty. I don't believe he was, but I'm willing to run that risk."

"It's more than that, Callie. Eddie used to say that people poking into a hornet's nest usually get stung."

"I appreciate your concern, Ella, but I can't let this go. I have to find out what happened to my mother. Or at least try to." That much was true, and by now it went way beyond just fulfilling a codicil.

Ella nodded. "Very well, if you're sure, then I'll do what I can to help you. Just promise me you'll be careful."

"I promise," I said, and opened the folder. I took out the printout showing the group shot of the Canada Day tree-planting volunteers.

"There are ten people in this photograph. I can pick out my mother and father, but I don't know any of the other people." A slight detour on the truth, since I recognized Reid as the man from the locket. Though technically, it wasn't a lie, since I didn't actually know him. "Can you put a name to any of these faces?"

Ella slid her glasses down her nose and peered over them. She traced her finger from one face to the next, first on the top row then the bottom. She pointed out a man who appeared to be in his early fifties. He was tall and thin, with angular features, a generous nose, and a bushy brown *Magnum PI* Tom Selleck mustache. He wore a Toronto Blue Jays baseball cap, the red and white Canada Day tree planting tee shirt, khaki shorts, and work boots.

"The man next to your father is Eddie. He and your father volunteered at the tree planting to support your mother. I looked after you that afternoon."

I made a note that the third man in the bottom row was Eddie Cole. "Anyone else look familiar?"

Ella studied the photo a while longer, but finally shook her head. "No, sorry."

I was disappointed. I'd hoped she would be able to identify the man I knew to be Reid, but if she could, she didn't say. "Do you recognize the name of the person doing the reporting? G.G. Pietrangelo."

Ella glanced down at the names and shook her head again. "I remember being interviewed by a young woman from the *Post*, but I don't remember her name. It could have been Gigi, I suppose. I'm sorry I couldn't be more helpful."

"That's okay. It was a long shot." I put the printout back inside the folder and removed the Christmas Drive at the food bank article. The photo that showed my mother, a young Misty Rivers, the man I knew as Reid, the man I now knew was Dwayne Shuter, and the woman I suspected was Maggie Lonergan.

"What about in this picture? It was taken in December during a holiday drive for the food bank."

Once again Ella studied the photograph, this time with better results. She looked up, a perplexed look on her face. "Lord love a duck, the woman with the curly hair is Misty Rivers. I almost didn't recognize her."

"I thought it might be her, but it's good to have confirmation. It does make me wonder, though, why she didn't tell me that she knew my mother. It also makes me wonder why she rented the house in the first place."

"I have to admit, I wondered about that myself. When she lived there, she claimed the house was haunted, that a woman who lived there had died an unnatural death. At the time I assumed she was a psychic, but now it looks as if she was well aware of the circumstances. I wish I could help you more, but I never really got to know her, beyond what she told me, and that seems suspect at this point, doesn't it?"

"It does, but there may be a perfectly plausible explanation." I didn't believe for a moment that there was a plausible explanation, but I didn't want Ella gossiping about it. "It's probably best if you don't mention this to anyone, just in case."

"Of course. My lips are sealed."

It was the best I could hope for. "Do you recognize anyone else in the photograph?"

"The red-haired woman is the busybody I told you about. Maggie Lonergan."

"So that's Maggie Lonergan. Does she still live in Marketville, do you know?"

Ella shook her head. "She moved up north, good riddance to bad rubbish. Somewhere in the Muskokas. I'm thinking Gravenhurst or Bala, but I could be wrong. That had to be at least twenty-five years ago. I haven't

seen or heard from her since. No reason I would have. I
didn't care for her and I'm sure the feeling was mutual."

It wasn't much of a lead, but it was more than I knew
before I came here. "What about the man with the fair
hair? I noticed him in the Canada Day photo." I pulled
it out and showed Ella.

Ella squinted over her glasses and nodded. "Yes,
that's definitely the same man, but I don't know who
he is. Eddie might have known him, since he was at the
Canada Day tree planting, but if he did, he never mentioned it to me."

"It's okay, you're doing great. What about the guy
with the beard?" I asked, pointing to the man I now
knew was Dwayne Shuter.

"Sorry, no. I think I would have remembered that
scar. When you talk to Misty, you might ask her since
she was in the picture with him."

"I plan to do just that. I have one more group shot.
A volunteer appreciation night hosted by Terrance
Thatcher at the Thatcher House. I remember you told
me it was fine dining when it was open. Can you tell
me which one of these people was Terrance Thatcher?"

Ella glanced at the photo and pointed to a short, ro-
tund man. He was balding in that "horseshoe" bald hair-
cut men used to wear before shaving their entire head
became the norm. "That's Terry. He died about a year
after the restaurant closed. Drowned in a boating accident in Lakeside. There were strong suggestions of sui-
cide. The failure of the Thatcher House haunted him,
but nothing was ever proven, and he had no real family to speak of."

Which meant Terrance Terry Thatcher was quite literally a dead end. "Is there anyone else in the photo

that you recognize? Besides my mother and Maggie Lonergan?"

"I wish there was, Callie, but no. No one else looks familiar to me."

"Okay, thanks. That's it for photos." I closed my folder. "May I ask you something else?"

"Of course."

"The newspaper mentioned that when my mother didn't pick me up on Valentine's Day, the school telephoned the emergency contact. They didn't mention any names, but I know from what you've told me that person was you. Do you know the names of the principal or my teacher? They aren't named, but I thought maybe—"

"That maybe they had some information that never came out?" Ella shook her head. "I don't think I ever knew their names, not having any kids of my own. The school board might be able to help you with that, if you can get by all the privacy rules they have these days."

"I suspect both the teacher and the principal are probably long retired, but it's a good suggestion nonetheless."

I got up, thanked Ella for the almond streusel cake—even drier than expected—tea, and her time. Then I headed back to Sixteen Snapdragon Circle, hoping that Leith or the Construction Company had returned my call.

TWENTY-FIVE

THERE WERE THREE messages on my phone. One from Leith, one from Southern Ontario Construction, and one from Constable Arbutus, noting that she'd picked up my number as a hang up and hoped everything was okay. "Call me back, Callie, or I'll feel the need to stop by and check on you."

As nice as it was to know Arbutus was in my corner, I cursed myself for calling her in the first place. How could I explain my investigation to her?

I called her first and apologized for the hang up. "Nothing is wrong, Officer. I've just been working on something and thought you might be able to help me find someone. I shouldn't have bothered you."

"Now that you have, you might as well fill me in."

"It's not a big deal. Mostly I was hoping you could tell me where Detective Rutger Ramsay might be now. I understand he's no longer with the force."

"Rutger Ramsay? The name doesn't ring a bell, but then again, I only started five years ago. Why? Does this have something to do with the skeleton and coffin in your attic?"

"No, nothing. In fact, I've since come across a letter from my father. Turns out he put the skeleton and coffin in the attic." I paused. "He had an idea for a stage play, Agatha Christie style." Not exactly true but a reasonable explanation.

Arbutus chuckled softly. "Good old Agatha Christie.

If only the police could gather a bunch of suspects together and get the killer to confess. But let's get back to Rutger Ramsay. Why are you looking for him?"

I sighed, knowing I'd brought this inquisition onto myself. "It's a long story."

"Maybe I should come over."

"Honestly, there's no need for that. I was only trying to find Detective Ramsay. It's a personal matter. I should never have bothered you in the first place."

There was a long silence. Finally, "Okay, Callie. I'm busy enough without looking for cases. Call me if you change your mind."

"I will. Thank you."

I hung up, feeling grateful and stupid at the same time. Next I called the Southern Ontario Construction Company. After navigating my way through the same series of annoying prompts, I finally got through to a live person on reception. A bored voice asked how they could assist me. I could almost imagine her filing her nails at the same time.

"My name is Callie Barnstable. I phoned earlier."

"Yes, I was the one who returned your call."

Was that a yawn I heard on the other end? "I'm hoping I can get a direct number for Dwayne Shuter. I understand he's a site supervisor for your company."

"Sorry, we don't give out that information. The company has a very rigid privacy policy. I can pass along your name and number. If Dwayne wants to call you back, that's up to him. Can I tell him what it's about?"

"I believe that my father, James David Barnstable, worked for Dwayne. Or at least that Dwayne knew my father. My father—"

"Of course. I should have recognized your last name. Jimmy was a great guy. He didn't have much cause to come to the office, but whenever he did, he'd bring a box of Timbits with him." The receptionist chuckled. "He used to say there were no calories in a donut hole." I smiled, remembering. He used to tell me the same thing.

"The thing is," the receptionist continued, "we're under strict orders not to talk to anyone about Jimmy, especially the press. I probably shouldn't even be talking to you. I can't afford to lose my job."

"I'm not the press. I'm Jimmy's daughter. Besides, all I'm asking is that you pass along my name and number to Dwayne Shuter."

"I suppose that would be okay. He usually pops by the office on Friday mornings to verify payroll. I'll tell him then."

It was the best I could ask for. My last call was to Leith Hampton. This time, I was put through right away.

"Callie, what's up?"

"Why didn't you tell me that Misty Rivers knew my mother?"

A long pause, then, "I assure you there is a very good reason for not doing so. Unfortunately, I have to cite solicitor-client privilege. I'm sure you understand."

"Not really. My father is dead. Surely the agreement is null and void." Leith remained silent.

I could feel my blood pressure rise and forced myself to take a deep breath. "I can always speak to Misty and see what she has to say."

"You're certainly free to do that."

Exasperating, but I could tell I was fighting a losing battle. "What about a man named Dwayne Shuter? He's the site supervisor where my dad worked."

"Dwayne Shuter?" I heard some flipping of paper and then, "Here it is. His name is on the official accident report as site supervisor, though his statement says he was off the premises at the time of the accident. Why are you looking for him? Surely he won't know anything about your mother's disappearance."

How could I tell Leith my reason for wanting to talk to Dwayne Shuter without telling him about the marriage certificate? Or the two suspicious accidents my father had described in his letter? I thought fast and came up with what I hoped was a plausible explanation.

"I just thought if Shuter was the site supervisor that he might have been friendly with my father."

Leith cleared his throat. "I appreciate how invested you've become in this whole business, Callie, but it's time for me to tell you exactly what I told your father when he came to me with the idea of this cockamamie codicil."

"And that is?"

"Sometimes people leave and don't want to be found. They start a new life with someone else, someplace else. I know it's not what you—or he—wanted to hear, but it's entirely possible that's what happened with your mother."

"You're saying she left of her own volition?"

"You're missing the point."

"Which is?"

"That finding out the truth after all these years might cause you more heartache than happiness."

"What if finding out the truth is important to me? Regardless of how much it might hurt. What then?"

Leith let out one of his theatrical sighs. "I'm trying to tell you, Callie, that you're going to be digging into a past that will in all likelihood only bring you heartache, regardless of the outcome. Don't do that to yourself. In a year's time, the condition will be lifted, you'll get the full inheritance, and you can do what you want with the house."

My B.S. meter sprang into action, a skill honed during my time in the fraud unit at the bank's call center. What did Leith know that he wasn't telling me? Who was he really trying to protect?

TWENTY-SIX

I WENT BACK to my computer and pulled up my Maps app. According to the directions, 127 Moore Gate Manor, Lakeside, was fifty minutes northeast of my current location. I printed off the route.

I thought about ways to visit my mother's parents—if they even still lived at 127 Moore Gate Manor. My attempts of finding a telephone listing for an Osgoode in Lakeside had come up blank, but that didn't mean much. Folks with money almost always had unlisted phone numbers, and besides, lots of people had ditched their landlines for cell phones. I was still mulling things over when the doorbell chimed. I went to the door and looked out the peephole.

It was Chantelle, holding a gallon of paint in each hand. I opened the door.

"Chantelle, you didn't have to buy my paint for me. C'mon in."

She came in and set the paint down in the foyer. "It's just primer. They had it on clearance at the hardware store, five dollars a can, so I figured I'd grab it for you. Some folks don't use primer, but I've always found it makes a difference."

"Thank you. What do I owe you?"

"A lasagna dinner? I ran into Royce. He told me how delicious your recipe is. I gather he was here the other night."

What exactly did Royce say, and why? Was Chantelle being sincere, jealous, or merely curious? I didn't know her well enough to make an accurate assessment.

"I'm always happy to make lasagna and making it for one means I'm eating it for a week, so it's a deal. I'm away this weekend, but one night next week?" I knew I should have said I was going to be with Royce, visiting his parents at their cottage. But I didn't. I wanted to see if she already knew.

If Chantelle knew, she didn't say. Instead she agreed to one night next week and started to leave. I have no idea why, but I stopped her.

"Chantelle, maybe you could do me another favor?" I waved my hand in the direction of the living room, and the papers on top of the coffee table. "If you've got a minute."

Her face lit up and my conscience took over. "Before we do that, there's something I need to tell you."

"What?"

"I'm going to the Ashfords' cottage this weekend with Royce. To meet his parents." I felt the heat rise in my face. "That came out wrong. It's just his parents might have known my mother. Anyway, I didn't want you to find out later on and think I was holding out on you."

"Like you did with the lasagna dinner?" Chantelle grinned at my discomfort. "Lighten up, Callie. I'm just messing with you. Royce is a friend of Lance the loser. Even if we both wanted a relationship—which we do not—Royce is too much of a good guy to cross that invisible line. I actually respect that. Of course, it doesn't stop me from flirting." She shrugged her shoulders as if to say *no big deal*.

"So what's the favor?"

"You mentioned you were into genealogy."

"Not just genealogy. I'm also trying to develop a re-lated business as an information broker. They seemed to be interconnected." She smiled. "Teaching yoga and spinning is great fun, and it was enough money when Lance was supporting me, but I need to find something more lucrative. Plus I like the idea of helping people connect with their past."

An information broker. The very thing Leith had recommended.

"Are you taking on clients?"

"Not officially, at least not until I can develop a web-site and get together with my accountant. All on my to-do list. I could use the practice, though, not to men-tion a client reference. Why? Are you looking for some-one?"

Now was the time to trust her and accept her offer of friendship or shut her out completely. Maybe more time passed than I realized, or maybe, once again, Chantelle had some sort of sixth sense that let her read me. All I know was that she reached over and gave me a brief hug, the scent of her herbal shampoo calming as magic elixir.

"You can trust me," she said, letting go. There was something in the way she said it, an undertone of plead-ing. I realized, for the first time, that for all her flirta-tion and seeming self-confidence, Chantelle was one very lonely lady. The offers to help me paint, to take me shopping, to get me a reduced gym membership, were all an effort to fill the void left by Lance, a man who, based on her reaction in the Italian restaurant, she still very much loved and missed.

What can I say? I'm a sucker for a sob story.

"You'd better come on in, Chantelle. This might take a while."

TWENTY-SEVEN

I PUT OUT a tray with homemade hummus, peppers, and naan wedges on the coffee table and poured us each a glass of wine, red for Chantelle, white for me. After a sip for courage, I got started with my story.

"I don't know either set of my grandparents; I never even met them. My folks got married when I was on the radar. Apparently that didn't go over so well." I pointed to the photo album. "There are some photos of the wedding in there. Take a look for yourself."

Chantelle picked up the album and flipped through it, pausing occasionally to study a photo at greater length.

"I see what you mean," she said, putting it back on the table. "No photos of anyone outside of your parents on their wedding day. It's unusual to say the least, but it backs up the theory that your grandparents hadn't approved. Otherwise, there would have been at least one obligatory group photo, don't you think?"

"What else do you notice?"

"Even after you were born, there are no photos with anyone else in them. Unless you consider Santa Claus." She looked up at me, her eyebrows raised in a question. "That, and the photos stop when you're six."

"That's the year my mother left. February 14, 1986."

"Valentine's Day."

I nodded. "The jury's still out on where and why she went. The police suspected foul play. I've been doing some research, reading old newspaper accounts at the

Reference Library." I grinned. "I've also been talking to Ella Cole."

Chantelle laughed. "Ella's probably better than any library. What about your dad? What did he believe?"

"He never talked about her when I was growing up. We moved to Toronto a few months after my mother's disappearance, not that I remember moving. My father put this album and a few of her personal belongings in the attic, padlocked it, and rented out the house. I didn't even know about this place until after he died."

"Not even a hint that it existed?"

I shook my head. "Furthermore, I have no idea why he never sold it. Why he just kept renting it out. Unless—"

"Unless he thought she'd come back here, but didn't want to get your hopes up. Telling you about the house might have raised too many other questions." Chantelle bit her bottom lip. "Which means, your father believed she might still be alive."

"I think he might have kept hoping, despite any evidence to support it, at least. I don't think he believed she was still alive at the time of his death."

"The letter you mentioned. The one in the safety deposit box."

"That, and some other things." I wasn't ready to talk about the will or the letter in any detail, at least not yet. I considered showing her my folder of printouts from the library but decided that, too, could wait. Baby steps.

Thankfully, Chantelle didn't push it.

"So what about your grandparents? The ones on your father's side?"

"All I know is that their names are Peter and Sandra Barnstable, that they used to live in Toronto, and that they moved decades ago, address unknown. To be honest, I haven't done much to find them yet. I've been so busy with everything else."

"Let me see what I can find out. What about your mother's parents?"

"There, at least, I have an old address. At least I think it's their address." I took the marriage certificate out of the envelope and handed it to Chantelle.

Her eyes scanned the document. "Your mother came from Lakeside. Should be easy enough to find them." She grabbed my laptop, and before I could blink, her fingertips were flying across the keyboard. I dipped a red pepper slice into the hummus and nibbled on it, toyed with the stem of my wineglass, and stayed silent. Less than five minutes later she glanced up, a triumphant grin on her face.

"They do. Still live there. Corbin and Yvette Osgoode. It looks like they're a bit of a high society couple, which would explain the nosebleed address." Chantelle turned the screen towards me to show a *Toronto Star* newspaper photo of a distinguished couple at some sort of charity gala, him in a tux, her in a long gold lamé gown with rhinestones around the bodice.

I felt a catch rise in my throat. I'd always thought I'd inherited a mix of features from my parents, the black-rimmed hazel eyes and unruly hair from my father, the slightly too-wide nose and heartshaped face from my mother. But with the exception of the eye color—hers were a molten chocolate brown—the aristocratic woman in this picture could have been me, forty years in the future. I wondered if Yvette fought with her hair, now short, curly, and iron gray, the same way I did.

Physical resemblance aside, the fact remained that they probably wouldn't welcome me with open arms, no matter how much time had passed. I told Chantelle so.

"Maybe they will, and maybe they won't, but there's no law against taking a stroll around the neighborhood. Lots of people do it. I suggest we park at the public beach on Winding Lake Drive and go from there."

Chantelle was right. No one would find it unusual to see a couple of women walking. The area attracted runners and walkers and cyclists in equal measure. I had dated a guy one summer, a triathlete with a fantastic body but not much else to offer. We'd spent more than a few days at that beach while he practiced open water swimming and I admired his form. Unfortunately, I discovered the only thing he was faithful to was training. "You'd go with me?"

"Sure, why not? I love an adventure." She picked up the photo album again. "We should probably take along a couple of the wedding pictures. Just in case."

"Just in case?"

"In case we meet someone who remembers them or end up talking to your grandparents." It wasn't much of a plan, but at least it was a plan.

"When do you want to go?"

"How's tomorrow morning sound? Bright and early, say nine o'clock? I don't teach classes at the gym until tomorrow afternoon. As long as I'm back by three I'm golden."

I didn't have anything specifically planned for Wednesday, with the exception of trying to reach Dwayne Shuter again and checking in with Shirley at the Reference Library. I nodded my agreement, finished my wine, and poured another glass.

Ready or not, it was time to face the past.

TWENTY-EIGHT

CHANTELLE WAS IN my driveway promptly at nine a.m. Wednesday. Dressed in what I hoped would pass for acceptable walking clothes—shorts, a *Run for the Cure* tee shirt, and running shoes—I climbed into her pickup truck, a zippered hoodie in my hand in case it was cold by the lake. I saw a flicker of movement in the curtains at Ella's front window and suppressed the urge to wave. Let her believe she'd been furtive.

The drive to Lakeside was enjoyable. Chantelle took the back roads, "the scenic tour," she called it, versus the faster commuter route which tended to be more heavily traveled, albeit at this time of the day in the direction headed towards the city, not away from it. We chatted about everything but the mission at hand. I appreciated Chantelle's attempts at diversion.

Parking for Winding Lake Beach was tucked behind a white clapboard convenience store. There was a hand-painted sign in the near empty lot directing us to pay the five-dollar daily charge inside Ben's Convenience. I knew from my days with the two-timing triathlete that come July the fee would be twice as much for half the time.

We made our way to the front of the store, pausing to look out at Lake Miakoda. It was still early in the season and only a handful of diehard swimmers in wetsuits and brightly colored caps were out in the choppy water. A cool breeze drifted onto the shore. I shivered just watching them, knowing the water temperature in late May wouldn't be much over fifty-eight degrees.

Inside, Ben's Convenience had the usual selection of soda, chips, chocolate bars, and—catering to the avid three-season cyclists that frequented Winding Lake Drive—an impressive variety of energy bars and sports drinks. There was a chest filled with plastic bags of ice and a freezer stocked with an assortment of ice cream bars. The owner stood behind a counter filled with scratch-and-win tickets safely stored behind Plexiglas. I remembered him from a decade ago, a grizzled man with bushy white hair, a permanent suntan, and a perpetual scowl. Come summer, he'd be out front grilling hot dogs, sausages, and burgers—beef or veggie— the price of each going up or down, depending on the temperature and the number of tourists and triathletes. I handed him the money for the parking and two overpriced bottles of water.

"You ladies heading out for a walk?" he asked, handing me my change.

"We are," Chantelle said with a brilliant smile. "You must be Ben."

"You read the sign." The scowl remained firmly in place.

I wanted to throttle him. Chantelle wasn't dissuaded.

"You owned this place long, Ben?"

"Coming up to forty years."

"That's a long time."

"A lifetime. Where you planning to walk?"

"We thought we'd head over to Moore Gate Manor," she said, "see how the other half live."

"You mean the other one percent," Ben said, but his scowl had lifted a little. I swear Chantelle could unfreeze an igloo in the Arctic.

"Yeah, I guess you're right about that." Chantelle paused, as if debating something with herself. After a few moments, she leaned forward onto the counter and stared up at the storekeeper with her intense charcoal gray eyes. She stopped just short of fluttering her eyelashes, possibly realizing that might be overkill.

"Look, between us, my friend here thinks she might have a relative on Moore Gate Manor. Remembers visiting there when she was a kid."

"So now she's hoping to find a pot of gold?" Spoken as if I weren't in the store.

"It's not like that. She's just looking for family."

Was it my imagination or did the shopkeeper flush beneath his tan?

"I didn't mean anything—"

Chantelle waved away his apology and pulled out one of the wedding photos from a pouch around her waist. "Maybe you recognize the woman?"

Ben barely glanced at the photo. "Can't say as I do."

"Let's go, Chantelle," I said, wishing I were anywhere but here. I flashed a look at the man. "Sorry to have bothered you."

To my surprise, the ingrained scowl softened a little bit more. "The one thing I can tell you is that the residents of Moore Gate Manor don't frequent the poor side of town. They even have their own private beach, completely gated, security cameras, the whole nine yards. No need to come here and spend time with the great unwashed."

"Well, it was worth a shot," Chantelle said, and flashed Ben another bright smile.

We were halfway out the door when he called out after us.

"Why don't you leave the picture here and stop in on your way back? Maybe something will come to me."

"Do YOU THINK he knows anything?" I asked Chantelle as we headed northeast along Winding Lake Drive. I was wearing my hoodie, glad that I'd had the foresight to bring it. The sun had yet to peek out of the clouds, and the wind was getting brisker by the minute. I hated to think what my hair looked like.

Chantelle shrugged. "It's hard to say. He barely glanced at the photo. Maybe if he takes the time to really look at it."

We walked the rest of the way in silence, pausing occasionally to look out at the water or a particularly nice home. No cookie cutter houses on Lake Miakoda. Every one was different, from the tiny original clapboard cottages dating back to the fifties, to the mega-windowed mansions that were gradually replacing them.

The further east we got, the nicer the houses became, until about three miles along, when we finally arrived at a stone archway and elaborately painted sign that indicated we were now entering the community of Moore Gate. There wasn't a locked gate, per se, but it felt as if there should be. You got the feeling you weren't welcome here unless you belonged, preferably from birth, though I expected new money was welcomed with a jaundiced eye.

The main thoroughfare was Moore Gate Manor, which wound its way through a maze of homes that dwarfed anything on Winding Lake Drive. Despite what Chantelle had told the convenience store owner, I'd never been here, not now, and not as a child. Not even when I'd been dating the two-timing triathlete.

The homes on the north side of Moore Gate Manor

sported a spectacular view of Lake Miakoda and a series of islands beyond. A half-dozen streets ran off of it; the homeowners there would have to walk a bit to get their view, but the homes were equally impressive, with immaculate gardens and copper weathervanes atop cupolas on cedar-shingled roofs.

We meandered along each side street first, as if in unspoken agreement that we leave my grandparents' house for the last. The day was blustery enough to keep folks inside, though they might also have been hard at work earning more millions. Whatever the reason, the only people we saw were a couple of young guys doing yard work, and a cable repairman doing something with wiring at a small green box.

We arrived at 127 Moore Gate Manor about fifteen minutes later. Located at the end of a cul-de-sac, it was by far the largest on the block, with a generous lawn groomed to perfection, a plethora of spring flowers in full bloom, and an interlocking brick driveway. The house itself reminded me of a medieval fairy tale castle, with its fieldstone façade, turrets, and two-story towers. The only thing missing was a moat.

So this is where my mother had grown up. Opulence on steroids, it was a far cry from the humble two-bedroom bungalow in Marketville she'd shared with my father and me.

Had it all gotten to be too much? The penny pinching on a sheet metal apprentice's salary, baking cookies instead of having them baked, the dreariness of a commuter town growing on the backs of those who wanted the dream of home ownership and couldn't afford anything better? Had the man I knew only as Reid been her Prince Charming, ready to offer her a happier ending?

There was a Persian cat resting in the front bay window, its emerald eyes watching our every move. A white toy poodle wearing a pink collar studded with colorful jewels lay sprawled next to the cat. I wondered if the baubles were real, and suspected they just might be. The dog hopped away, making room for an elderly woman who came to the window. She stared at us long and hard before closing the blinds.

My grandmother.

"This was a stupid idea," I said to Chantelle. I turned around and ran back to the convenience store, tears streaming down my face, my heart pounding, my breathing ragged. By the time I got there, I was dry-eyed and angry. I sat down at a bench in the park and looked northeast towards the community of Moore Gate. "Damn you, Yvette Osgoode. You're going to meet me. Like it or not."

TWENTY-NINE

Chantelle caught up with me a few minutes later. She plopped down on the bench and draped her arm around my shoulder. "If it's any consolation, Callie, I doubt she recognized you. She probably just wanted to make a point. Uninvited visitors need not come by."

It would have been some consolation if I believed it, but I didn't. There had been recognition in her look. Recognition and something else. Anger? Annoyance? Fear? I couldn't be sure, but knew I had to find out. I summoned up a smile and nodded. "You could be right. Look, I'm going to go in, talk to the convenience store owner. See if his memory has improved any. I'd like to do it alone, if that's okay."

"I'll be here if you need me," she said, and gently removed her arm from my shoulder.

There were a couple of cyclists in the store, replenishing their supply of sports drinks and energy bars. The cleats of their shoes clicked across the linoleum-tiled floor as they made their selections. I waited until they'd paid for their purchases and left.

Ben slid the photograph over the counter in my general direction. "I do remember them," he said. "It was a very long time ago. I can't imagine what good the memory will do anyone, least of all you."

"It's been thirty-five years," I said. "As for whether it will do any good, why not let me be the judge."

He appeared to give that some thought then nodded.

"Thirty-five years would be about right, though it doesn't seem that long ago. I would have been in my early twenties, a few years older than these two. The guy in the photo used to come here every night, not that he ever bought anything outside of the occasional pack of gum. Wasn't much more than a kid. He'd just wait outside on the bench until the girl came along. They'd hug and kiss then the two of them would get in his car and drive off. It was an old beater, lots of rust on the rocker panels. From the way she dressed and carried herself, I got the impression she came from Moore Gate Manor. Those folks walk different than the rest of us. I always figured they arranged to meet here on the sly."

"You've got a good memory, Ben."

"Not really. It's unlikely I would have remembered either one of them, except one night a middle-aged man drove up in a white Mercedes. The girl hadn't arrived yet. The man went ballistic, started shouting at the guy, shaking him by the collar, screaming obscenities. He told the kid to stay away from his daughter, that he was going to make sure he took care of things once and for all. The kid mouthed back, said they were in love and no one could stand in their way. That snapped any sense of restraint the man might have had. He put his hands around the guy's throat and started choking him."

Ben shook his head at the memory. "That's when I called the cops. First time I'd ever done that, though certainly not the last. I honestly thought the man in the Mercedes was going to kill that kid. I still think he would have, given half a chance."

"What happened when the police arrived?"

"They seemed to know the man. They certainly treated him with deference. My guess is he was a Moore Gate Manorite who donated plenty to the police fund coffers. At any rate, after a while they managed to calm him down."

"What about the kid?"

"One of the cops took him off to one side. The cop must have convinced him it was in his best interest not to press charges, because after a few minutes, the kid got in his beater of a car and drove off. I never saw the man in the Mercedes again. Or the kid and the girl. Based on this photograph, they got married."

"They did. They had me about five months later."

"What about the grandparents? The man with the Mercedes?"

"Never had the pleasure of meeting them."

"I'm not surprised. It's sad, the things snobbery and stubbornness can cost a person." I didn't say anything to that. What was there to say?

"Where are they now? Your parents?"

"My father's dead."

"And your mother?"

"The jury's still out."

CHANTELLE AND I didn't talk on the way back to Marketville. I wasn't ready, and she seemed to understand that. Once again, I appreciated her sense of decorum. She pulled into her driveway and I hopped out of the truck.

"Thanks for coming along with me. Sorry I wasn't better company on the ride back."

"Any time." She paused for a moment, as if debating something, then forged ahead. "I probably won't see you until you get back from the Ashfords' cottage. Do me a favor, okay. Be careful of Royce."

"What? Where's that coming from?"

Chantelle blushed. "It's just that Lance always said… no, forget it. You just have fun up there."

"Lance always said what?"

She sighed and then spit it out. "He always said Royce was a player, but maybe that was just to keep me disinterested. There was a time when both of them showed an interest in me. I picked Lance, but he was always a little bit jealous of Royce and his family's money."

So Royce was a player with family money. I couldn't reconcile the image with the man who'd help me lug out bundles of carpet, or the man I'd had to my house for dinner, though I suppose anything was possible. It was also possible that Chantelle actually had a thing for Royce, as I'd first suspected.

My head was too full of other stuff to process it. "I'll be on guard," I said, and walked across the street.

A RED LIGHT flashed on my landline, indicating a message. I was bone-tired and wanted nothing more than a glass of white wine and a long soak in a hot lavender-scented bubble bath, but curiosity got the better of me. Maybe Dwayne Shuter had finally decided to return my call.

The message was from Shirley the librarian.

"Callie, it's Shirley. I finally had a chance to go through the back issues of the *Toronto Sun* and *Toronto Star* for the month or so after your mother's disappearance. I found a couple of articles that might be of interest. If you can, pop by tomorrow and I'll show you."

That was the end of the message. I was impatient to find out what she'd discovered, but there wasn't much I could do about it and another day wouldn't kill me. In the meantime, I was starving.

A tuna salad on rye hit the spot. I decided to prepare my email to Leith ahead of time to free up my morning. The sooner I could get to the library and meet with Shirley, the better.

To: Leith Hampton
From: Callie Barnstable
Subject: Friday Report Number 3

Went to the attic and found a trunk containing some clothes and jewelry—nothing of value—of my mother's, including her wedding dress. There was also a photo album with a few wedding pictures. They were taken in a studio and there are no photos of guests. There are also pictures of me as a baby and young child. Nothing brought back any memories, or offered any clues.

I stopped and thought about what to tell Leith. I decided not to mention finding the marriage certificate. Of course, not mentioning it meant I also couldn't mention finding out where my grandparents lived, or that I knew Dwayne Shuter had once been more than my dad's site supervisor at work, or enough of a friend to be a witness at my parents' wedding. I remembered the hesitation when I told him about Misty knowing my mother, that slight intake of breath on the phone when I mentioned Dwayne. I wasn't sure how much I could really trust him. I certainly wasn't ready to tell Leith I'd gone and scoped out the Osgoode house with Chantelle. I damn sure didn't feel like getting into the story Ben had told us.

The decision made not to go into those details, I continued.

I also went to the Regional Reference Library and sifted through the archives for the Marketville Post from the time of my mother's disappearance. I made copies of any story that referenced my mother or father to review in more detail at home, but so far, it looks like there isn't much to go on.

Another omission, insomuch as I'd gone far beyond just looking at the time of my mother's disappearance, and I had Shirley scouring the *Sun* and *Star*. It was true, however, that I'd made copies. I was storing tidbits to share if I ran out of news, like squirrels hiding their nuts for winter.

I read over my report. Satisfied I'd met the codicil condition without causing any suspicion, I saved the email as a draft, ready to send the next morning.

Job done, I reviewed the printouts again, but couldn't summon up the energy to do another online search, this time for G.G. Pietrangelo. Instead, I took another look through the photo album, hoping to remember something more.

I didn't.

It was almost seven by the time I felt hungry enough to make myself a light dinner and was contemplating scrambled eggs and toast when the doorbell rang. I ran through the possibilities. Royce? Ella? Chantelle? Or maybe Misty Rivers had decided to pay me another visit. I sighed. As much as I needed to talk to her, after the day I had, I didn't feel like having company.

I got up and looked through the peephole to see a refined woman in her early seventies standing on the stoop.

Mrs. Yvette Osgoode.

My grandmother.

THIRTY

I OPENED THE door and took note of the black Cadillac parked in my driveway. A man with a cap sat in the driver's seat. Her chauffeur, I assumed. "Yes?"

"Good evening, Calamity. My name is Yvette Osgoode, although I suspect you already know that. I'd like to come in. To talk." She licked her lips, a quick flick with the tip of her tongue. "Corbin…my husband…your grandfather. He doesn't know I'm here."

"What about him?" I pointed to the guy in the Caddy. That was sure to get Ella's curiosity up.

She shook her head. "He won't say anything, and he's used to waiting for me."

I'm sure he was. I stood away from the doorway and waved her into the living room. "Have a seat. Can I get you anything? Tea, coffee, water, something stronger? I have red and white wine and some fairly decent double malt scotch. I've also got some chocolate chip cookies and some shortbread. Both store bought but quite good." I realized I was babbling and shut up.

"I'd love a scotch rocks. Thank you."

I went to the kitchen and put a few cookies—my dinner now—on a bone china plate, poured two fingers of scotch into a tumbler filled with ice, and then poured myself a generous glass of chardonnay. I put everything on a tray, including some of my fancy napkins saved for guests, took it into the living room, and set it down on the coffee table.

Yvette was sitting ramrod straight in the chair. The photo album and folder with newspaper printouts lay where I had left them. If she had been curious about either, she'd had the good manners to refrain from snooping. I picked them up, put them on the end table next to the sofa, and took a seat.

"Please, help yourself," I said, taking a shortbread and nibbling on it. "Forgive me, but I was just about to make a light supper."

"I'm sorry, I should have called first. Perhaps I should come another time."

"Not to worry. You've given me an excuse to have cookies for dinner." She smiled at that, and I recognized my smile in hers.

"I wouldn't mind a cookie myself," she said, and took one of the chocolate chip ones. We sat in semi-companionable silence and munched and sipped. Three cookies and half her scotch later, Yvette spoke again.

"I saw you this morning. Outside of my house on Moore Gate Manor. You were with your friend."

There was no point in denying it. "I was."

"Why now? After all these years?"

It seemed like an odd question, given that my grandparents were the ones who rejected my parents, and by extension me, but I opted for the truth. Or at least a version of it. "My father died recently and left me this house. I haven't seen my mother since I was six. I'm an only child. I suppose I just felt the need to find out if I had any other family."

The explanation seemed to satisfy her, because she nodded.

"How did you know it was me?" I asked.

That really seemed to amuse her. "I'd say there was rather a strong family resemblance between us, wouldn't you? I have to admit that it was a bit of a shock to see myself, forty years younger. Of course, you have your father's eyes, or at least his eye color. Otherwise, the resemblance is uncanny." She licked her lips again. "I told Corbin that Abigail would never forgive us for turning her out when she told us about the pregnancy. I told him she'd never agree to adoption, and most certainly not abortion. But he was…*is* a stubborn, prideful man, too concerned about appearances, about what the neighbors might think."

She let out a harsh laugh. "As if a young girl in the family way is somehow worse than tax evasion, insider trading, or embezzlement. All crimes committed by some of our upstanding neighbors over the years. Not that everyone who lives in the neighborhood is a criminal. There are plenty of hardworking folks who earned their way into the Manor, and plenty more who inherited their way there. I'm sure that even those families have their fair share of skeletons. I tried to reason with Corbin, but he wouldn't listen. Maybe because before your father came into Abigail's life, she had always been Daddy's little girl. Suddenly, she'd fallen madly in love with one of his construction workers. Even worse, she was carrying that man's child."

I remembered what Ben, the Lakeside convenience store owner had said. "It's sad, the things snobbery and stubbornness can cost a person."

"I always believed Corbin would come around, given time," Yvette continued. "Then one day, the police came to see us. I knew then that we'd lost Abigail forever." Yvette—I couldn't quite bring myself to think of her as my grandmother—leaned back in her chair, as if exhausted from her monologue. Her face was pale, and there was a faint bead of perspiration on her brow. She reached into her pink Birkin handbag and pulled out a small pot of lip balm. If I hadn't been so freaked out by everything she'd told me, I might have laughed out loud. "When did the police come to see you?"

"It was a few days after Abigail disappeared. Of course, we'd read about it. It was in all the papers." Yvette took another sip of her scotch before continuing. "Corbin was sure she'd finally come to her senses and left your father. I didn't know what to think. The police seemed to think she might find her way back to us. The officer in charge implied there may have been difficulties in the marriage." Another sip of scotch. "I have no way of knowing if that was true."

I knew I had to ask, even though I wasn't sure I wanted to know the answer.

"Did she? Come back to you?"

Yvette shook her head. "No. I wish she had. The police interviewed us on a couple of occasions. Actually grilled is more like it. Corbin…let's just say Corbin had a temper when it came to your father and there was an incident once, at the convenience store on the lake. He tended to be overprotective. Abigail was our only child."

Ben's "man in the Mercedes." Corbin Osgoode might have skated on that particular altercation, but six years later, when his daughter had disappeared without a trace, the police must have dug up an old report.

"Can I ask you another question, Yvette?"

"Of course."

"Why didn't you try to connect with me, especially after my mother disappeared? I was an innocent child, your flesh and blood." I heard the catch in my voice and cursed myself for it.

Yvette's eyebrows shot up in surprise. "I did try, Calamity. It was harder back then to find someone, to get in touch. There was no Internet, no email, no texting. I hired a private investigator to find out what day you were born, and where you'd moved to after leaving Marketville. All without Corbin's knowledge, of course. I sent letters by mail, birthday and Christmas cards, left messages on your father's answering machine. I finally gave up when you were about thirteen. It was just easier to pretend I'd never had a granddaughter."

All these years, I'd been led to believe that my grandparents didn't want me, and now Yvette was saying it wasn't true.

"Are you telling me that my father didn't return the calls, cards, or letters?"

"That's exactly what I'm saying, Calamity." She gave a very sad smile and drained the rest of her scotch. "I can't really blame him, especially since the letters and phone calls only came from me. Corbin and I both reacted rather badly to the news of your mother's pregnancy. I think your mother might have forgiven us, with time, but your father was a very stubborn man." That much I knew to be true.

Yvette continued. "Perhaps if I'd managed to get Corbin on board things might have been different. I blame myself for not pushing harder. But we've found each other now. Perhaps we can start over. Maybe in time, Corbin will come around."

I was exhausted and more than a little bit hungry, with a wine and cookie headache threatening to crack open my temples. I leaned forward and leveled her with my best black-rimmed hazel-eyed stare, the one my father used to bestow on me when he was good and angry.

"Perhaps it would be best if we didn't meet again. I don't want to put you in any difficulty with Corbin.

After all, I've managed for thirty-six years without you. I'm sure I can manage another thirty-six."

I don't know what I expected. Maybe that Yvette would beg for a second chance, or at the very least ask me to reconsider, but instead she stood up, smoothed an invisible wrinkle from her immaculately pressed and pleated pants, thanked me for the scotch and cookies, and walked out the front door without so much as a backward glance.

I watched from the window as the Cadillac pulled out of the driveway. Then I sat back down, put my head in my hands, and cried, the kind of hard sobbing that leaves you splotchy-faced, mascara-streaked, and out of breath.

I was still crying when the doorbell rang. I looked out the window and saw that the Cadillac was back. Went to the door and opened it. Yvette stood there, her face pinched and pale.

"What now?" I asked.

"I'm going to have a long talk to Corbin," Yvette said. "Force him to listen." She gave me a weary smile. "He has to, doesn't he? If he wants us both back." With that, she left.

THIRTY-ONE

I GOT UP Friday morning feeling groggy and out of sorts after a virtually sleepless night. I don't often drink coffee, but I needed the caffeine. I made a pot, extra strong, and felt almost human by the end of the second cup. I even managed to choke down a slice of toast with peanut butter.

I pulled up my report to Leith and briefly considered sharing the news of my grandmother's visit with him. In the end I decided there was more than enough information to satisfy him for another week. I hit send and shut down my computer. It was time to head over to the library.

TRUE TO HER WORD, Shirley had reviewed the microfiche records from both the *Toronto Sun* and *Toronto Star* from February 14 through to the end of March 1986. She handed me a file folder with a handful of printouts, patted me on the arm, and left me to review them on my own.

The first mention of my mother's disappearance was on February 16 in the *Sun*, and February 17 in the *Star*. Both had clearly cribbed from the *Marketville Post* with nothing new to add. Thereafter there was the odd mention in both papers under a "Woman still missing" type of headline, but you couldn't help but get the impression it was considered a bit of a non-event, at least in a city the size of Toronto.

It wasn't until the March 2nd issue of the *Sunday Sun* that things got interesting. The headline read Missing Women's Parents Attend Political Fundraiser. There was a photograph of Corbin and Yvette Osgoode, both smiling widely for the camera, he in black tie and tails, her in a heavily beaded midnight blue gown. Even without the headline, I would have been riveted to the picture. With the exception of the color of her eyes, looking at Yvette Osgoode was like looking at a photo of myself. Well, myself if I took the time to dress up in fancy clothes and have my hair professionally styled in an elaborate up-do.

It was only on closer inspection that you could see the tautness in Yvette's chin, the way Corbin's arm was wrapped around her waist, the knuckles white, as if his fingers were gripping a little too tightly.

The story went on to say that Abigail Barnstable, the only child of Corbin Osgoode, president of the Osgoode Construction Company, and his wife, Yvette, had been missing since Valentine's Day. There were a few rehashed details culled from previous reports. Corbin asked that the public respect their privacy during "this difficult time."

They had disowned her when she got pregnant with me, rebuffed any attempt at reconciliation, but were more than willing to go to a three-hundred dollar a plate political party fundraiser and have their photo taken by a reporter during their supposed "difficult time." I felt like flinging the printout across the room. I despise hypocrites.

Then again, maybe they'd regretted it, once she went missing. I thought about Yvette, how the police had suggested Abigail might come home to them. Maybe they had tired of answering questions from the police and nosey neighbors. Based upon this photo, there were definitely signs of visible tension in both of them. I turned the page over and went onto the final printout in the pile.

The article was in the March 14th issue of the *Toronto Sun*, exactly one month after my mother's disappearance. It took less than an eighth of a page, relegated to the back end of the paper. Filler on a slow news day. A photograph of a young woman holding a reward poster was aligned to the left of a brief recap of the circumstances surrounding my mother's disappearance.

I wondered what Shirley had recognized first—the photograph of Misty Rivers, or the reward poster. Not that it mattered.

Because it wasn't so much Misty and the poster that made me feel as though I'd just been punched in the gut.

It was the man standing next to her.

He was thirty years younger, and there was no trace of a paunch, but the eyes were every bit as electric blue as they were today.

My father's lawyer.

Leith Hampton.

THIRTY-TWO

LEITH HAD CITED attorney-client privilege as the reason he'd neglected to tell me that Misty had known my mother. At the time, I'd assumed he was talking about betraying my father's confidence. Now it appeared as though the client he was protecting was Misty Rivers. I wondered whether representing my father and Misty at the same time could be considered a conflict of interest.

It also made me wonder about his connection to Dwayne Shuter. I closed my eyes and remembered the way Leith had flipped through some pages. "Dwayne Shuter?" he had said, and then, "His name was on the official accident report as site supervisor, though according to Shuter's statement he was off the premises at the time of the accident."

Not, "No, I don't know him," or "Yes, I know him," but, "His name was on the official accident report," and later, "Why do you ask?" I was getting a very bad feeling about Leith Hampton.

"It's the reward poster I was telling you about," Shirley said, interrupting my thoughts. "I recognize the woman in the photo as well. She was definitely the one who came by the library and asked if we could post it. I can't think of her name, though, and I've never met the man. I'd remember those eyes."

"The woman was in a couple of the *Post* photos," I said. "I've since identified her as Misty Rivers. She still lives in Marketville. She used to volunteer at the food

bank with my mother. They must have been friends. I
don't think the man is from around here." I felt badly
about not telling Shirley the whole truth, but it was just
too complicated. Fortunately, she seemed satisfied with
my explanation. Or at least she didn't push for more information. Either way, I was grateful.

I thanked Shirley for her hard work, promised to
keep her posted on any progress, and headed home with
printouts in hand, determined not to let my concerns
over Leith ruin my upcoming weekend in the Muskokas.
True, I was going to the Ashford cottage to talk to Mr.
and Mrs. Ashford and hopefully find out more about
my mother, but I was also in dire need of a bit of rest
and relaxation. The opportunity to get to know Royce
a little better was a bonus.

ROYCE AND I left for Lake Rosseau about ten o'clock
Saturday morning with the idea of arriving about noon.
We spent the drive discussing our favorite authors, and
debating which was the stronger series, Michael Connelly's Harry Bosch or John Sandford's Lucas Daven-
port *Prey* novels.

Despite the northbound cottage country traffic, we
made good time on the 400 to the Highway 69 cutoff
towards Muskoka. Thirty minutes and a few cutoffs
later we came to a meandering chip-tarred road, which
in turn led to a dirt-packed single laneway that would
surely not be navigable during mud season or winter.
If you happened to meet an oncoming car, there was—
occasionally—a narrow shoulder that barely allowed
the other vehicle to pass. Fortunately, it didn't look like
there was any traffic to worry about. The only life we'd
seen so far was a flock of wild turkeys in no hurry to

get out of our way. I was wondering if a GPS could even read a location when Royce seemed to read my mind.

"A GPS will only pick up as far as the paved road. Once you turn onto Ashford Road, you pretty much lose the signal. It's good and bad. Good, because it's mercifully private in an increasingly public world. Unless one of us invited you, you're not about to find the place." Royce chuckled. "That said, it's bad if you want pizza delivery."

We arrived at the cottage to find a fine-boned pony-tailed woman, about my age, waiting in a slant-backed Muskoka chair outside a large log cabin. She got up to greet us, flicking a stray strawberry blonde hair away from her face. There was enough family resemblance for me to peg her as Royce's sister.

"It's about time you got your arse up here, Royce. Mom's been driving me crazy since I got here last night. If I'd have known, I'd have waited to come until later today."

"I told Mom about noon," Royce said.

"Yeah, yeah, yeah." She turned to me, her dark eyes twinkling, and stuck out a ringless left hand. "Allow me to introduce myself, since Royce seems to have forgotten his manners. Porsche Ashford, kid sister extraordinaire."

I shook her hand somewhat awkwardly; I was used to shaking with my right. "Pleased to meet you, Portia."

"Not Portia, as in de Rossi. Porsche, as in the luxury automobile."

Of course. Royce as in Rolls. The connection had never occurred to me before. Before I could say anything else, Porsche grabbed me by the arm and proceeded to steer me in the direction of the cottage.

"Royce can schlepp in whatever luggage you

brought," Porsche said. "C'mon and let me introduce you to our mom and Auntie Maggs."

"Where's Dad?" Royce asked. "I thought Mom told me he wouldn't be traveling this week."

Porsche rolled her eyes. "He wasn't supposed to be, but apparently he had some sort of last minute business trip. The usual story. He got back late last night. The first thing he did was arrange a golf game. Mom is none too pleased, let me tell you, but he promised to be back in time for cocktail hour. Now enough of your dilly-dallying. Go fetch the luggage. I'll show Callie around and introduce her."

I followed Porsche inside and barely suppressed a gasp. The interior of the cottage could best be described as rich rustic. The room was filled with leather chairs, sofas, and love seats in earth tones ranging from pumpkin and puce to brown and ochre, with coordinating throw pillows, woven from what appeared to be strips of fabric, tossed casually here and there. Solid oak coffee and side tables were scattered throughout the space. It shouldn't have worked, it should have looked cluttered, but instead it looked cozy and cottagey and inviting. There was a faint smell of pine lingering in the air, emanating from artful arrangements of freshly cut evergreens mixed with daisies and sunflowers.

With the exception of a massive stone floor-to-ceiling wood-burning fireplace, the walls were covered with wildlife art. I'd studied art for two semesters in college and switched majors when I realized I would never be good enough to make a living at it, but I could still recognize an oil painting of a loon family by Robert Bateman, frequently reproduced, as well as an impressive collection of chipmunks, squirrels, and barnyard birds by Carl Brenders, all original oils from the looks of it.

There were other paintings as well, by artists I couldn't instantly identify, along with several hand-woven tapestries. The overall effect was striking.

But nothing could compete with the million-dollar view. A full bank of windows with glass garden doors overlooked Lake Rosseau and the forests and rocky shores that surrounded it. Two women lay on recliners on an immense wooden dock that took up most of the frontage. I estimated it at about 300 feet, possibly more. The taxes on this place were probably close to what I earned in a year. There were still a few original old cabins, but those were gradually being bought up and transformed into places like this one. Muskoka was money country with a capital "M," especially Lakes Rosseau, Joseph, and Muskoka. This is where professional athletes, celebrities, and CEOs went to get away from it all.

"It's spectacular," I said.

"Daddy was a stockbroker. He did quite well in the market," Porsche said. "Fortunately he got out of the business before the big crash." She gave an impish grin. "Unfortunately neither Royce nor I inherited his financial acumen or his love for the cutthroat world of buying and selling on margin, much to Daddy's deep disappointment. Of course, at least Royce has his contracting business. I'm the starving artist in the family."

"Dad has never considered my work dignified enough for an Ashford," Royce said, coming into the room, a small suitcase in each hand. "Porsche is being modest. She wove all the pillows and tapestries in this room, and she has very successful shops in both Yorkville and Muskoka."

Toronto was sometimes referred to as Hollywood North by the movie industry. Yorkville was the place celebrities shopped when filming in Toronto. If Porsche

could make the rent there with her tapestries, they sold
very well indeed, and for a high price. I went over to
one and admired the intricacy of her work. "You're very
talented," I said, and meant it.

Porsche laughed. "You can stay." To Royce she said,
"Why not show Callie to her room so she can unpack.
I'll try to get Mom and Auntie Maggs up from the dock."

The plan in place, Royce led me to a spacious bedroom with a double bed, pine dresser, and a four-piece
ensuite bath. The white eyelet lace bedspread and curtains were brightened up by a colorful array of hand-
woven pillows. More of Porsche's handiwork, I assumed.

I put away the few things I'd brought to wear, fresh-
ened up, and sat on the bed, trying to calm the butterflies that had taken up residence in my stomach. Along
with the "four seasons" photographs, I'd brought my
folder with the printouts from the library. I wasn't sure
whether to show them or not. I was still assessing the
pros and cons when there was a soft rap on the door. I
opened it to find Royce on the other side.

"Ready?" he asked.

I nodded, trying to show a confidence I didn't feel.
He took my hand and gently led me back into the living room. I left the folder behind.

An older version of Porsche was comfortably en-
sconced in one of the leather recliners. She had the same
delicate features, the same almond-shaped brown eyes.
Her strawberry blonde hair had been subtly colored and
highlighted to hide any gray. This, then, would be Mrs.
Ashford. There was no sign of the woman Porsche had
referred to as Aunt Maggs.

"Callie," Royce said, "I'd like you to meet my mother."

"It's nice to meet you, Mrs. Ashford. Thank you for
inviting me."

"Melanie. Mrs. Ashford is my mother-in-law." She waved a French-manicured hand. "It's our pleasure. My sister, Maggie, went back to her own cottage across the bay for a little nap, but she'll be joining us for dinner. Porsche went off to her shop in town. She's got retail help, of course, but it's always good to have the artist present. Folks like that. I also thought you might want to reminisce without them, at least initially."

"That's very considerate of you."

"Nonsense." Another wave of the hand. "Royce tells me you're trying to learn more about your mother. I'll tell you what I can, not that it's much."

"Actually, Melanie, it's more than that. You see, my mother was last seen walking me to school on Valentine's Day, 1986. I'm hoping to find out what happened to her. If she's dead or alive." I surprised myself by the open admission. I could tell by the quick arching of his eyebrows that I'd surprised Royce as well.

Melanie, however, didn't appear the least bit surprised. She merely nodded. "It must have been difficult, growing up and not knowing why she left or what happened to her."

"I suppose it should have been, but the reality is, it wasn't. Not really. My father was a good parent. He made sure I was fed and clothed, and put me in the obligatory skating and swimming lessons. We never talked about my mother. After a while I just stopped thinking of her. I was six when she left. Almost seven. Old enough to remember at least some things. And yet…" I glance over at Royce. "Maybe I've suppressed the memories to protect myself. To protect myself from what, I have no idea."

"So you don't remember anything?"

I didn't want to tell her that the memories were

starting to come back, bit by bit, like disjointed movie scenes. At least not until I could put enough scenes together to create a story. "Not really."

"There were no pictures of her when you were growing up?"

I shook my head. "Not a one. I'm not sure if my dad didn't want the reminder, or if he couldn't bear the reminder. Regardless, the first time I saw a picture of my mother was when I found some in the house. I showed them to Royce when he was over for dinner. He thought he recognized her as the cookie lady who'd come to your house a couple of times. Hence my imposition on your hospitality."

Melanie smiled. "It's no imposition. Royce doesn't visit nearly enough, and his friends are welcome anytime. As for remembering the 'cookie lady,' Royce always did have a sweet tooth."

"What about Porsche?"

"It's unlikely she would remember. Porsche would have been about three at the time. But, yes, the woman who Royce thinks might have been your mom did come by a couple of times to drop off baked goods for the school library fundraiser. We were trying to buy a full set of *Nancy Drew* and *Hardy Boys* books for the library. Those stuffed shirts on the board were only interested in purchasing textbooks and encyclopedias. They couldn't understand that getting a child to read is the most important thing. Who cares if it's a mystery story or the back of hockey cards?"

I smiled at her candor. Melanie Ashford might have money but she wasn't a snob. "I brought the photographs. May I show them to you?"

"I'd love to see them."

I went back to the bedroom and pulled out the four

seasons photos from my folder. I left the printouts behind. One thing at a time.

Melanie studied the photographs carefully, first one
by one, then by laying them out in a row. "It's interesting
that she chose the same place for four pictures in four
different seasons. Royce told me he thought they were
taken at the elementary school. I'm sure he's right, not
that I would have made the connection. I wonder what
motivated her to do that?"

"I've been wondering the same thing. More importantly, is this the woman you remember as Abby?"

"Almost certainly." Melanie looked up. "I wish I
could help you more, but I never really got to know her."

I was no further ahead. I collected the photographs,
placed them back in their envelope and summoned up a
smile, trying to hide my disappointment. After all, the
weather outside was glorious, and I still had a weekend
away at Lake Rosseau.

Melanie, however, seemed to sense my disappointment. "Perhaps my husband or my sister will remember
more about your mom. Marketville's still a small town,
but in 1986 it was positively incestuous."

"In the meantime, Callie," Royce said, speaking up
for the first time, "we can go for a tour of the lake. The
boat's all ready to go. I'm sure Mom won't mind being
left to her book."

"Not only won't I mind, I insist," Melanie said.

I had to admit a tour of the lake sounded like fun. Especially with Royce. Despite my best intentions, I found
myself falling for him with each passing minute. I just
hoped my loser radar had gone on hiatus.

"Far be it for me to argue with my hosts," I said, and
followed Royce out to the dock.

THIRTY-THREE

IT HAD BEEN years since I'd visited the Muskokas, but it felt as though time had stood still. Royce was an accomplished boater, navigating around the numerous inlets and islands with ease as I took in the craggy granite bluffs dotted with pines, the cottages ranging from small cabins to magnificent summer homes, their docks sporting canoes, kayaks, jet skis, yachts, and boats of every size and color. Even the cell towers had been disguised to look like trees. I could imagine myself spending a summer here, and felt an unexpected twinge of envy for those who did.

We arrived back to the cottage about four p.m., giving us plenty of time to get ready for what Royce called Happy Hour.

"A long standing Ashford family tradition," he said. "We all meet for drinks at five in the sunroom. Casual attire only. Shorts and tee shirts or jeans and sweatshirts, depending on the temperature. Right about now, everyone will be napping or getting cleaned up."

"Getting cleaned up sounds good to me," I said, knowing my hair would have gotten that wild windblown look that sounds sexy on paper but in reality looks like a bird's nest. "So does Happy Hour."

I took extra care with my appearance, making sure my hair was tamed into a tidy French braid, adding a light touch of mascara to my lashes. I donned white capris, a multi-colored tee shirt in shades of pink, plum, and purple, and amethyst stud earrings. I'd just slipped on a pair of white sandals when Royce knocked on the door.

"You clean up nice," he said, his eyes scanning me from top to bottom and back again.

I felt the color rise on my cheeks. It had been a long time since anyone had looked at me that way, let alone paid me a compliment.

"Thank you. I'll admit I'm feeling a bit nervous about meeting your father and Aunt Maggie. I want to make a good impression."

He put an arm around my waist and led me into the hallway towards the sunroom. "They're both going to love you. Especially my father, though I have to warn you. He can be an outrageous flirt when it comes to beautiful women. My mother pretends to ignore it. Sometimes I think she finds it vaguely amusing, as if it's a game the two of them play with each other. Sort of like cat and mouse, except with humans."

"I'll consider myself forewarned. I just hope one of them remembers something about my mother. As great as this day has been, that's the main reason I'm here."

"The main reason, Callie? I'm shattered." Royce gave an exaggerated frown, then smiled warmly. "All joking aside, I'm sure they will. What was it my mom said? About Marketville being a small town?"

"She said back then, Marketville wasn't just small, it was incestuous."

"Then you're in luck. When it comes to incestuous, Aunt Maggs is a bit of an expert."

THE SUNROOM WAS actually a screened-in porch that took up the entire west side of the cottage.

Once again, the view was nothing short of magnificent, taking in forest, granite rock formations, and a large swath of Lake Rosseau. The sunsets would be spectacular.

White wicker dominated the space, although once again Porsche's handiwork was in evidence throughout in the colorful pillows and casual throws. I wondered how much of her commercial success had to do with purchases by her parents and their friends. A lot, I expected, although there was no doubt she had talent.

Porsche and Melanie Ashford were curled up in matching wicker rockers, each with a martini in hand. Melanie gestured to a stainless steel bar, complete with built-in refrigerator. "Welcome to Happy Hour, Callie. My sister and husband should be here shortly. In the meantime, there's a pitcher of vodka martinis already made. There's also a decent selection of spirits, soft drinks, sparkling water, wine, and beer. Royce, pour the lady a drink."

I settled on an Australian chardonnay and took a seat in a comfy looking settee, absurdly pleased when Royce sat next to me. I had just taken my first sip of wine when a heavily bejeweled woman in her mid-fifties strolled in. She'd gained a few pounds, and her red hair was no longer entirely dependent on nature, but there was no question about it. Aunt Maggs was Maggie Lonergan. The woman Ella Cole called Magpie.

The woman who accused my father of murdering my mother.

"Aunt Maggs, I'd like you to meet my friend and neighbor, Callie Barnstable," Royce said, giving her a peck on the cheek. "Callie, this is Maggie Lonergan, my mother's sister. Also affectionately known as Aunt Maggs."

"Royce, darling, you know how much I hate Maggs,"

the woman said, but there was indulgence in her tone. To me she said, "Please, call me Maggie. It's lovely to meet you, Callie. Any friend of Royce's and all that."

I made an effort to be polite. I was, after all, a guest, and I only had Ella Cole's version of Maggie's accusations. "It's nice to meet you, too, Maggie. Melanie says you might have known my mother. Abigail Barnstable."

Maggie poured herself a martini, added six olives, one at a time, then slid into a lounge chair. She reminded me a bit of a lizard slithering into the sunlight.

"I knew her as Abby. We volunteered together at the food bank. Or should I say, I volunteered and your mother ran the place. Her rules and all that." Maggie smiled, but I detected a trace of irritation, as if something still bothered her after all these years. I could almost feel her trying to shake it off.

She took out one olive with a toothpick, picked the pimento into a napkin, popped the olive in her mouth, munched on it slowly, and then gave another cold smile. "I'm afraid that sounded rather unkind. Without your mother, Marketville wouldn't even have a food bank, at least not at that time. She was relentless in her efforts to get it off the ground. It's just that people with that kind of drive or vision, they sometimes forget that other people have feelings."

Had my mother truly been like that? A person who didn't care about other people's feelings? Ella Cole hadn't suggested as much, but she may have been trying to spare me. Then again, Maggie struck me as the kind of person who needed to be center stage. The way she came in to Happy Hour, fashionably late and dripping with jewelry, as if trying to make a grand entrance. Maybe my mother didn't kowtow to her. I was debating on how to respond when Melanie chimed in.

"I'd forgotten you volunteered at the food bank," Melanie said, chuckling at the memory.

"I have no idea what you find so amusing," Maggie said with a disdainful sniff. "The food bank is a very worthy cause."

"Oh for heaven's sake, Maggie, it's been thirty years. Why not admit you were a reluctant volunteer at best?" Melanie folded her arms in front of her and glared at her sister. I got the impression there was more than a little sibling rivalry between them.

Maggie rolled her eyes dramatically and fished another olive from her martini, repeating her earlier pimento-removing ritual. "I wouldn't say I was reluctant, Mellie. True, I was there because I'd been assigned a hundred hours of community service, but I did get to pick the charitable organization."

"Aunt Maggs. Community service. I had no idea." Royce grinned. "What ever did you do?"

"Yes, do tell, Auntie Maggs," Porsche said, leaning forward.

"What did our father do, is more like it," Melanie said. "Without his involvement in the auxiliary police department, and the Lonergan name, your Aunt Maggs could have wound up with a lot more than one hundred hours of community service."

"Your mother is exaggerating, as is her custom. It was a minor shoplifting incident, a couple of baubles from the jewelry store." Maggie waved a ring-laden hand. "What can I say, I've always liked shiny things."

"You actually got arrested?" From the tone of his voice, the thought of it seemed to amuse Royce more than offend him. I gathered Aunt Maggs was the black sheep of the family and worked hard to maintain her reputation.

"Of course not. The store called the cops and they detained me, but your grandfather was able to convince everyone that the entire mishap was just an unfortunate misunderstanding. I returned the jewelry and agreed to do the community service. Willingly."

"Did you do all one hundred hours at the food bank?" I asked, hoping to drive the conversation back to my mother.

Maggie nodded. "Roughly eight hours a week for three months. Unpacked boxes, sorted the donations, stocked shelves. Whatever Abby asked, the volunteers did."

"Did you get to know her very well?"

This time Maggie shook her head. "Can't say as I did. She tended to keep her private life private, at least when it came to me, although I got the impression she wasn't particularly happy at home." She pressed her lips together. "I'm sorry, that was insensitive."

"Not if it's what you believed. I'm looking for the truth, not some candy-coated version of the past. Did anyone else who worked there feel the same way you did?"

"I can't speak for anyone else."

I knew that Misty Rivers, Dwayne Shuter, and the man only known to me as Reid had also worked at the food bank, but I didn't want to tip my hand. There were likely more volunteers who hadn't been photographed.

"At this point I'm just trying to find out who else might have worked there. Do you recall the names of any of the others?"

"Hmm… I'd have to give it some thought. As Mellie was so quick to point out, it has been thirty years, and my memory's not what it once was. But there is one person who definitely should remember your mother."

She shot a malicious grin in Melanie's direction. "As I recall, he and Abby were quite friendly."

"And who was that?"

"Why, Melanie's husband, also known as my brother-in-law, and Royce and Porsche's father. He should be here any minute, fresh off a hard day on the golf course. Why not ask him yourself?"

As if on cue, the screen door opened and an athletic-looking man in his early fifties sauntered into the sunroom. He leaned over, kissed Melanie on the cheek, and murmured something in the ear. She blushed slightly and gave him a playful tap on the shoulder.

If I felt nervous before, it was nothing compared to what I was feeling now. The fair hair might have turned a silvery shade of gray, and the chiseled chin might have softened somewhat over time, but the brown eyes had stayed the same—dark, serious, intense.

It was the man from the locket.

Reid.

THIRTY-FOUR

IT OCCURRED TO me that the reason Reid had looked familiar all this time was because of Royce. It wasn't so much that Royce was a younger version of Reid, as was the case with Porsche and Melanie, as a general similarity in the overall features. Standing in the same room, however, it was overwhelmingly obvious and I couldn't imagine how I'd missed it. I made a concerted effort not to look shocked and must have succeeded because no one looked at me oddly.

In fact, no one looked at me, period. All eyes were on Reid. He had a commanding presence, the sort that comes with power and wealth. I could imagine him, thirty years younger, handsome, charismatic, more than a little bit arrogant, on his way to making his first million in the markets, yet somehow still finding time to volunteer an hour or so here and there.

I could equally imagine my stay-at-home mother, a leader and go-getter by all accounts, trying to find new meaning in her life by taking charge of volunteer initiatives while scraping by on my father's income as an apprentice sheet metal worker. A decent living, to be sure, one with promise, but often seasonal. I know. I'd experienced enough of those times growing up. It had been feast or famine. Crazy overtime hours during a project on deadline, then nothing; maybe a few hours here and there.

Reid poured himself a generous scotch on the rocks

and made his way over to where I was sitting. "You must be Callie Barnstable. Royce has been telling me about you. It seems you've made quite an impression on my son." He flashed an ultra-white smile and winked in Royce's general direction.

Porsche grinned and hugged her knees to her chest as if waiting for a show. Melanie stared into her martini. Royce looked mildly embarrassed, not that I blamed him.

"Guilty as charged," I said, attempting a smile. "Thank you for inviting me."

"Our pleasure. Melanie tells me you're hoping to find out more about your mother."

"That's right. Abigail Barnstable." I studied his face for any sign of discomfort. Nada.

"Abigail Barnstable, yes, although I knew her as Abby. I volunteered with her on a couple of initiatives. I first met her at a Canada Day tree planting sponsored by the town. When she wanted to start up a food bank, she called me and asked if I could help."

"So you stayed in touch after the tree planting?"

"Not really. I suspect that she called everyone on her volunteer list. Maggie volunteered at the food bank as well, although as I recall her time there may not have been completely voluntary." He took a sip of his scotch and winked.

I forced another smile. "Maggie's already shared her reason for volunteering. What about you? Surely a successful stockbroker wouldn't be in the position of enforced community service. Were you friends with my mother?"

"Friends?" Reid narrowed his eyes and tilted his head to the side as if in deep concentration.

Waited a few moments, then, "No, I wouldn't say we were friends."

More like lovers, I thought, thinking about the tarot cards and the locket. But I couldn't call him on it, not here in his own cottage country sunroom with his wife, son, and sister-in-law present. Besides, he wasn't likely to admit it. "So if you weren't friends—"

"Let's just say your mother could be very persuasive, and the food bank meant a lot to her." Another ultra-white smile. "Abby was a very passionate woman."

I wasn't sure whether Reid meant the double entendre or not, but I couldn't help but notice that the color had drained from Melanie's face, while Maggie looked positively like a cat with the cream. Royce looked oblivious. I plunged ahead.

"I'm afraid I don't know much about her. My mother left when I was six, and my dad didn't talk about her much as I was growing up."

"I can understand that. There was a lot of gossip after your mother's disappearance, much of it directed in his direction. It must have been extremely difficult for him. For both of you, I expect. Of course, I never knew your father at all. My association was strictly with Abby, and it was a very long time ago." Reid cast a sideways glance at his wife. "That chapter of my life is long behind me."

"I wish we could tell you more, Callie," Melanie said, a faint flush staining her cheeks, "but the reality is none of us knew her very well. I'm sorry we can't be more help."

Did Melanie really believe that? Because I was convinced there had been an affair, and Reid's innuendo and body language suggested his wife knew all about it. Maggie's earlier offhand comment just confirmed my suspicions.

I thought about the locket. Surely if my mother had left that day to meet or be with Reid she would have worn the locket, not hidden it inside an envelope under the carpet. But if she'd left to meet with his wife, possibly worried about what might happen during the meeting… until now I'd suspected that Reid was the one who sent the tarot cards. Now I wondered if Melanie had been the orchestrator of that particular symphony.

I took a generous sip of my chardonnay and contemplated my next step. Reid claimed he didn't know my father but the truth was both men had been at the Canada Day tree planting, and without a doubt my mother would have introduced them. That meant he'd lied. Showing Reid the tree planting photo would make me look sneaky. It would also put Reid on the defensive, something I didn't want. But if I just showed the photograph from the food bank, maybe I could find out more about Dwayne Shuter and Misty Rivers.

"Earth calling Callie, come in Callie." Royce's voice, a soft buzz in my ear. I flashed him a sheepish grin. I knew I'd been alone in my thoughts but I hadn't realized it had been so obvious.

"My apologies. It's just that I was thinking about the printout I'd brought along with me. It's in my room."

"Printout? What sort of printout?" Royce and Melanie spoke in unison. Maggie's eyes narrowed. Reid's face was inscrutable.

"I've been doing some research at the Regional Reference Library. I found a photograph of my mother at the food bank during a holiday drive. It was in the *Marketville Post*. I didn't realize it until now, but I'm sure both Maggie and Reid are in the picture. May I show it to you? There are a couple of other people in the photo. Maybe you can tell me who they are."

"I'm not sure what good identifying people we knew thirty years ago will do, Callie, but we'd all be happy to take a look." Melanie looked at Reid and Maggie. "Isn't that right?"

"Goes without saying," Maggie said, picking the pimento out of an olive.

"Whatever we can do," Reid said, but judging by the sudden twitch in his jaw, I wasn't entirely sure I believed him.

THIRTY-FIVE

ANY CONVERSATION WAS quickly silenced when I sauntered back into the sunroom, printout in hand. Maggie
went and stood behind Reid, ending any indecision on
my part as to who to show it to first.

"You can see my mother is in the foreground," I said,
pointing to her. "There are four other volunteers in the
photograph. There you are, Reid, and the striking red-
head would be you, Maggie. I'm not sure who the other
two are. The man with a beard and a small crescent-
shaped scar above his left eyebrow, and the woman with
dark eyes and curly brown hair."

"I really was striking, wasn't I?" Maggie said, without a trace of humility. "So were you, Reid. I'd forgotten how handsome you were."

"Were? Are you saying I've lost my looks, Maggs?
Because that might be a bit like the pot calling the kettle
black." Reid softened his words with a smile, but I could
tell by Maggie's quick flinch and tightened grip on the
back of Reid's chair that the words stung.

"The years have been kind to both of you," I said,
determined to keep the peace. "How else would I have
recognized you from a thirty-year-old photograph?"

That seemed to mollify Maggie; her fingers relaxed
and her face lost its painfully pinched expression. A
brief smile played at the corners of Reid's mouth, and
he gave me an almost imperceptible nod. I was left with
the feeling that I'd passed some sort of litmus test.

"What about the other two?" I asked again.

"The woman with the unbecoming perm is Misty Rivers," Maggie said. "She claimed to be a psychic, used to do tarot card readings for those of us at the food bank. A lot of hogwash if you ask me, but as I recall, your mom used to ask her questions about tarot."

"What sort of questions?"

Maggie shrugged. "You're asking me after all these years as if I might actually remember? I suppose something along the line of what does this or that card mean, that sort of thing."

"What about Misty Rivers? Have you kept in touch?"

"You're kidding, right? I had less than zero in common with her."

"So the answer is no."

"You catch on fast," Maggie said, attacking another pimento. "I haven't seen or heard from Misty Rivers in years. Do you remember her, Reid?"

Reid shook his head. "Can't say as I do, but then again my contribution came from trying to solicit corporate donations, either in the form of food or cash. Most of my dealings with Abby fell outside of the food bank hours, when everyone else had left. She liked to keep the financial aspect of things on a need to know basis. Besides, at the time I was working on Bay Street in the city. I don't even remember this photo being taken."

I wasn't sure I believed him about not remembering the photo shoot, but his admission that he met with my mother outside of food bank hours to discuss finances certainly provided the opportunity to carry on an affair.

"What about the man? Do you recognize him?"

Reid gave the photo another cursory glance. "Sorry, he doesn't look familiar."

"Maggie?"

"He was only there a couple of times when I was there and I don't remember his name." Maggie scrunched up her face in concentration. "Might have been William, Warren, Wade. Something with a W. Maybe Mellie can ID him. She's great with names and faces, and she was always doing some sort of charity drive or another. It's possible she ran into him."

"I'm certainly willing to take a look," Melanie said.

I wandered over to Melanie's wicker chair and had just handed her the photo when Maggie piped up again.

"Wayne, that was it. His name was Wayne. I can't remember his last name."

Melanie looked up from the photo, her face pale beneath her tan. "Not Wayne," she said, "Dwayne. His name is Dwayne Shuter."

It wasn't so much what she said, but how she said it. That's when I realized Reid wasn't the only Ashford who'd had an affair back in 1985. "Dwayne Shuter," I said, as if I'd never heard the name before.

Porsche leaned over to take a look. "He looks very handsome and that scar over his eye lends a hint of mystery. However did you meet him, Mommy?"

"Yes, do tell, Mellie," Maggie said, toying with the pimentos she'd placed on her napkin. I noticed her hands had the slightest tremor and realized she'd known who Dwayne Shuter was all along. Had she been trying to protect her sister, or put her on the spot? I glanced at Reid, but his face was an impenetrable mask. This was a man used to hiding his emotions.

Melanie handed the printout back to me, the color back in her face. She'd had time to recover. "I'm afraid it's rather a dull story. I met him while I was getting things ready for the school library fundraiser. There were a bunch of tables and folding chairs in the basement, and he was down there doing something with the ductwork." She smiled at the memory. "I wasn't expecting anyone to be down there, and certainly not a guy in coveralls and a hard hat. He gave me quite a scare. Anyway, he was kind enough to help me take the tables and chairs upstairs."

"Probably paid by the hour," Reid said, getting up to pour another scotch. "Kindness likely never factored into it. Any excuse to bill the school and its taxpayers for more time. I know the type."

Melanie flushed and I could tell she was trying to formulate a response when Royce spoke up.

"What type is that, Father? The contractor type?" Royce said it quietly, but the underlying anger was unmistakable. What was it he'd said? That his father had never considered Royce's line of work dignified enough to be worthy of the Ashford name. I thought he'd been exaggerating at the time. Now I realized he'd been dead serious.

"Everything isn't always about you, son," Reid said. "I was merely stating an opinion. Most of these construction workers overcharge and underwork. I'm sure this Dwayne person was no exception."

I knew I should have kept my mouth shut. After all, I was a guest in Reid's cottage, and I wanted to find out more about Dwayne Shuter. But I couldn't let it go. "My father was a construction worker, Mr. Ashford, and to the best of my knowledge, he was as honest as the day is long, as were, I'm sure, the majority of his co-workers. The same cannot be said for your former profession, as history has told us on more than one occasion, the recent economic crisis being a notable example."

To my surprise, Reid clapped. "You've found yourself a feisty one here, Royce. I like a woman who's not afraid to speak her mind."

"I didn't *find* Callie, Father. She's not some stray dog or cat. She's my next-door neighbor, and we're becoming friends. I brought her to the cottage so she could learn a little bit more about her mother, and by extension, possibly some of the people who might have known her. I'd rather hoped we could avoid playing dysfunctional family just this once."

"Honestly, bro, why do you let Daddy bait you like that? You know he's just trying to get to you." Porsche got up and poured another martini, took a long, generous swig, then topped up her glass. "Callie, on behalf of the entire Ashford clan, let me apologize for our poor behavior."

"There's no need, Porsche, but thank you." I probably should have uttered some sort of apology back, but it would have been insincere, and I don't do insincere well. What I really wanted was to know more about Melanie's version of Dwayne Shuter, though I knew this wasn't the time or place for it. Whatever Melanie knew or didn't know, she wasn't about to say it around her husband, children, or sister. I was thinking of ways to get her alone when Royce came to the rescue.

"Mom, Callie's also a runner. Do you think she could join you tomorrow morning for your Sunday run?"

Melanie smiled gratefully at Royce, the tension draining from her neck and shoulders. "It would be lovely to have company for a change. Did you bring your running gear, Callie?"

"I did. I wasn't sure if I'd get a run in, but I packed with the idea it might be possible. I'm not especially fast though."

"Neither is Melanie," Reid said.

Melanie glared at him. "As if you'd know. The only exercise you get is getting in and out of a golf cart."

"I'm only basing my observations on how long it takes you to get back to the cottage, darling."

This time, Melanie ignored the barb. "I have a lovely five-mile route, Callie, very scenic. Most of it's along the trail behind the golf course, which sometimes slows the pacing down to an absolute crawl. Have to be mindful of rocks and roots and the inclines are as steep as stepladders. I usually have a bowl of oatmeal and then head out at eight o'clock. I stop and have coffee at the local café when I'm finished."

"A very long coffee," Reid said.

"It sounds great, the run and the coffee after," I said, hoping to put an end to the bickering. "I would love to join you."

"It will be nice to have someone to talk to." She looked pointedly at Reid and her blatant hostility chilled the room.

"Mommy, shouldn't we be getting ready for supper? You know how Bianca hates it when we're late," Porsche said, trying to play peacekeeper.

"You're right, Porsche, and besides, we're being rude to our guest." Melanie summoned up a smile. "Bianca's our cook and she most definitely does not like to be kept waiting. Dinner's at seven o'clock sharp."

Melanie got up and strolled out of the sunroom. Reid, Maggie, and Porsche followed close behind. No one spoke.

"I tried to warn you," Royce said after they'd left. "Cat and mouse. You should be able to find out more about Dwayne Shuter tomorrow. Based on Father's behavior—worse than usual—I'm fairly certain there's more to that story than some tables and chairs in the school basement."

So he had the same impression as I did. I wondered what else he knew or suspected. I had the feeling it was more than the vague memory of a kind cookie lady.

How much more, I was about to find out.

THIRTY-SIX

WE WERE ABOUT three miles into our run, the terrain as rugged and scenic as Melanie promised, when she took the pace down to an easy jog. I didn't see anything treacherous about this particular stretch of trail, but I was willing to follow her lead. After all, I didn't know what lay ahead.

"Look, Callie," Melanie said, slowing down even more. "You came here looking for the truth. I think after thirty years of living without a mother, you deserve that much." She attempted a smile, failed miserably. "Reid disagrees with me. We've had more than a few harsh words since Royce called asking if he could bring you here."

"I'm sorry. I never meant to cause you any grief." By now we were walking and our stride was anything but brisk.

She waved her hands in dismissal. "If we weren't arguing about you, we'd be arguing about something else. That's just who we are, or at least, who we've become."

I didn't know what to say to that, so I didn't say anything.

"Your father seems to have done a fine job of raising you."

Not the direction I was expecting, but once again my call center training kicked in. Let people tell the story in their own way.

"He was a good man. Sometimes a little lost when

it came to girly things, but he did his best. I still can't believe he's dead."

"You must miss him very much."

"I do. That's one of the reasons I want to find out what really happened to my mother in 1986. My father was convinced she came to a bad end, that she didn't leave voluntarily."

Melanie stopped dead in her tracks and turned to face me, her brown eyes serious. "Can I trust you, Callie?"

"I suppose that depends on what you want to tell me. And why."

Melanie didn't answer. Instead she started jogging, her steps getting faster and less cautious. Once again, I followed her lead. We'd covered about a mile when she stopped dead in her tracks. If I hadn't been paying attention I would have fallen ass over teakettle, but I didn't complain. Instead, I waited for what she had to say. I didn't have to wait long.

"You're a smart girl, Callie, and so I think you know that Dwayne Shuter was more than some guy I met at the library."

"I didn't know when I came here."

"But now?"

"Let's just say I suspected."

Melanie nodded and started walking again. I tagged along.

"We had an affair. I was lonely. Reid was working long hours. Royce was a restless child, so we'd put him in every available activity. Swimming, Boy Scouts, soccer, baseball, hockey. You name it, he was in it. Porsche was only in Junior Kindergarten, but we had her in swimming, tap, and ballet. I would have loved to organize it all, but Reid insisted we hire a nanny. Appearances were—are—important to him. Having a live-in nanny fit the image he wanted to project."

Just like having a cook at a summer cottage, I thought. Other folks barbecued hamburgers and had wienie roasts over a fire pit. We'd feasted on prime rib, Yorkshire pudding, green beans with toasted almonds, asparagus with hollandaise, and wild blueberry pie with homemade vanilla bourbon ice cream for dessert. An aperitif before dinner, wine with, cognac and espresso after.

"I'm sure you're thinking, 'Poor little rich wife,' and I wouldn't blame you," Melanie said. "Maybe I should have asked Reid for a divorce and left when Dwayne begged me to. I told myself I stayed for the sake of the kids, but…but there was something so delightfully sordid about sneaking around, and if I'm being perfectly honest, I'd gotten used to the luxury lifestyle, something Dwayne would never be able to supply. Long story short, I wouldn't leave and Dwayne wasn't satisfied with being the other man. He left me on the same day as your mother left you."

"The same day?"

"The same day. Valentine's Day 1986. How's that for a coincidence?"

THIRTY-SEVEN

I DON'T BELIEVE in coincidence any more than I believe
in psychics. But what did it mean? I stumbled over a tree
root and righted myself before I ended up face down
in the dirt.

"But Dwayne Shuter, he's still alive—" I blurted out
the words before I could stop them. Idiot.

"So you knew who Dwayne Shuter was before you
showed us that photograph." Melanie's tone was one degree up from sub-zero. "I thought as much, though I'll
admit you played it well. I think even Maggie was convinced. She may be a fool, but she doesn't fool easily."

"Yes, I knew who he was, but I didn't know that when
I first came across the photo in the *Marketville Post*."

"I believe you. However did you learn who he was?
There were no names mentioned in the paper."

I told her about finding my parents' certificate of
marriage. How Dwayne Shuter had been listed as a witness. That I'd found him and a recent photo on LinkedIn.
The way the crescent-shaped scar had been the giveaway. Ended with the fact he'd been the site supervisor
on the job site where father had died.

"That's a lot of six degrees of Dwayne Shuter," Melanie said.

"That's what I'm thinking."

"I take it you now believe Dwayne was responsible
for your mother's disappearance and your father's accident?"

"I don't want to jump to any conclusions, but I'm leaning in that direction. Especially now that I know he left Marketville on the same day she did."

"I'll admit it looks bad for him, but the Dwayne Shuter I knew would never have hurt anyone. He broke my heart, yes, but I deserved that."

"Then why did he leave on the same day?"

"We'd had a huge fight a couple of days before. Dwayne wanted us to celebrate Valentine's Day together. It would have been impossible. Reid always made a big deal about Valentine's Day, the best restaurant, two dozen long-stemmed red roses, some sort of expensive jewelry, the more bling the better. It was all part of his idea of appearances."

"So you think Dwayne picked Valentine's Day to leave as the ultimate good-bye?"

"It's what I've believed for thirty years." Melanie's voice caught. "I had no idea how close he was. Toronto. Rumor had him going out west, not that I can remember how that started."

"I don't buy it." I'm not even sure I bought her version of the story, not that I was going to tell her that. "There's something that connects the two of them leaving on the same day. Maybe they even left together, but if so, I don't believe my mother went with the intention of not returning. Neither did my dad. He was digging into her disappearance when he had his accident. Maybe he found out something to incriminate Dwayne."

"I refuse to believe Dwayne would have been a party to your mother's disappearance or your father's death. Besides, you're missing some facts."

"Oh?"

"Abby—your mother—and Reid had been having an affair. Reid told me all about it. Gloated about it even.

He likes to do that, makes him feel like a man. Just one more reason I didn't feel guilty about my relationship with Dwayne. One day, your mother dumped him. Apparently she wanted to make things work with your father." Melanie laughed, a harsh guttural sound that didn't fit with the refined woman in designer running gear. "No one leaves Reid and lives to tell about it. Why do you think I'm still with him?"

I thought about the locket and the tarot cards. "Are you implying that it was Reid, not Dwayne, who killed my mother?"

Melanie stopped walking and turned to face me. "I think it's possible."

We were nearing the end of the trail and I doubted either one of us wanted to sit inside a café and sip on cappuccino. "I appreciate the confidence. I'm just not sure what to do with it. Are you asking me to prove that Reid killed my mother?"

Melanie gave another harsh laugh, wiped away a few stray tears with an impatient hand. "Is that why you think I told you all this, Callie? Why I invited you to our summer home when Royce told me your pathetic tale about your long-lost mother? To get even with Reid for some long ago indiscretion?"

An affair might be considered an indiscretion, but murder? "If not that, then why?"

"Simple, Callie. I want you to stop investigating." Melanie stared at me, manicured hands on hips, her brown eyes hard, any trace of tears long gone. "I want you to bury these secrets so deep that nobody will ever come looking again. Leave Marketville. Go back to Toronto. Forget all about the past, all about my son. Hell, if you need some money, we can arrange that, too. Just

name your price." I stepped back as if I'd been slapped
in the face.

"What if I can't do that? Leave here, forget all about
it. What if I don't have a price?"

"Then I suggest you find a way, and an amount, and
find it soon. Oh, and Callie?"

"Yes?"

"It's best if you and Royce leave when we get back
to the cottage. Make up some sort of forgotten appointment, a migraine headache, whatever it takes."

Melanie started running again, quick and nimble as
an eighteen-year-old, her burden unveiled. I kicked a
stone and watched her go.

THIRTY-EIGHT

WE'D BEEN DRIVING forty-five minutes before either one of us spoke. "What happened during your run with my mother?" Royce asked. It was the first thing he'd said to me since we'd started the two-hour drive home.

"Nothing happened. I just thought it was time to go home. I didn't want to overstay my welcome. Besides, I already told you. I have a bit of a headache."

"Bullshit."

"You're saying I don't have a headache?"

Royce shot me an exasperated look. "No, I'm saying that I don't believe nothing happened. The two of you were like peas in a pod heading off this morning. My mom gets back without you and promptly goes for a nap—something she never does. You arrive almost ten minutes later, say you've got a headache and want to leave. I may not be the most perceptive guy in the world, but even I can connect the dots."

What was I supposed to tell him? That Melanie believed Reid had murdered my mother? That she wanted me to bury any proof I might find? That she'd all but ordered me to stop investigating?

"There are no dots to connect."

"If you say so, Callie." Royce's face tightened and his chin jutted out. I pulled my cocoa butter lip balm out of my purse, slathered it on, and proceeded to stare out the side window.

We drove the rest of the way in silence. By the time

we reached Snapdragon Circle the tension between us was almost palpable. I wished things could have been different, that I could confide in him, but it simply wasn't possible. From this point on, I had to keep Royce at arm's length. The less he knew about my investigation, the better. Despite Melanie's orders, I had every intention of continuing it.

I'd just have to be a little more careful.

I SPENT THE better part of the afternoon going through every single printout, over and over and over again, always reverting to the photo of Leith and Misty and the reward poster. Why hadn't he admitted he knew Misty from way back when? Why hadn't he told me he'd been involved in trying to find out what had happened to my mother? I'd always known that my dad and Leith had been unlikely friends, given their vastly different occupations and rungs on the social ladder, but was there a deeper connection? Some reason that Leith had taken my father on as an "estate" client when his specialty was criminal law?

I didn't have the answer, and I still wasn't sure how to confront him. Sometimes the best way to come up with a plan was to think about something else, let the subconscious work. What I needed was a diversion.

I thought about phoning Chantelle to see if she wanted to go out for dinner or maybe order something in, but she'd want to know how it went at the Ashfords' cottage and I wasn't ready to talk about it. I thought, briefly, of calling Royce but dismissed the idea just as quickly. Ella Cole was also out of the question. Her snoop radar would be on full alert, and I was feeling too vulnerable to dodge her questions effectively. Unfortunately, that was the extent of my "friends" in Marketville.

I pushed my pen and notebook aside, turned on the TV, and started channel surfing and found a *Location, Location, Location* marathon on BBC. There was something about watching Phil Spencer and Kirstie Allsopp touring the UK looking for the ideal home for their latest hard-to-please clients that always made me smile. Maybe it was trying to translate the British terminology. No one seemed to want "new builds." Everyone seemed to want "character features." A nearby "High Street" meant a Main Street with pubs and shops. A "lovely kitchen-diner" meant an eat-in kitchen, most of them painfully miniscule by North American standards. "Two reception rooms" meant a living room and family room. Whatever the reason, the show entertained me without requiring any effort on the part of my brain. Exactly what I needed.

I was midway through the third rerun of *Location, Location, Location*—this time in Glasgow where they talked about the Scottish "offers over" real estate system—when the doorbell rang. Part of me wanted to ignore it, but I paused the show, went to the door and peered out the peephole.

The last person I expected to see stood there, a baseball cap shielding his face.

THIRTY-NINE

REID ASHFORD WAS dressed in blue jeans, a plaid shirt, aviator sunglasses, running shoes, and a Toronto Maple Leaf baseball cap, which he'd pulled down low over his forehead. If he was looking to be inconspicuous, he was doing a halfway decent job of looking like a guy trying to look inconspicuous. Despite the effort I was pretty sure Royce would recognize his own father. I checked the driveway and the road, but didn't see a car.

I opened the door and asked him in. What else what I supposed to do?

"I parked at the mall," Reid said, removing his running shoes, sunglasses, and ball cap in the foyer.

The mall was a couple of miles south of Snapdragon Circle, and the parking lot was typically packed, regardless of day, time, or occasion. Suburbia, it seemed, loved to shop. It would be easy to hide a car there. Parking at the mall would explain the lack of a vehicle in my driveway, though not the reason for his visit. Whatever it was, clearly he didn't want Royce to know about it. Reid went into the living room and watched while I cleared the coffee table.

"Can I get you something? Tea, coffee? Something stronger?"

"I could use something stronger, but I'll settle for coffee. Black, one sugar."

I fled to the kitchen and busied myself with the cof-feemaker. Took a couple of mugs out of the cupboard, along with the sugar bowl. Put a few cookies on a plate. Reid didn't strike me as a cookie kind of guy, but it only seemed polite to offer. Put everything on a black lacquer tray. By the time I got back to the living room, Reid was sitting in my recliner watching baseball. He turned the sound down but left the TV on when I set the tray down.

"Thanks for inviting me in." He stirred a teaspoon of sugar into his coffee mug, took a sip, one eye on the Jays game. I couldn't blame him. They were playing the Yankees, always a good rivalry.

"Good coffee."

"Thank you. Now let's get to what brought you here."

Reid managed a rueful smile. "I'm afraid Melanie can be overly dramatic, especially when it comes to your mother. I came to apologize."

"And yet, you don't want your son to know you're sorry. Otherwise, why the subterfuge?"

"It's not so much that I don't want Royce to know, as there is no need for him to know. The story goes back three decades. He was just a boy when your mother disappeared. This has nothing to do with him. I'd rather it stayed that way."

I nodded. "You're asking me not to tell Royce what you're about share with me."

"Something like that."

Exactly like that. "So tell me the story." I wasn't going to make any promises, any more than I was going to run over to Royce's front door the minute Reid left. He seemed to understand that.

"My wife believes that I murdered your mother, though I don't think she's ever come up with a plausible method. Regardless, I can assure you that I did no such thing."

"Assuming my mother was murdered, why should I believe you?"

"Because I loved your mother, Callie. I would have done anything for her."

"Does doing anything for her include leaving your wife and two kids?"

"I'm not proud of it, but yes, including that."

I took a sip of my coffee and wished I'd poured a generous dollop of Bailey's Irish Cream in it.

"You have my attention."

"At the cottage, I told you I had met your mother on Canada Day, but the truth is that we were first introduced at the volunteer meeting for Marketville's Canada Day tree planting initiative," Reid said. "I didn't want to be there, but Melanie insisted I do something to give back to the community. She was always volunteering for something or the other. Then again, she wasn't commuting to downtown Toronto and working sixty-hour weeks. There was an ad in the *Marketville Post* for the tree planting initiative. The town wanted to plant one hundred and eighteen maple trees, one for every year of Canada's confederation. It sounded like physical labor, something I got far too little of as a stockbroker."

I thought about the newspaper photograph showing the Canada Day volunteers, my father included. Surely they wouldn't have started an affair when he was there? "When did you first meet, do you remember?"

"I'll never forget it. It was March 14, 1984. A Tuesday evening. I had answered the ad, and turned out to be the only one. I met your mother at the Tim Hortons in the strip plaza across from the mall." Reid smiled, and his eyes had a faraway look. "Abby was beautiful, with shoulder-length blonde hair and sapphire blue eyes that sparkled when she talked, but it was more than that. It was the passionate way she presented her vision for what planting trees could do for the town and for the environment. In that your mother was well ahead of the curve. Folks didn't talk about the environment back then, with the possible exception of acid rain. Looking back, I suppose it was love at first sight. On my part, anyway."

"And on her part?"

Reid smiled. "I'd like to say the feeling was mutual, but your mother was strictly business. She had come prepared with a list of tasks that needed doing, from where to purchase and pick up the saplings to finding sponsors for the shovels and gardening gloves, to recruiting enough volunteers to do the actual planting. We split the list down the middle and agreed to meet the following Wednesday. That's when things started to change."

"How so?"

"It was clear Abby was upset. She couldn't seem to focus and it was obvious from the swelling around her eyes and nose that she'd been crying. After a few minutes, she apologized and confessed that she'd had an argument with her husband. I remember saying something like life with my wife was one constant argument, which was, and still is, sadly true."

"Just two people unhappy in their marriages." The sarcasm in my voice sounded sharp, even to me, but I couldn't help it.

"You make it sound so tawdry. It wasn't like that. Your mom needed to talk to someone. I was there. Right place at the right time."

Or maybe the wrong place at the wrong time. "Did my mother tell you why they argued?"

Reid nodded. "Abby wanted to try and reach out to her parents, and Jim—your father—was dead set against it. Apparently they were less than supportive when she told them about her pregnancy. Abby thought it was time to let the past go. You were going to be four, she told me, and enough time had passed. It was time you met your grandparents."

So my mother had wanted to make peace with Corbin and Yvette. My father, stubborn soul that he was, was having none of it. But sharing the family secrets with a virtual stranger? What sort of desperate person did that?

"Let me get this straight. My mother had met you once before, at Tim Hortons, and on the second meeting, she's telling you all of this?"

"It sounds odd when you put it like that, but I got the impression your mother didn't have anyone else to talk to."

How lonely must she have been, with parents who had disowned her and no real friends? Ella Cole might have been a good neighbor, but her gossipy tendencies would rule out any real confidences. I imagined my mother in the beginning, getting married, having a baby, hopeful as she tried to find her way as a young wife and stay-at-home mom. How long before she missed the luxuries of Moore Gate Manor? Before she realized what she had with my father wasn't enough?

I was still mulling it over in my mind when Reid's voice interrupted my thoughts.

"If it's any consolation, we didn't plan to have an affair. It's just that we were both going through a difficult time in our marriages. Your father wouldn't give in on the whole grandparents business, and Melanie had become increasingly fixated on appearances, right down to wanting to enroll Royce in boarding school. She'd even talked about sending Porsche to a private JK. As if. I told her the public system had been good enough for me. I wanted the kids to have a family life, the kind where you watched *Hockey Night in Canada* together on Saturday evenings and played board games like *Monopoly*, *Snakes and Ladders*, and *Clue*."

I couldn't imagine the woman I met playing board games. Bridge, maybe. Or roulette in Vegas. "So you confided in one another and one night…" I couldn't bring myself to say the words. "When did the affair start?"

"A few weeks before Canada Day."

So my mother and Reid had been sleeping together when the Canada Day tree-planting photo had been taken. The one with my father in it. I wondered if he suspected at the time. "How long did it last?"

"We had a handful of 'wrap-up' meetings after Canada Day, but without the volunteer initiative, it was hard to get together without creating suspicion. In hindsight, I realize that Melanie knew something was up. I can't speak for your father."

"So you broke up shortly after Canada Day."

"Yes and no. We'd break up and then find a way to reconnect again. Then one day Abby said it was over for good." Reid's voice broke a little. "She said she owed it to both of you to make the marriage work. I agreed to walk away."

I thought about the photos. Four seasons of a happy family. Ella had said my mother approached her with the idea in February 1985. "Do you remember when that was?"

"As a matter of fact, I do. It was on my thirty-fifth birthday. January 14, 1985."

January 14, 1985. Exactly one year later, Reid had given my mother a locket. A month after that, my mother disappeared.

FORTY

I STARED AT Reid for a moment, trying to keep my emotions in check, then said. "I found the locket."

"What locket?"

"Don't play games. I found the locket with your photograph inside it, a photograph signed by you, with love always, to Abby. I found it in the house, shortly after I moved in."

Now Reid stared at me, his face a mask of bewilderment. Either he was one hell of an actor, or he truly had no idea what I was talking about.

"You can believe me or not, but I don't know anything about a photograph inside a locket," Reid said. "Why would I lie about that when I've admitted to everything else?"

"First of all, you haven't admitted to everything else. I've been doing some research, and I found a photograph of you in a December 1985 issue of the *Marketville Post*. You were volunteering at the food bank with my mother."

"Okay, so I volunteered at the food bank. Maggie was volunteering there and she told me they were desperate for help during the holidays. The only day I was there was the day of the photo shoot." Reid frowned at the memory. "I wasn't expecting undying gratitude, but your mother was positively rude to me, implied that I had an underlying motive. I couldn't understand that. We'd parted amicably, had seen each other in passing several times after that. We'd always been pleasant to one another. Then out of the blue, when I come to help her out, she treated me like some sort of a stalker."

"Maybe she didn't appreciate receiving the tarot cards."

That netted me another blank look. "What tarot cards?"

"Are you trying to tell me that you didn't give my mother a locket and you didn't mail her the tarot cards?"

"I'm not trying to tell you. I am telling you. You said Abby received tarot cards. Clearly they represented some sort of threat to her and she believed I'd sent them." Reid rubbed his chin and nodded. "That would explain her behavior towards me, but I swear I didn't send them. You said you found the locket in the house. Where?"

"In an envelope. The locket was inside it, along with the tarot cards."

"Doesn't it strike you as odd that the house was rented out since 1986 and yet no one found the envelope before now?"

"It was well hidden."

"Or maybe someone left it for you to find, knowing you'd be moving in."

It was a possibility I hadn't considered. I went to my purse and pulled out my cocoa butter lip balm. The ritual of dabbing it on gave me time to think about the options. Had Misty hidden them for me to find? As the last tenant, she had the most opportunity, outside of my dad, and I didn't think he'd hide anything under the carpet. Not when he had a safety deposit box at the bank. Maybe Misty had hidden them for my dad to find, knowing he was planning on renovations. Either way, if someone other than my mother had left them, Misty was the star candidate.

"Why would someone do that?"

"I don't know, but clearly someone believed they were important enough to hide. Will you show me what you found?"

I thought about it. Part of me was reluctant. On the other hand, if Reid were lying, maybe I'd notice something in the way he reacted. "I'll be right back."

I went to the kitchen, opened up the cupboard over the fridge, and pulled out a box of bran flakes, now devoid of cereal and acting as a filing cabinet for the envelope and its contents. Then I went back to the living room, grateful that my open concept floor plan wasn't yet in place.

I pulled out the tarot cards first, tapping each one with my index finger as I placed them side-by-side on the coffee table. "Five tarot cards. The Empress, The Emperor, The Lovers, the Three of Swords…and Death."

Reid picked up each card and studied it before placing it back down on the table. "I'm afraid I don't know anything about tarot."

"I don't understand it either, but I visited a tarot card reader who believes whoever sent these used a five-card spread that represented the Past, Present, Future, the Reason, and Possible Results, and that whoever sent them to my mother took the images at face value. For example, The Empress, with her long, flowing blonde hair represented my mother in the present."

"And the Emperor is in the past," Reid said. "Abby's father."

"Exactly. Which means—"

"Whoever sent these cards knew that part of your mother's history."

"Yes."

"What about The Lovers? You said that represented the future."

"Randi didn't seem to think it represented my parents."

"Meaning the card might have represented me and Abby."

"I think it's possible." I pointed to the Three of Swords, the image of a red heart with three steel blue swords driven through it, storm clouds overhead, rain in the background. "According to Randi, this card represents sorrow, deep sadness, and heartache, but she was especially interested in the three swords. As if the unhappiness was shared."

"And the Possible Results—"

I nodded. "Death."

Reid didn't say anything for a good few minutes. Finally, "Who do you think sent them to Abby?"

I shook my head. "I wish I knew. Until today, I assumed it was the same person who gave her the locket. I also assumed that the person was you."

"Why me?"

I took the locket out of the envelope and passed it to him across the table.

Reid turned the locket over and over in his hands. "It's lovely. It also looks old. And expensive."

"My friend, Arabella, owns an antiques shop in Lount's Landing. I sent her photos of the locket. She tells me the style is Art Deco, likely made in the nineteen-twenties. The opaque glass is something called camphor glass and based on the mark at the back, the silver is actually fourteen-karat white gold. The clear stone in the center is probably a diamond, but of course, she can't verify that from photographs."

"Based on the quality and the use of white gold, I think your friend is right. I still don't understand why you think I gave Abby this. Wouldn't it be more probable that the giver was your father?"

"I think you need to open it."

Reid did just that, taking care not to damage the delicate opening. I could hear the breath catch in his throat when he saw the photograph of himself.

"There's a note on the back of the photo." I watched as Reid popped the picture out and turned it over.

"To Abby, with love always, Reid. Jan. 14, 1986," he read out loud.

He looked at me, his dark eyes serious. "Who would do this? It's like a bad joke."

"Are you saying this isn't your handwriting?"

Reid shook his head. "It's a good imitation, overall, but my uppercase A is more rectangular. If you give me a pen and paper, I'll show you what I mean."

I got both and waited while he rewrote the same words, then compared the two examples side-by-side. The handwriting had strong similarities, but he was right, the uppercase A on the back of the photograph had slightly rounder edges. Even the lowercase letters had subtle differences. I don't know if I'd spot either unless I was looking for it, however. I massaged my temples. There was something else about the handwriting, but I couldn't put my finger on it. Hopefully it would come to me.

"Did you send my mother letters?"

"Never. It would have been too risky."

"So she wouldn't know if this was your handwriting."

"I can't say for certain. I wrote up all of our notes when we were prepping for the Canada Day tree planting initiative. Would she spot the differences a year and a half later? It seems unlikely. Then again, I never heard from her about the locket. If Abby truly believed I sent it, why didn't she get in touch?" Reid's shoulders slumped and for the first time since I'd met him he looked every year of his fifty-some years. "I don't know what to think."

"The obvious answer is that someone was trying to frame you, mess with my mother's head, or both."

Reid put the photograph back, closed the locket, and handed it back to me. "I don't know what to tell you, Callie. I know all signs point to me. All I can tell you is I didn't give the cards or the locket to your mother."

I wasn't ready to let it go. "You admitted that you loved my mother."

"I also told you I loved her enough to let her go."

"Maybe I'm being naïve, but I actually believe you." And I did. Unfortunately, the realization didn't bring me any closer to the truth about my mother.

"Thank you, though I can't help but wonder who was behind all of this."

"I'm going to do everything in my power to find out."

"Be careful, Callie. Whoever it was has kept the secret for thirty years. They aren't going to give it up willingly."

"I'll be careful." How many times had I promised that already?

Reid didn't look convinced, but he nodded anyway. "Fair enough. I'll call you if I think of anything that might help."

"I think Maggie might remember more than she let

on. She worked at the food bank every day for a month. I just don't know how receptive she'll be to my phoning her up and interrogating her."

"I'll try to talk to her. I'll tell her it's important that she gets in touch with you. She'll listen to me."

"I appreciate it."

"It's the least I can do. I should have done more—no, done something—when your mother disappeared, but I didn't want Melanie to know about the affair and I was afraid it would come out. Now I find out she knew all along." Reid shook his head. "All these years, we've been tiptoeing around a secret."

I wasn't about to tell Reid about his wife's affair with Dwayne Shuter. Maybe Melanie would confess, or maybe not. Either way, it wasn't any of my business. I looked outside, saw that it had started raining. "The weather's turned. Do you want a ride back to the mall?"

"No, thanks. I'm only going next door. I need to talk to Royce. It's time that he learns the truth after all these years."

"Why now?"

"Because it should have been done a long time ago. Because as long as the past remains buried, none of us will have a chance in the present. Not me and Mel, and not you and Royce."

"Royce and I are just neighbors."

Reid smiled. "I saw the way my son looked at you. Those weren't neighborly thoughts he was having. I got the impression the feeling was mutual."

I felt myself blush. "Somehow I don't think your wife would approve."

"Leave Melanie to me. You just follow your heart. I'm going to encourage my son to do the same."

I walked Reid to the door and watched as he made his way over to Royce's house, the baseball cap shielding his face from the rain.

FORTY-ONE

I GOT UP at five a.m. Monday morning, tired of tossing and turning. What with Melanie, Reid, Royce, my grandparents, and Leith all battling for top position in my head, sleep had been elusive. If this kept up, I'd have to invest in some serious under-eye concealer.

I still hadn't decided how best to approach Leith, although I was very glad I'd kept my weekly email communications to him at a minimum. I thought about contacting Misty Rivers. I just wasn't up to it. When I finally sat down to talk to her, I needed as much knowledge as possible. The same would hold true for Leith.

But where to get that knowledge? I fired up my laptop and typed G.G. Pietrangelo into the search bar. A LinkedIn listing popped up for a Gloria Grace (G.G.) Pietrangelo, photographer. Her job at the *Marketville Post* was listed in the resume as "staff writer/photographer" from 1983 to 2008. So she'd stayed with the *Post* for twenty-five years. Had the decision to leave been hers, theirs, or mutual?

There was a link to a website for Gloria Grace's Nature Photography. I clicked on it and spent the next hour immersed in a world of stunning photographs, mostly birds, butterflies, fauna and flora, with the occasional insect, turtle, and snake. I wasn't an expert, but even I could recognize when something was really good, and these were truly exceptional. A quarter of a century taking shots of smiling politicians and kids on toboggans, writing blurbs that most people never read, must have seemed like a life sentence. My guess was twenty-five years at the *Post* was about all Gloria Grace could tolerate.

In addition to taking breathtaking shots, Gloria Grace offered pre-planned group outings, all geared exclusively to wildlife and nature photography. The last one had taken place a month earlier at the Bruce Peninsula National Park in Tobermory. There was an online form to arrange for private or semi-private lessons.

A list of recommended cameras included a selection of point and shoot and digital SLRs in a wide range of prices. I printed off the list and got ready to go shopping. It was time to buy myself a camera.

CHANTELLE WAS JUST getting in as I was going out. She was wearing yoga gear and toting a pale green mat, probably just back from teaching a class. I called out to her before taking the Ashford cottage weekend into consideration.

"I'm off to buy a camera. I noticed a huge camera shop in the Nature's Way plaza. I thought I'd check it out. Want to come? I'm terrible at making decisions, and you *are* the self-proclaimed shopping expert."

She grinned, opened the door to her truck, tossed the yoga mat inside, and crossed the road in less time than it took me to extend the invitation.

"I don't know a darned thing about photography, besides taking really horrible pix with my phone, but I'm all in. My plans today included cleaning the house and paying bills." She slid into the passenger seat of my Civic and closed the door. "There's a great all-day breakfast place in that plaza. I love all-day breakfast, don't you?"

"Sure."

"Perfect. We can go there afterwards. I'm dying to find out what happened with Royce and his parents."

"I'm not sure what to tell you," I said with a laugh, thinking about that old adage—more truth is told in jest.

THE CAMERA STORE had an overwhelming selection. Thankfully, I'd brought my list.

"I don't want anything too pricey," I said to the associate. "I'm not sure photography is something I really want to get into. I do have a list of recommendations."

"What sort of photography are you planning?"

"Flowers. Birds. That sort of thing."

Chantelle raised an eyebrow but didn't say anything. I knew I'd be grilled at the all-day breakfast place. Another pun intended.

The associate looked over my list, nodded, then asked me to wait while he found a couple of camera candidates. He came back with three.

"Each of these is a point and shoot. They have the advantage of being compact and lightweight, at a much lower price point than an SLR. Of course the quality of the photos won't be quite as good, but for a novice, any of these three cameras would suit your needs." He smiled. "You can always upgrade."

I made my decision based on the case color—black; price—midpoint; and size of LCD display—largest, while Chantelle dickered with the associate on the price. After a bit of back and forth, he reluctantly knocked a few dollars off.

I grinned as I watched them. They both played the game well. Far better than I could have.

"Thank heavens that's done," Chantelle said as we took our seats at the breakfast place. "Totally boring, even with that little debate thrown in." She leaned forward. "So tell me, just when did this interest in wildlife photography come on? Was it at the cottage?"

"Not exactly."

"Hmm. Okay, then what did happen at the cottage?"

"I'm not quite ready to talk about it yet."

"I can wait. That brings us back to your sudden interest in nature photography. At least I'm assuming it's a sudden interest."

"It is," I said, and updated Chantelle with an abbreviated version of the articles found in the *Marketville Post* while we ate our breakfast—to-die-for French toast with powdered cinnamon sugar, sliced bananas, and real Ontario maple syrup—promising to show her the printouts back at the house.

"Let me get this straight," Chantelle said, after I'd finished. "All of the articles and photographs in the *Post*—at least those ones relating to your mother's disappearance— were by G.G. Pietrangelo, who has since retired and now goes by Gloria Grace Pietrangelo, and who now specializes in nature photography."

"That's right."

"Your idea is to arrange for a private lesson, casually mention your mother, and hope she remembers something that will help you?"

"Put like that, it does sound ridiculous."

"I'm just not sure how you're planning to introduce the topic."

"I suppose I hadn't really thought that part through." I pushed my plate aside, my appetite gone. "Plus it was thirty years ago. The chances of her remembering anything are remote."

Chantelle considered this for a few moments then shook her head. "I don't agree. This would have been at the beginning of her career. Long before she got tired and jaded. It would also have been a big news story in a very small town."

"But that brings me back to your original point. How do I ask Gloria Grace about it?" I sighed. "I don't know what I was thinking. Maybe I should just send the contact form with the truth. Tell her I'm trying to find out the truth behind my mother's disappearance."

"You could do that, I suppose, although you run the risk of coming across like a bit of a nut. She might also remember and decide she doesn't want to get involved."

"What do you suggest?"

"You need to meet with her in person, use the element of surprise. Taking a lesson is a good way to do that." Chantelle drummed her fingers on the table, a look of concentration on her face.

"I've got it," she said after a couple of minutes. There was a glint in her eye that hadn't been there before.

"Meaning?"

"Meaning I'm about to get back to nature with you. C'mon, let's get out of here. It's time to buy another camera. A pink one. Black is so pedestrian."

AFTER CHANTELLE PURCHASED her camera from the same associate—at an even deeper discount than the one she'd negotiated for me—we headed back to Snapdragon Circle, where we spent the next couple of hours at my kitchen table, going over the printouts from the *Post*.

Well, most of the printouts. I held back the ones from the *Toronto Sun* and *Toronto Star*. With the exception of the photo of Misty Rivers and Leith Hampton, they were nothing more than a rehash of what was in the

Marketville paper. I wanted to confront Leith and Misty before I showed Chantelle that one.

For her part, Chantelle studied each printout, listening to my explanation of who was who with an intensity I hadn't expected. She also asked a lot of questions, especially when it came to Reid Ashford and Maggie Lonergan. Maybe that's what information brokers did, but her unabashed curiosity about Royce's father and aunt put me on my guard. I decided not to share Melanie Ashford's confidence about her affair with Dwayne Shuter, partly because I didn't think it was my secret to tell, and partly because I didn't want it to get back to Royce. It wasn't that I didn't trust Chantelle, necessarily, so much as I hadn't quite figured out their relationship.

"There's absolutely no way G.G. Pietrangelo won't remember your mother," Chantelle said when we'd gone through the lot of them. "You need to make that appointment."

I filled out the online form with preferred dates and times, working around Chantelle's fitness class schedule. "Now we wait," I said, hitting send.

"Now we wait," Chantelle agreed, checking her watch. "I should go, unless there's something else you want me to help you with."

There was, though it surprised me to realize it.

"Can you help me find my father's parents?"

"I can certainly try, but from what little you've told me, they may not welcome hearing from you. Are you sure you're ready for that sort of rejection after all you've been through?"

I thought about Yvette's claim that she'd tried to reconnect with my father. Possibly his parents had as well. Even if they hadn't, I needed to find out for myself.

"I'm ready."

No sooner had Chantelle left, promising to get started on the search for Sandra and Peter Barnstable, when my phone rang. The call display said *Private Caller*, and the number was from area code 705. Not local, and not Toronto. *Probably a telemarketer.* I answered it anyway.

"Hello."

"Calamity Barnstable, please."

"Speaking."

"This is Gloria Grace Pietrangelo. You filled out my online form for semi-private nature photography lessons."

"I did." The hair on my arms prickled. I'd filled out the form as Callie. I was sure of it.

"There's no need for the pretense of lessons, Calamity. I recognized your last name. You're Abigail and Jim's daughter. I'm just wondering what brings you to me after all these years."

I'd been going over my cover story since the camera store. Knowing I could simply tell the truth was both terrifying and liberating.

"I'm trying to find out what happened to my mother."

"Why now?"

It was a fair question. I opted for transparency, with some boundaries. "My dad died recently. An occupational accident. I inherited the house in Marketville."

"He kept the house? I'm confused. I was under the impression you'd moved to Toronto."

"We did. He'd been renting the house since 1986. I didn't know about it until the reading of the will. It's raised a lot of questions about the past."

"I appreciate your candor. What can I do for you?"

I told Gloria Grace about going through the *Marketville Post* articles and photos, finding her name as writer and photographer. I stopped short of telling her about my dad's letter, the tarot cards, Reid, and the locket. "I suppose I hoped you'd remember the case," I finished, and heard the hint of desperation in my voice.

"Remember it? It's haunted me every day since the first day I wrote about it. A loving mother and wife who simply vanishes into thin air? I did a lot of research. Most of it never ended up in the paper. My job was to report the facts, not get into conjecture. But there were a few things that just didn't make sense."

I took a deep breath. "Would you be willing to share your research, what you remember?"

"I'm not sure how much help it will be to you after all these years, but, yes. I still have all my notes and photographs. For some reason, I could never bring myself to throw them out. I suppose part of me always thought you'd call one day."

"When can I come and see you?"

"I'm free tomorrow morning, but you'll have to come bright and early. Say eight a.m.?"

"Eight a.m. would be great."

Gloria Grace gave me directions to her studio in Barrie. "It should take you about forty minutes if you take the 400."

"I'll factor that in so I'm not late. And Gloria?"

"Yes?"

"Thank you."

"Don't thank me yet, Calamity. Digging into the past might sound cathartic, but in my experience, it seldom is."

FORTY-TWO

I PUT THE tarot cards, locket, and letter from my father in my purse. I wasn't sure if I would show them to Gloria Grace, but it made sense to bring them along. Just in case.

Gloria Grace's studio was tucked in the middle unit of a small strip plaza that also included a pizza place, sub shop, chiropractic clinic, combination Laundromat/dry cleaner, and convenience store. It didn't strike me as the ideal location for a nature photographer, but what did I know?

Inside the studio was entirely different matter. Every wall was plastered with stunning photographs, each one more vibrant and detailed than the other. My breath caught at a picture of a blue jay fighting off a hawk, claws against talons, the abject fear in the jay's eyes as palpable as the merciless will to kill in the eyes of the hawk. How long did Gloria have to sit in waiting to capture that image?

"*Birds of Prey*. That's one of my favorites. I'm Gloria Grace Pietrangelo." A woman of generous proportions, mid- to late-fifties, sauntered out from behind a screened off area. Unlike many of her size, she wasn't wearing a flowing caftan or leggings with a long sweater. Instead, she was dressed in olive green cargo pants, matching vest, and black turtleneck. From the various lumps and bumps, it appeared that every pocket in the pants and vest held something. Her hair was shoulder length, rust-colored, and heavily streaked with gray. Pale brown eyes that might have been amber in another light. Not a scrap of make-up on a face that, based on the ruddy complexion and deeply etched lines, had experienced decades of the great outdoors. An unapologetic face. An unapologetic woman.

"You're very talented," I said.

"It's a passion."

"It must have been challenging, working for the *Marketville Post* all those years. Kids on toboggans and ribbon cutting ceremonies." I felt my face heat up. What right did I have to speak to her like that?

Gloria Grace laughed, a soft throaty sound that seemed to echo in the small room. "What can I say? The checks cleared. I saved every dime I could. Spent every free moment outside, studying that world. It made living life as G.G. Pietrangelo a little easier. Had to go by G.G. back when I started. A woman working in a man's world. Things have changed. It's easier for women, now. For photographers, what with digital, though I do miss film and the darkroom." She offered up a sad smile. "Of course, every nincompoop with a smartphone thinks they're a photographer these days, but you're not here to listen to me rant. C'mon. There's a kitchenette at the back. We can talk over tea and scones."

I followed Gloria Grace behind the screen, passing a closed door marked "Office," one marked "Washroom," and a stark white room with a basket of dog and cat toys. "Pet sittings," she said, waving her hand in the general direction. "I don't do a ton of it, but I love animals and it helps pay the bills."

I remembered seeing some photos of dogs and cats on her website. Even here, her talent had shone through, the dogs looking proud and pampered, the cats sleek and smug.

Unlike the front of the studio, the kitchenette's soft green walls were devoid of any photographs or other ornamentation. A small, rectangular wooden table, painted white, was tucked against one wall. Gloria Grace gestured for me to sit at one of the two chairs, plugged in the kettle, then pointed to a plastic-covered plate with four scones.

"Lemon cranberry or blueberry? I bought both kinds since I didn't know your preference."

"Blueberry."

She nodded, took out one blueberry and one lemon cranberry scone, wrapped each in a paper towel, and popped them in a microwave for ten seconds. "Heated. Makes all the difference. Butter? Preserves?"

"No, thanks."

"Earl Grey okay?"

"Earl Grey sounds great."

"Anything in it?"

"Just the tea. No milk or sugar."

She nodded again, got everything ready and placed it on the table in front of me. "First we eat. Then we talk."

"You said you expected my call." We'd finished our scones and Gloria Grace had topped up our tea.

"Will you allow me to tell the unvarnished truth? I believe you deserve to know that much, but only you can tell me if you're ready for it. I think you are, otherwise you wouldn't have gone to the trouble of contacting me under the guise of photography lessons, but I need to be sure. Not everything I tell you about your mother or your father will paint a pretty picture. Either I tell it to you the way I'd tell someone with no ties to the story, or I won't tell it at all. It's your choice, and it's not too late to walk away."

I took a sip of my tea, wishing it were something stronger. "I'm not walking away."

Gloria Grace studied me for a few moments. Apparently satisfied, she got up, opened a deep kitchen drawer, and pulled out a thick black binder. She turned to the first page and began reading, flipping through notes and newspaper clippings. I waited while she stood there and read the first few pages, trying hard not to signal my growing impatience. By the time she sat down, I was positively wired.

"It was early on Saturday, February fifteenth when I got the call from my assigning editor at the *Post*," Gloria Grace began. "Word was that an Abigail Barnstable had gone missing the day before, with possible suspicious circumstances. I knew Abby from her volunteer efforts. Some folks, they do these volunteer things because they have community service hours to serve, or because they want the photo op, but your mom seemed like the real deal, and she always treated me with respect whenever I'd come to cover one of her events. Believe me, in the newspaper business, you meet all kinds, and there are plenty of folks who are complete assholes the minute the camera is turned off."

Gloria Grace took a deep breath. "Anyhow, just up and leaving without a word, that didn't sit with me as the sort of thing a woman like Abby would do. Not in a million years. Besides, I knew she doted on you, although in the vein of full disclosure, and not wanting to speak ill of the dead, I think your parents' marriage had its share of challenges. Nothing I knew for fact, at least in the beginning, but I'm good at reading people. I couldn't reconcile her leaving you behind of her own volition. I want you to know that, to believe that, before I go on."

I pulled my cocoa butter lip balm out of my purse and dabbed some on, nodding but unable to speak. Gloria Grace forged ahead with her story.

"As I was saying, I got the call on the Saturday from the editor-in-chief at the paper, a pompous ass I'd been putting up with for more than a decade, but I digress. He told me that the police suspected foul play and that the husband might have been involved. I didn't know Jim Barnstable well. I'd met him at the Canada Day tree planting the year before and he was what best could be described as reticent. At the time I put it down to him wanting to let the limelight shine on his wife." Gloria Grace flushed and fidgeted as if looking for the right words.

"I found out about her affair with Reid Ashford recently," I said, and watched her eyebrows rise in surprise. "Was that what you were worried about telling me?"

Gloria Grace admitted it was. "It makes it easier for me, knowing that you know."

"How did you find out?" I asked, before she could ask me the same thing.

"I interviewed a lot of people. Marketville was even sleepier then than it is now, and your mother's disappearance was big news. It wasn't long before the innuendo of an affair surfaced, thanks to a couple of women who volunteered at the food bank with your mom."

"Let me guess. Misty Rivers and Maggie Lonergan."

"That's right." Gloria Grace gave me an appraising look. "You're remarkably well informed. I'm not sure what I can tell you that you don't already know."

"You can tell me if you believe my father knew about the affair."

"I'm sure he did, Callie. I know that's not what you want to hear, but I'm certain that Maggie Lonergan would have told him."

"Because she was Reid's sister-in-law."

"Hell no. Because she was a woman scorned."

FORTY-THREE

I STARED AT Gloria Grace. "A woman scorned? Are you saying that Maggie Lonergan had an affair with her sister, Melanie's, husband?" Talk about the Bermuda triangle of sibling rivalry.

"No, but not for lack of trying. Maggie had been in love with Reid for years, though he'd always declined her advances. She probably could have dealt with the rejection as long as Reid stayed faithful to her sister. When he had the affair with Abby, it became a personal rejection."

It also meant that when Maggie selected the food bank for her community service hours it had been more with the eye towards stalking than a gesture of goodwill. Then again… "But the affair was over by the time they were all volunteering at the food bank together."

"Your research really is impressive. Yes, it *was* over by then. To Maggie, that made it even more personal. How dare someone like Abby reject someone as wonderful as Reid? I got the distinct impression Maggie had a very vengeful streak in her."

"Meaning?"

"Meaning that I've always wondered if Maggie Lonergan was behind your mother's disappearance."

The statement caught me by surprise. During our run in Muskoka, Melanie had demanded I stop investigating. At the time I believed she was protecting Reid, but it was equally possible she'd been protecting her sister. Another thought occurred to me.

"Who told you that Maggie was in love with Reid?"

"Another volunteer at the food bank. A woman by the name of Misty Rivers. Claimed to be a psychic."

Misty Rivers. Again.

"How would Misty Rivers know?"

"They grew up on the same street in Marketville, back when it was a really small town. Reid and Melanie were high school seniors when they started dating. Maggie and Misty were a year younger, and close friends at the time. By the time I interviewed them, the friendship was over. From what I could gather, neither sister had much time for Misty's so-called mystic abilities."

I rubbed my temples, trying to fight off the headache I knew was coming, and trying to make sense of everything Gloria Grace had told me so far.

"You believe Maggie might be behind my mother's disappearance. Where do you think my mother went that day?"

Gloria Grace shook her head. "I wish I knew. I tracked down every lead, no matter how slim. Nothing. The police also came up empty-handed. It was as if she just vanished in thin air."

"But people don't just disappear into thin air."

"No, they don't."

"What do you make of Dwayne Shuter leaving on the same day?"

Now it was Gloria Grace's turn to look surprised. "Dwayne Shuter? I don't recall any Dwayne Shuter."

I filled her in. Told her how he'd been a witness at my parents' wedding. How he'd had an affair with Melanie. How he'd left the same day as my mother. How I'd seen his picture in the Christmas food bank photo, and later on, on LinkedIn, where his occupation was listed as site supervisor at the same company as my dad had worked when he died. How, despite repeated efforts, he was not returning my calls.

By the time I was done talking, I realized that Dwayne Shuter looked very guilty indeed.

Gloria Grace reached the same conclusion, although she was none too happy about it. "I don't know how I missed Dwayne Shuter," she lamented, buttering the other blueberry scone and offering half to me. I waved it off. The last thing I needed was more starch and sugar.

"Well, to be fair, he had left Marketville," I said, dabbing on the balm. "In all likelihood he and Melanie kept the affair a deep secret. I don't even think Maggie knew. And if Misty knew—"

"You're right. If Misty had known, she'd have told me in a heartbeat." She sighed and took a bite out of her scone. "We need to find a way to get this Dwayne Shuter to talk to you."

I had to smile at that. "We, Gloria Grace?"

"Yes, we. I always finish what I start, Callie, and I've been waiting to write the ending of this story for thirty years. Now, what else can you tell me, so *we* can get started?"

I thought about the tarot cards. The four seasons of a happy family photographs. The silver locket from Reid. The letter from my father. The photo in the *Sun* of Misty with Leith Hampton. For the first time since I'd started on this journey, I was ready to show my collection of clues to someone. Who better than the reporter who'd been there at the beginning of it all?

"It's not what I can tell you, so much, Gloria Grace, as what I can show you."

"These things, did you bring them with you?"

"I did."

"Then what are we waiting for?"

"I FOUND THESE in the attic," I said, laying out the four seasons photographs of our family on the kitchen table. I left out the part of finding them inside a coffin in the attic. There were some things just too weird to try and explain. "The next-door neighbor, Ella Cole, took these in 1985. The location is the elementary school where the Canada Day tree planting took place. You interviewed Ella for the *Marketville Post*."

"I remember her," Gloria Grace said. "She was a bit of a gossip, as I recall."

"Still is, though I don't think there's anything mean-spirited about her."

"Why did she take the photos?"

"Ella claims to be an amateur photographer. According to her, my mother asked her if she'd do the series. Ella said she didn't question why, that she was honored to be asked."

"She's a good photographer. Caught the nuances of each face, used the lighting to her best advantage. None of that explains the why of it."

"It's possible my mother was trying to create a time capsule. It's also possible she just wanted to reassure herself everything was back to normal. From what Reid told me, she'd broken up with him in January 1985. From what Ella told me, my mother approached her that February."

"Hmm... I suppose that's one possible explanation. What else do you have in that bag of tricks?"

I put the photographs back in my purse and took out the envelope containing the tarot cards and the locket. "I was stripping out the old carpet in the living room—

there's hardwood under there I want to get refinished. Anyway, I found this envelope."

"How old was the carpet?"

"Original to the house, if you can believe that. I'm sure whoever hid this envelope either expected to come back or expected someone to find it long before now."

Gloria Grace nodded. "That's a valid point. I take it that you think your mother hid the envelope?"

"I do, though I don't have anything concrete to back that up."

"Okay. Let's see what you have in there."

I started with the five tarot cards, laying them in the order listed on the paper they were wrapped in. "I've consulted with a tarot card reader, a woman by the name of Jessica Tamarand, goes by the name of Randi, who coincidentally, was also a tenant at Sixteen Snapdragon Circle about four years ago."

"You're sure it's a coincidence? Did it ever occur to you that she might have been the one to hide the cards?"

I shook my head. "I don't see it. Randi was just twelve when her family moved to Marketville. She didn't even realize that the house she was renting was the house my mother had disappeared from, though she remembered the story because it made her parents second-guess their decision to move to Marketville. She said the house had a bad aura, made worse when Ella Cole came around, so she broke her lease agreement early and moved out. She seemed very sincere."

"I'm sure she did."

I looked down at my shoes and tried to think of something to say. Gloria Grace took pity on me.

"Let me go through my notes. The Tamarand name doesn't sound familiar, but I might have something on the family."

"Thank you."

Gloria Grace fingered the cards, tapping the images one at a time. "The Empress, The Emperor, The Lovers, The Three of Swords, and the Death card. What did Randi have to say about the cards?"

"She said whoever sent them selected them for their obvious imagery, versus any real knowledge of tarot. I thought perhaps Reid had sent them, because of this." I handed her the locket. "There's a picture of Reid inside, with an inscription to Abby. When I confronted Reid about it, he said he'd never seen it before. Furthermore, he claims the note isn't his handwriting, but an attempt to copy it."

"Let me guess," Gloria Grace said with a smile. "He seemed sincere."

I felt the color rise in my face. "I must seem like a complete fool."

"No, just someone very trusting, and perhaps a little naïve. But let's take Reid at his word. If he didn't give your mother the locket, who did, and why would they go to the trouble of making her believe the locket came from him? What purpose could it serve?"

I shook my head, my frustration mounting. "I don't know. The cards might have been sent to scare her, but the locket wouldn't do that. It doesn't make sense."

"Exactly. When I was a journalist, if something didn't make sense, it usually meant I was looking at the situation in the wrong way."

I mulled over the possibilities. Earlier Gloria Grace had suggested that Randi might have hidden the tarot cards. I still didn't believe Randi would have done such a thing, but I could think of one person who had the means, motive, and opportunity. Misty Rivers.

The only question was whether Leith was her accomplice. "I have an idea of who might have hidden the envelope," I said.

"I thought you might, once you considered the possibility that it wasn't your mother," Gloria Grace said. "Care to share?"

I wanted to, I really did. I also knew it wouldn't be right to make unfounded accusations. I needed to confront Misty Rivers first. How I was going to do that remained to be seen. What Misty told me would also determine how, or if, I approached Leith about his prior relationship with the self-proclaimed psychic. It might even be possible that Misty hid the envelope on Leith's instruction.

"I'm sorry. I dragged you back into this and now I'm being secretive, but I need to speak to the person first."

"I respect your position, Callie. Just be careful."

I was tired of being told to be careful, but I nodded anyway. I'd come here hoping to learn something, anything, that might help me, and I'd learned a lot. I didn't want Gloria Grace to think I was ungrateful. Besides, there was more that I wanted to show her.

"I have one final printout. It's from the March second issue of the *Toronto Star*." I slid the photocopy across the table and waited while she read the article.

"You can almost feel the tension," Gloria Grace said. "I'm guessing they weren't too pleased with the coverage, but they probably didn't want to make a scene." She flipped the copy back to me. "You take after your grandmother."

"Did you ever meet them? My grandparents?"

"No. In fact, that was one of the things about this story that bothered me."

"In what way?"

"It didn't take me long to find out that your mother's

parents were Corbin and Yvette Osgoode of Moore Gate Manor in Lakeside. I'll admit I was surprised. Nothing about your parents' house indicated coming from that sort of affluence."

"They were estranged. Didn't approve of my dad, the wedding, or my being born."

"That would explain the quash."

"The quash?"

"I told my editor I'd found another angle for the story, and that the Osgoodes were it. At first he seemed enthusiastic. A couple of hours later he came back and told me in no uncertain terms to back off. There was to be no mention of either Corbin or Yvette. Nor was I to approach them."

"Why would he want to stop an interview? If nothing else, it could have strung the story along."

"A large media conglomerate owns the *Marketville Post*, along with a number of other regional newspapers and magazines. Osgoode Construction was a big advertiser in *Home and Builder*, one of its major trade and consumer publications—when it comes to print, it's usually trade or consumer, but *Home and Builder* had a glossy magazine format for each market. I suspect Corbin threatened to stop advertising if the *Post* went down that road. At the time, I figured the Osgoodes just wanted privacy during a difficult time, and since my editor assured me they knew nothing, I let it go. It rankled, but I had to drop it if I wanted to keep my job. Which I did. I've never felt right about it."

"Did your editor make a habit of interfering in your articles?"

Gloria Grace shook her head. "Never. That was the one and only time."

Now that was interesting. I filled her in on Yvette's

impromptu visit. "I don't think she was involved in stopping your investigation or your story," I finished. "Corbin, on the other hand, it's entirely plausible."

"Makes you wonder what he was afraid I'd find out."

"Do you think you'd be willing to try now, all these years later? I mean, you're not working for the *Post* any longer."

Gloria Grace smiled, a glint brightening her pale brown eyes to amber. "I thought you'd never ask."

FORTY-FOUR

GLORIA GRACE'S PROMISE to follow through on Corbin Osgoode had done wonders for my peace of mind. For the first time since I'd moved to Marketville, I woke up ready to face Misty Rivers. She answered her phone on the second ring.

"Hello, Callie."

Damn call display. Ruined any element of surprise. "Hi, Misty. I'm wondering if you had some time to stop by. I have some questions. About my mother." *Among other things.*

"You're in luck. I've got nothing planned for today that can't be shifted to another. I can swing by this morning if that works."

"It does. Thank you."

Misty was at my door within the hour. She had managed to squeeze into a pair of black jeans that were ten years and ten pounds away from the present. The jeans were topped off with a rainbow-colored crocheted sweater that looked homemade and probably was. The inky blue nail polish had been changed to black with silver glitter at the tips.

"Misty. Thanks for coming." I led her into the kitchen. "Can I offer you something to drink? Coffee or tea?"

"Do you have milk yet?" Said with the hint of a smile, but it was a definite dig in reference to our first meeting. What Misty was telling me in a not-so-subtle way was that she remembered how dismissive I'd been. I let it go.

"I do indeed. I also have some store-bought chocolate chip cookies."

"Then coffee, please. One sugar. I'll pass on the cookies, much as I'd love one. I should probably pass on the sugar, too, but can't seem to manage it." Misty looked down at her too-tight jeans and shifted in her seat. "I'm trying to lose a bit of weight. Unfortunately, it keeps finding me."

Could this woman actually read my mind? Or had I stared at those jeans without realizing it? I got the coffeemaker going, put the mugs, milk, and sugar on the bistro table, all the while trying to steady my nerves. Watched as the coffee dripped, dripped, dripped.

Misty reached for the milk and sugar, poured some of each into her empty mug, and stirred the contents into a thick paste. "On the phone you said you had some questions for me."

I poured the coffee, tried to keep my hands steady and my voice calm. "Actually, I have some things to show you if that's okay."

"I'm more than happy to help."

I went to the cupboard where I'd hidden everything inside the cereal box—admittedly feeling a bit 007. I took out the locket and tarot cards and placed them on the table. "I found these in an envelope, hidden under the living room carpet. At first I thought my mother had hidden them there but I no longer believe that."

"What *do* you believe?" Misty's black eyes narrowed.

"That you placed them there, knowing I'd rip up the carpet in short order."

Misty clapped softly, her silver-tipped fingernails sparkling in the kitchen's soft light. "I wondered when you'd figure that out. I thought I might have given myself away when I mentioned the envelope the last time I was here. I saw you'd been tearing up the carpet and knew you must have found it."

"So you covered up the slip by claiming to have psychic vision."

"Guilty as charged, though in my defense, I do have some psychic abilities. What I don't understand is why you didn't show me the locket and tarot cards there and then. Why wait until now?"

"I'd just found the envelope. I didn't even have a chance to process what I'd seen, let alone show it to anyone. I didn't know whether I could trust you. I knew my father had, but he was dead, and I'm not convinced that his fall was an accident. Add to the mix that Leith seemed skeptical about you and your psychic abilities and you can understand my hesitation."

"Leith was skeptical?"

"Yes," I said, not sure why that was the point Misty had zoned in on. "Why, does that matter?"

"No, I'm just surprised. He never seemed like a doubter to me. Go on."

"After you left, I checked the peephole in the door. I could see right into the kitchen. I figured you'd seen me hiding the envelope in the cupboard. That really gave rise to my suspicions."

"I didn't look through the peephole and see you hide it, but I can certainly see where you would have arrived at that conclusion." Misty leaned back in her chair, her eyes piercing in their appraisal. "You trust me now, though. At least enough to invite me here and do a show and tell. What's changed?"

"I met with Gloria Grace Pietrangelo yesterday." No reaction beyond a shrug.

"You might remember her as G.G. Pietrangelo." Still no reaction from Misty.

"She used to write for the *Marketville Post*. She covered my mother's disappearance extensively."

A flicker of recognition in the inky black eyes. A nod. "I remember her now. Weird eyes. Pale brown, a hint of amber. Skinny. She was very intense."

"She's chilled out some," I said, trying to imagine a skinny Gloria Grace. I couldn't. "The way I figure it, there was only one person with the means, motive, and opportunity to hide that envelope. That was you. You lived here. You were into tarot. You worked with my mother at the food bank. What I haven't been able to figure out is why."

Misty nodded her approval. "I admire your powers of deductive reasoning, not to mention your investigative research. As for the why, it's a long story that goes an even longer way back. I think I'll take you up on the offer of chocolate chip cookies after all."

"I FIRST MET your mother in the spring of 1984," Misty said. "It was a blustery day in late March, the kind of day where you start to think winter will never let go. We were manning the Canada Day tree-planting booth at the Marketville Home Show. It was held indoors, but we had set up the display outside the front doors. It was your mom's idea. She figured we could get people coming and going. Mostly I remember how we just about perished from the cold."

A memory. Me, tobogganing down a hill, laughing, my mom clapping and cheering me on, her face red from the cold. I wondered if I could find the hill again.

I saw Misty looking at me with open curiosity.

"Sorry, you were mentioning the cold. It made me remember tobogganing with my mom."

Misty nodded. "That would have been the hill over by Tom Flanagan Park. Sorry to say that it's no longer there. It's all houses now, with fenced-in yards."

Another lead gone. If I could have walked that hill, maybe another memory would have come to me. As it was—

"Back to the day I met your mom," Misty said, interrupting my thoughts. "The idea was to hand out brochures about the initiative and get more volunteers for the big day. We also handed out maple seedlings for local residents to plant on their own property on Canada Day. Your mom was a born leader, and I've always been more of a follower, so we were well suited. By the end of the day, we'd formed the beginning of a friendship."

"If you were friends, then why didn't my dad know who you were?" I thought about Misty standing beside Leith with the reward poster. "Or maybe he did, but for some reason Leith didn't bother to share that information when he was going over the terms of my dad's will."

"You mustn't blame Leith. Your father was insistent. If anything happened to him, you were not to be told about our past history. To say Leith was unhappy about that condition would be an understatement, but your father was not to be swayed. He truly wanted you to go at this with a completely unbiased eye." Misty smiled. "He also knew you, Callie. If you thought some swindling psychic was after his money, you'd work tirelessly to find the truth on your own. The fact that you've learned as much as you have in such a short time proves him right."

"But you'd been living here when he drew up the

will. When he had the accident. He'd hired you when he was alive. He must have trusted you."

"He did. He trusted me enough to know I'd do what I could to help you. Even if you didn't want my help."

"The locket and the tarot cards. You hid them under the carpet, knowing I'd find them."

"I knew you were being left a bit of money to renovate the house. The carpeting was well past its prime and there was hardwood underneath. I figured you'd remove the carpet sooner rather than later. Putting the locket and the tarot cards in an envelope there would lend a hint of mystery. Nothing like a good mystery to motivate a curious mind."

"Where did you find them?" I asked.

"In the attic."

"You were in the attic?" I said, incredulous.

"It's not like I broke into it," Misty said, her tone indignant. "Your dad gave me the key and asked me to take a poke around. He knew I'd been a friend of Abigail's and he thought I might find something that he had overlooked but didn't add up. The locket was in a blue trunk, in a small enameled box with some other jewelry."

"Was the photo of Reid inside when you found it?"

"Why do you ask?" She was staring down at her fingernails.

"Because I showed the locket and the photograph to Reid, and he claimed not to know anything about it. I'm inclined to believe him. He was very forthright about his affair with my mother. He had no reason to lie about the locket."

Misty looked up and stared at me with those piercing dark eyes. "No reason to lie about the photograph, maybe. The locket…that's a different kettle of fish entirely."

"What are you saying, Misty?"

"That maybe I added the photo of Reid and faked his handwriting."

Faked? Sounds more like forged to me. "Maybe?"

"All right, fine. I did add the photo. But I know for a fact that Reid gave that locket to your mom." I thought about what Reid had said. *I don't know anything about a photograph inside a locket. Not, I don't know anything about a locket.* I realized how easily he had played me. "The locket is old, from the nineteen-twenties. Was it some sort of family heirloom?"

Misty nodded. "Reid told Abby it had belonged to his mother, or was it his grandmother? It doesn't matter. It was some sort of family heirloom. He'd kept it hidden from Melanie because she wouldn't have appreciated it. Melanie liked new things. She would have viewed the locket as a hand-me-down. Your mom loved anything vintage."

I thought about the Calamity Jane poster in the attic. "That still doesn't explain your duplicity."

"I wanted you to know about Reid. The locket alone wouldn't have done that, now would it? You'd just have thought your dad gave it to your mom. Or that it was something passed down from your grandmother."

That much was true. In fact, without the photo of Reid, it's likely I would never have connected him to my mother. "I assume you selected the tarot cards for the same reason."

Misty nodded. "I'd hoped that you would come to me for an explanation. When you didn't…well, I could hardly ask you about them, now could I?"

"I wasn't sure I could trust you. I'm sorry."

"I probably would have felt the same way, if our roles were reversed. What did you end up doing about the tarot cards?"

"I visited Randi at Sun, Moon & Stars. It turns out she used to live here, just before you, as a matter of fact. Though back then she went by the name of Jessica Tamarand. She broke her lease—claimed the house was haunted and she wanted no part of that."

"Ella told me about the previous tenant. I gathered she and Ella didn't get on too well."

"She saw Ella as a busybody, and Ella saw her as standoffish. But it was Ella that told me that Jessica worked as a psychic at that 'new-agey' place behind the whole foods store. I checked and saw that a Randi worked there. I figured Randi might be Jessica Tamarand. I was right."

"You don't need psychic abilities," Misty said with a smile. "You're much better at playing amateur detective than I am. I'd heard of Randi, of course, but I never connected the dots. What did she tell you about the cards?"

"Essentially, she felt that whoever had sent them had chosen cards that would represent a literal meaning. She didn't think that they were from an actual reading. That's when I began to think you might have been behind the cards, though at the time I thought they had been sent to my mother and she'd hidden them so my dad wouldn't find them. It never occurred to me that you might have hidden them for me to find until I spoke with Gloria Grace."

"Randi was right. I did select them based on the imagery. I didn't think you knew anything about tarot cards, and as I said before, I assumed you'd come to me for an interpretation."

"I appreciate what Randi told me about them, but

she was quick to point out her reading was subjective." I pointed to the cards on the table. "Will you tell me what you meant them to represent?"

Misty tapped each card with a silver-tipped fingernail then gently pushed The Empress and The Emperor in my direction. "The Empress, of course, represents your mother, The Emperor your grandfather. Notice how The Empress looks as if she might be pregnant, how The Emperor is so stern and authoritative. Your grandfather, the obstinate old goat, could never forgive your mother for getting pregnant as a teenager. He refused to speak to her or your father, let alone acknowledge you. Then something happened just before she disappeared. It made me think he might have had a change of heart."

I started in surprise. This was something new. Yvette believed that Corbin had been too stubborn to change his mind, and I'd found no evidence to the contrary. "What happened?"

"She received a phone call one day at the food bank. That in itself was surprising. None of us had ever received a call there. She seemed flustered during the call, not that it lasted long. When she hung up she said something along the lines of forgiveness coming at a high price, but she wouldn't elaborate." Misty sighed softly. "That phone call rattled her to the core. A week later, she was gone."

"What made you think the call came from my grandfather?"

"I'll admit it's a leap. But who else could it have been?"

I didn't have an answer. I only knew that if it was my grandfather, my grandmother hadn't been aware of it. "What about the next two cards, The Lovers and the Three of Swords? Randi told me that the Three of

Swords represents sorrow, deep sadness, and heartache. What interested her were the three swords, as if the unhappiness was shared between the lovers and a third party. Is that what you meant? That the affair between Reid and my mother was causing pain to all of them?"

"Randi is very astute. Your mom tried to break it off with Reid, I can't tell you how many times. She just couldn't seem to make a clean break. She'd go a few weeks, even a few months without seeing him, but he was like opium to her. It was only a matter of time until your father found out." Misty tapped the Death card. "That was the death of their marriage."

Another surprise. There had never been a whisper of my mother's infidelity, not when I grew up, and not in my father's letter to me. "He knew?"

"Not at first, not for a long time. Love truly can be blind. Of course, once Maggie the mouthpiece got wind of it, there was no stopping her from going to see your father as a 'friend.'" Misty laughed. "Ella Cole used to call her Magpie Lonergan, an aptly fitting name."

I smiled, remembering Ella saying those exact same words.

"Your father had a tough time reconciling it," Misty continued, "and the strain of trying to work things out really seemed to wreak havoc with your mom's health. She'd lost a lot of weight, and she'd already been thin to start with. Her skin took on a waxy look, and her hair had all but lost its shine. I told her I was worried about her, and that's when she told me they were considering a trial separation. I suppose that's what made the police so suspicious of your father. They just couldn't prove anything, and without a body—"

"But you believed him, didn't you? So did Leith.

Otherwise why would the two of you hand out reward posters?"

"I'm not sure what I believed, Callie. I suppose I just wanted to find out the truth. Your mother might have been an adulterer but she was my best friend, and that meant something to me. It still does. As for Leith, we go back a lot further than that reward poster. You see, once upon a time, we were married."

FORTY-FIVE

IF MISTY'S REVELATION shocked me, it was mostly because she didn't strike me as a trophy wife.

Misty sensed my surprise. "I know. I'm not his usual type, which over the years has become younger, blonder, and bustier. We met as teenagers at the beach in Lakeside, had a hot and heavy romance, got married without a lot of forethought, and rented in Marketville while Leith finished university in Toronto. When he graduated a couple of years later, he moved to the city and I stayed up here. It was all very amicable."

"So you've remained friends."

"A more apt description is that we're friends between wives. When he's married, we're cordial. How cordial depends on how secure or insecure the current wife is." Misty shrugged, resigned to the reality of the relationship. "We were already divorced by the time your mom went missing, but Leith was a friend of your dad's, and I was a friend of your mom's. We banded together. The reward poster was Leith's idea. I'm fairly certain he was planning to fund it. He was doing all right by then and your parents didn't have a bean between them."

Yvette and Corbin Osgoode had plenty of beans. Too bad they hadn't been willing to pony up a cent for their only child. Then again, if there had been more money available in the way of a reward, would the outcome have been any different?

I thought about the letter my father had left for me in

the safety deposit box. I'd read it so many times I could recall it verbatim.

Things changed when Misty Rivers rented the house. She told me the house was not haunted, but possessed by your mother's spirit. I know it sounds farfetched, but another renter had insinuated much the same thing. Misty was convinced your mother had been murdered, and she wanted to help me seek out the truth. I'll admit I was skeptical at first. I'm not a believer in spirits or psychics, but I've never been able to reconcile your mother's disappearance. I decided to put my trust in her.

At the time I read it, I assumed Misty had been a stranger who had rented the house. Now I realized the error of my assumption. A psychic-touting stranger would never have convinced my father to buy a coffin, let alone put a skeleton in it. That still didn't explain why Leith had kept his relationship with Misty a secret.

"You, Misty, I can almost forgive. After all, you did come here to talk to me and I sent you packing. But why didn't Leith tell me? Why all the secrecy?"

"Your father had expressly told both of us not to say anything to you unless it was absolutely necessary. He wanted you to look at this with an open mind."

"And now?"

"You've uncovered a lot in a short time. More than anyone expected. Better you hear the truth from me than from another source. To be honest, I figured Maggie Lonergan or Ella Cole would have said something, but I'm guessing neither one knew about Leith. Trust me, if they had, you would have heard. Regardless, it was only a matter of time. As I've said before, your investigative abilities are impressive."

"Not so impressive that I've found anything out to solve the mystery. When you think about it, I'm no further ahead than you were thirty years ago. Except that now I have a coffin with a skeleton in my attic."

"I'm sorry about that. One of my more lame-brained ideas. I'm actually surprised that your father agreed to it, let alone followed through with the purchase." Misty gave a sad smile. "It only goes to underline how desperate he was to find out the truth."

"So the séance—"

"I wouldn't know how to hold a séance if my life depended on it." I sighed, wondering what to do with them.

"If you like, I can see if my theater group would like it. They always put on a Halloween play."

"That would be great."

Misty got up. "I'll get back to you. In the meantime, I've taken up enough of your time. I just hope I've been some help."

"You have, thank you. Before you go, did my father tell you anything about the accidents he had at work?"

"Accidents?" Misty frowned. "No, why? Surely you don't believe his death was any more than an unfortunate industrial accident."

An unfortunate industrial accident. The exact words the caller had used to tell me about my dad's death.

"I don't know what—or who—to believe any longer, Misty. The more I dig, the more nothing is what it appears to be on the surface. One thing I do know. That skeleton I found in the attic isn't the only false clue. Of that much I'm certain."

CHANTELLE CALLED A few minutes after Misty left. Seeing her name displayed on the caller ID, I didn't bother with the formality of a hello.

"What's up?"

"I might have a line on your grandparents, Peter and

Sandra Barnstable. I still need to confirm some details, but it looks like they might have gone to Newfoundland a few years ago."

I thought about the travel brochure from Newfoundland and Labrador that I'd found in my dad's filing cabinet. At the time I thought it was because he wanted to go whale watching there someday. Could it be he had found his parents? "Newfoundland. Are you sure?"

"Well, no, if I were sure, I wouldn't be calling to ask you questions." Chantelle sounded more than a bit annoyed, not that I could blame her. She'd offered to help me—gratis—and here I was second-guessing her.

"I apologize. I just had a long visit with Misty Rivers and my head is spinning."

"Anything you want to talk about?"

"Not yet. Maybe tomorrow evening, over pizza and a glass of wine."

"Sounds like a plan. In the meantime, I'll try to find out a bit more about the Barnstables. Could be they just went there for a visit and left again. The thing is, I found a record of them going there about ten years ago, but there are no records of them leaving. Of course, they could have bought a car from the *Auto Trader* and driven to who-knows-where."

Who-knows-where. There was a lot of that going around.

THE PHONE RANG again less than five minutes later. According to the caller ID, it was the Glass Dolphin.

"Arabella, nice to hear from you. Any more information about the locket?"

"Not the locket, the poster."

I wandered into my bedroom and looked at the Calamity Jane poster hanging on the wall. "What about it?"

"I studied all the photos you sent to me and something seems a bit off. I checked with Levon, and he agrees. We'll have to remove it from the frame to be sure."

Levon was an antiques picker, Arabella's ex-husband and ex-business partner, and oddly enough, her best friend. "Be sure of what?"

"I think it's probably a very recent reproduction. Which means it wouldn't have any value beyond decorative."

A reproduction. I'd imagined my mother scouring around antique malls looking for the perfect gift. Now it looked as if my poster was just one more thing that wasn't all it seemed to be.

"I wasn't planning on selling it, so the value isn't really a concern to me. I'd like to find out either way."

"As long as you're sure you want to know the truth."

"I'm sure."

"Okay. Then why not bring it to the Glass Dolphin along with the locket?"

We went back and forth, comparing calendars and availability, and finally made arrangements for me to go to the Glass Dolphin the following week. At this point, I didn't see either the locket or the poster offering me any additional clues into my mother's disappearance, but it would be nice to see Arabella again. I was overdue to visit her new shop.

With Misty gone, Chantelle's possible news about my grandparents, and Arabella's suspicion over the Calamity Jane poster, my mind was a complete and utter mess. I decided to bake some peanut butter cookies. If they turned out well, I would bring a half-dozen to Royce and see where it might lead. I already knew he had a sweet tooth, and if I could cultivate that, more the better. I know it probably made no sense, but I was starting to feel ready for a relationship, and I couldn't get Royce out of my mind. The fact that his father complicated things...well, we could work around that, couldn't we?

That decided, I wasn't sure if the recipe I'd found online was the one my mother had used. Even so, the Old-Fashioned Peanut Butter Cookies recipe seemed easy enough, even for someone with my limited baking skills.

There was something therapeutic about mixing together the simple ingredients of peanut butter, baking powder, baking soda, white and brown sugar, eggs, flour, and vanilla—the real stuff, not the imitation kind that tasted like chemicals.

I'd just set the oven temperature to 350, dropped spoonfuls of cookie dough onto a greased baking sheet, and was about to flatten and put a crisscross pattern on the tops with the tines of a fork when the doorbell rang. I wiped my hands on a terrycloth tea towel, wondering if Royce had somehow sensed what I was doing and had come to share the experience. The idea of it made me smile and I found myself humming as I went to the door, knowing that I probably had flour on my face, and not caring.

The hum stuck in the middle of my throat when I saw who was standing there.

FORTY-SIX

I RECOGNIZED MY grandfather from the society newspaper photo Chantelle had shown me. He wasn't wearing a tux, but his crisply pleated khakis and pale blue button-down shirt reminded me of the sort of business casual attire the bank's executives used to wear on Fridays. Us call center types didn't tend to dress that well even on a regular day, but then again, we were tucked inside minuscule cubicles where no one saw us—or cared to.

I opened the door, wishing I wasn't covered in peanut butter and flour, and hoped my hair looked reasonably tame tucked inside its ponytail. "Can I help you?"

"Corbin Osgoode. My wife, Yvette, was here earlier. She insisted I pay you a visit. Here I am." His voice was the gravelly baritone of a longtime smoker.

I felt my face flush under the layer of flour and wanted to kick myself. "Please, come in. Forgive my appearance. I've been baking. Or trying to. Peanut butter cookies. They should be ready in a half hour or so. If you'd like a sample." I realized I sounded like a blithering idiot but I couldn't seem to stop myself.

Corbin merely nodded and walked stiffly into the living room. I got the coffee going using freshly ground Arabica beans, finished crisscrossing the peanut butter cookies, and put them in the oven, setting the timer for eight minutes. The last thing I needed was a burned batch. I took a few deep breaths until I was ready to face my company.

I put down a tray with two mugs of coffee, milk, and sugar. "The cookies will take a bit longer. They're still baking."

Corbin nodded, though his face was so tight it looked as if it had been placed in a vise and squeezed. I jumped up when the oven buzzer went off and darted into the kitchen, grateful for the reprieve. All this time I'd wanted to speak to this man. Now that he was here, I had no idea where to start and no idea what to say. I transferred the cookies to a wire rack to cool and tried to steady my nerves.

CORBIN—I COULDN'T think of him as my grandfather—was sipping coffee when I came back into the living room.

"I have to admit you've taken me by surprise, coming here," I said.

"Yvette can be very persuasive." He cleared his throat. "Let me start by saying how very sorry I am about your father's death."

"Are you? Very sorry? Because I happen to know that you had no time for either him or me while he was alive. I also know you stopped Gloria Grace Pietrangelo from writing about you. So you can spare me the false sympathy."

Corbin frowned. "Who is Gloria Grace Pietrangelo?"

"She was the reporter from the *Marketville Post* covering my mother's disappearance. Wrote under the by-line of G.G. Pietrangelo. She found out you and Yvette were my grandparents. When she told the editor about it, she was told to drop it."

At least he had the good grace to blush. "I admit I quashed the press. It's hard enough to run a successful business without having all your dirty laundry aired in public."

I stared at him open-mouthed. "You consider a missing daughter dirty laundry?"

"You misunderstood. What I meant is that reporter would certainly have put in our estrangement with Abigail. I didn't feel that information was relevant. I still don't."

"But with your money, your connections, surely you could have done more to find out what happened to my mother. Surely you could have gotten past her having a baby and marrying my father."

Corbin pressed his lips together in a thin line. "Thank you for the coffee and cookies." He got up and walked out the front door. He was halfway down the driveway when he turned around and spoke again.

"I'm going to tell you the same thing I told Yvette, then and now. Sometimes the truth can break your heart."

"What's that supposed to mean?"

The bastard drove away without answering.

AFTER WHAT COULD only be described as a restless night's sleep, I woke up to the sweet smell of lilac wafting through my open bedroom window. I pulled my blinds all the way up and admired the deep purple flowers juxtaposed against shiny dark green leaves. Not so pretty, perhaps, most of the year, but when in bloom, lilac bushes were truly spectacular, both in scent and in sight. Next year, if I were still living here, I would take Ella Cole up on her offer, plant a garden or two.

I grabbed a quick shower, pulled my hair into a messy ponytail, tossed on a pair of khaki shorts and an old race tee shirt. I was just about to go out and cut a few stems of lilac to put in a vase when the phone rang. I checked the caller ID. Shirley.

"Hey, Shirley, it's been a while. Are you calling to tell me you've finally retired?"

"Not exactly. The library asked if I'd stay on another year. I said yes."

"Well, good for you. Nice to know you're appreciated."

"It is, but that isn't why I'm calling."

"Then to what do I owe this pleasure?"

"I've been keeping an eye out for anything that might help you find out more about your mother's disappearance. Not just local papers, but across the country. Last night I found something. In a small town Newfoundland newspaper."

My stomach flip-flopped. "Newfoundland?"

"Newfoundland. But what I found, it isn't from the capitol of St. John's as you might expect. It was in a place called St. Bernard's-Jacques Fontaine. A small fishing village. Apparently the locals call it Jack's Fountain."

"Jack's Fountain."

Shirley laughed. "I know, eh? I might have found your father's parents, or at least a newspaper photo of the two of them. It isn't much, but who knows where that might lead? I'll make you a copy of it."

My curiosity was sufficiently piqued, and not just because of the Newfoundland connection. "I'll try to pop by later on."

I'd barely hung up when the phone rang again. This time the call display said "Private Caller." Probably a telemarketer but...

"Hello."

"Callie, it's me. Gloria Grace." Spoken in a rush.

"Corbin Osgoode had been sending your father money every month for the past thirty years."

That might explain how my dad had managed to save one hundred thousand dollars. "I had no idea. How did you find out?"

"My source is confidential. The bigger question is, why?"

What was it Corbin had said? *Sometimes the truth can break your heart.*

"I don't know. But I'm going to try and find out."

I was still mulling everything over when the doorbell rang out its sing-songy chime. After a couple of months in Marketville, I was almost getting used to having drop-in visitors. Almost being the operative word. I opened the door.

Dwayne Shuter was recognizable from his LinkedIn photo, the scar over his eye more prominent without any digital enhancements. The car in the driveway was also a giveaway, a black Mercedes coupe with the license plate DW*SHUTR.

A slender woman stood next to him. She was twenty or so years older than me. Good skin, shoulder-length straight blonde hair streaked with hints of silver. Clear blue eyes set in a heart-shaped face, the nose just a little too wide.

"Calamity," my mother said. "We need to talk."

FORTY-SEVEN

So THEY HAD all been wrong. My father. Leith Hampton. Ella Cole. Reid and Melanie Ashford. Misty Rivers. Randi Tamarand. I should have suspected. No one had ever found a body. The simplest explanation was that there had been no body to find.

What I didn't understand was why a mother—one who supposedly doted on her only child—could disappear without a word for thirty years. How she could let her husband and daughter believe she was dead. It was beyond cruel, even taking into account that the marriage had been in jeopardy.

My mother reached out to touch me. I flinched and drew back, one hand on the door. How dare she think she could turn up and pretend this was some sort of family reunion?

"May we come in before the neighbours come out?" Dwayne nodded in the direction of Ella's house, a silent signal that spoke volumes.

He had a point. I stepped back.

We made our way into the living room. I didn't bother playing hostess. If I had a glass in my hand I was likely to crush it. Or throw it. I certainly wasn't going to offer them cookies. "I'm sorry it's taken me so long, Calamity."

"Callie."

She bit her lower lip. "Callie."

"What do you want from me?"

"It's not what I want from you. It's what I want to tell you. Where I've been, why I left. I don't expect forgiveness."

What was it Misty had said? Your mother received a phone call one day at the food bank. She said something along the lines of forgiveness coming at a high price. "Why now?"

"I found out you were looking into the past. It was only a matter of time until you discovered I was alive. I thought that bit of news would be better coming from me."

"It's a bit late for true confessions, don't you think? Besides, why should I believe anything you have to tell me?"

"Because I no longer have any reason to lie. You see, once Jimmy died, the reason for secrecy died with him." She cleared her throat. "It was all my fault. I missed my parents. I wanted them to get to know their grandchild. More than that, I wanted you to have the opportunities they could offer. Jimmy was a hard worker, and a good man, but his vision for our future was limited. He was never going to be able to provide the finer things in life, or get you into the best schools."

"I did just fine going through the public school system. I even managed to get a business degree in college. I graduated not owing a dime, thanks to Dad and some part-time jobs." *Was that true? How much of Corbin's money paid for my education?*

"We're not here to debate your upbringing," Dwayne said. "Your father did a fine job of raising you. He loved you above and beyond anything or anyone. But if you want to hear the story, you have to be willing to listen."

Did I want to hear the story? I did, if only to get closure. "I won't interrupt again."

My mother twisted her hands in her lap. "I desperately wanted to reconnect with my parents. Jimmy couldn't understand it. He had no desire to see his own parents, and he couldn't forgive mine for turning me out when I became pregnant. I kept telling him it was time to let go of the past, to at least try to make amends. It caused a serious rift in our relationship. We fought about it day and night."

The affair with Reid probably didn't help, either. "Go on."

"Things came to a head on my twenty-fifth birthday. I shared the same birthday date with Ella next door, and so her husband, Eddie, wanted to throw a party for both of us. But just before going over there, my mother called. It was the first time I'd heard her voice in over six years. I'll have to admit it rattled me. All those years of waiting for absolution. I thought I was prepared for it. I wasn't."

I could relate. "What did you do?"

"Before I could say or do anything, Jimmy grabbed the phone and demanded to speak to Corbin, so my mother hung up. I never heard from her again."

That explained why my mother had been so twitchy on the night of her birthday party. It also went a long way in explaining the strengthening rift in my parents' marriage. My mother's next statement confirmed it.

"After that day, I could never love or look at Jimmy in the same way. There's being proud, and then there's being obstinate at the cost of everything else. Even so, I thought given enough time he might come to his senses. I suggested a trial separation. That's when he finally agreed to pay a visit to your grandfather. I wanted to go with him, but he insisted on going alone." My mother's voice broke.

"Not a day has gone by when I haven't regretted that decision."

"You can't blame yourself for what happened," Dwayne said, reaching for my mother's hand.

I was getting tired of the drama. "Can we cut to the chase, Mother? Dad went to see Corbin. Something happened that made you decide to leave. What I want to know is who, what, and why."

My mother nodded. "It was early February when Jimmy went to see my father. He waited down the street until my mother went out." She shook her head. "I'll never know what truly happened that day, but I do know that your grandfather has a temper. Years ago, he almost strangled Jimmy outside of Ben's Convenience. That time, Jimmy didn't fight back."

"But this time, he did?"

Another nod. "All those years of hurt and betrayal had festered inside of him like a poison. He went crazy, nearly beat my father to death. If Dwayne hadn't walked in on them, maybe he would have."

Dwayne picked up the narrative. "I worked for Osgoode Construction at the time, and I had some paperwork to deliver. I heard someone fighting when I got to the door. What I saw when I opened it…let's just say that a few more punches and Corbin might not have made it. I managed to pull Jimmy off of him and convinced him to get out of there while he still had a chance. The last time I saw him, he was driving his pickup down Moore Gate Manor."

"What happened next?"

"Corbin picked up the phone. I thought he was calling the police. Instead, he called Abby."

"He told me to get over there if I wanted to save Jimmy's life," my mother said. "I asked Ella Cole to look after you and drove to Lakeside as fast as our old station wagon would take me. When I got there, he gave me an ultimatum. If I didn't leave Jimmy and his bastard child—his term, not mine—he would press charges for attempted murder."

"Surely it wouldn't have come to that?"

My mother gave a thin-lipped smile. "Corbin Osgoode is a very powerful man. Back then, he all but owned Lakeside. He was very generous when it came to local initiatives, especially when it came to the police. The thought of leaving you behind broke my heart, but I couldn't let you grow up with your father in jail."

"So your solution was to give in to your father's blackmail and disappear?"

"Not at first. I thought with some time and distance, my father would come to his senses and drop the whole thing. Instead, the delay only served to enrage him all the more. One day, he called me at the food bank where I'd been volunteering. This time he threatened to call the police on Jimmy and report us to the Children's Aid. He convinced me that they would take you away and put you in foster care."

Dwayne picked up the narrative. "I'd been planning to move to Vancouver. I was trying to escape a rather destructive relationship and Vancouver seemed as good a place as any. I approached Corbin and told him that I would take care of Abby if he gave us enough money to start over. He laughed in my face and said he wouldn't give her a dime. Then he said that time was running out for Jimmy Barnstable."

"We left the next day," my mother said. "Valentine's Day. The only thing I took were the clothes on my back. I buried my wedding ring under the lilac tree. I'm sure it's still there."

"You make it all sound so simple," I said, unable to keep the bitterness from my voice.

"Simple? Is that what you think it was? Callie, leaving you was the hardest thing I've ever done in my life, but I did it because I loved you with every fiber of my being. I thought we'd be back after a few months, but by then, you'd moved to Toronto."

"Corbin told me that he was sending your father money every month to make sure you were well looked after," Dwayne said. "He said he'd keep sending it only if Abby stayed away. If she came back—"

"The threat of sending your dad to jail continued to loom large, even as time went by," my mother said. "Was there a statute of limitation on attempted murder? Would my father make good on his promise to call Children's Aid and have you sent to a foster home? I didn't know. I only know that I truly believed I was doing the right thing. Your father was a free man, and you were being well cared for."

My dad had led me to believe that my grandparents hadn't cared about me. I'd since come to learn that Yvette had tried sending cards and letters, and that Corbin had tried to care for me in the only way he knew: with money. And still my father's stubborn streak had stopped him from telling me.

"We hired a firm to give us an update on you and your dad," Dwayne said, interrupting my thoughts. "Jimmy was having a hard time finding a job in Marketville, thanks to Corbin putting the word out that he was unreliable. So when I moved back to Toronto and started working for Southern Ontario Construction Company, I made sure that they hired your father, and I was able to keep tabs on you at the same time. Not that your dad ever invited me to your house. It was as if he wanted to separate the past from the present. I respected that."

"What about you, Mother?" I asked, turning back to face her. "Did you stay in Vancouver?"

"No. I changed my name to Alison Lake. I moved around. A lot. Calgary. Winnipeg. Montreal. Halifax. Anywhere but Marketville or Toronto. I took odd jobs to make ends meet. Mostly I just drifted, although I stayed in touch with Dwayne."

She gave me a sad smile. "I always knew how you were doing. Then one day Dwayne called to tell me that Jimmy had died. I might have stayed away, but you started looking into the past. It was only a matter of time until you figured it all out. I needed you to hear the true story from me."

I leaned back in my chair. It was quite the story. It would take some time to process everything I'd learned. To decide whether I had it in me to forgive my mother. I hoped so, but I couldn't be sure.

There were still two unanswered questions.

"Do you think my father's death was an accident?"

"There is no reason to think otherwise," Dwayne said.

I wasn't about to tell them about my dad's letter. Besides, whatever I found out would only be conjecture on my part. It wouldn't bring him back.

I turned to face my mother. "Can I ask you one more question?"

Her face brightened. "Of course. Anything."

"I know that the Calamity Jane movie poster is a recent reproduction. What I don't know is how you managed to get it into the attic without anyone seeing you."

My mother stared at me, her face a complete blank. "I don't know anything about a movie poster."

I thought about the signature on the back of the poster, a backhand slant, sure, but a little bit spidery, just like my father's handwriting. I looked up towards the ceiling and smiled. It seemed the skeleton in the attic wasn't the only thing my father had left for me.

* * * * *

ACKNOWLEDGMENTS

Long before I was a writer, I was a reader, and I have my mother to thank for my love of reading, especially the mystery genre. When I was a young girl, she worked part-time at Zeller's department store. Every payday, she would bring home a new Nancy Drew book, which I would read, reread, and covet.

Long before I was published, I had friends who believed in me. Far too numerous to mention, for this novel I must thank Donna Dixon and Nina Patterson.

For her professional advice on a very rough first draft, thanks go to Marta Tanrikulu, a phenomenal developmental editor.

For their keen eyes, honest critiques, and never-ending encouragement, my profound gratitude to Michelle Banfield and Jennifer Grybowski.

Last, but certainly not least, thanks to my husband, Mike, for his unfailing belief in me, and my stories.

AUTHOR NOTE

I started writing *Skeletons in the Attic* while trying to find a publisher for my debut mystery novel, *The Hanged Man's Noose*, the first book in the Glass Dolphin Mystery series. I didn't want to stop writing, but I couldn't bring myself to write the sequel to a novel that hadn't yet found a home.

Just as the setting of Lount's Landing is loosely based on my former community of Holland Landing in Ontario, Canada, so too is Marketville loosely based on the town of Newmarket, which is situated just south of Holland Landing. Of course, I have taken great liberties with both locations as well as the surrounding area, and the characters are entirely fictitious, but therein lies the inspiration.

The idea for *Skeletons in the Attic* came to me while I waited with my husband, Mike, in our lawyer's office. We were there to update our wills, and his goldendoodle kept us company while our lawyer was detained at court. The opening scenes of this book are culled directly from that experience. (Let that be your takeaway from this: everything that happens in a writer's life may end up in one of their stories.)

ABOUT THE AUTHOR

Judy Penz Sheluk is the author of the Glass Dolphin Mystery and the Marketville Mystery series. Her short stories appear in several collections, including *The Best Laid Plans: 21 Stories of Mystery & Suspense*, which she also edited.

In addition to writing mysteries, she spent many years working as a freelance writer and editor; her articles have appeared in dozens of U.S. and Canadian consumer and trade publications.

Judy is a member of Sisters in Crime National, Toronto, and Guppy Chapters, International Thriller Writers, the Short Mystery Fiction Society, South Simcoe Arts Council, and Crime Writers of Canada, where she serves on the Board of Directors.